The Secret Lives of Copperheads and Fireflies

An Appalachian Mystery

Courtnee Turner Hoyle

Pale Woods Publishing

The Secret Lives of Copperheads and Fireflies

An Appalachian Mystery

Copyright © May 2, 2024

Erwin, TN

by Courtnee Turner Hoyle

Library of Congress Control Number: 2024909808

Paperback IBSN 979-8-9899846-2-6

Hardback ISBN 979-8-9899846-3-3

E-book ISBN: 979-8-9899846-4-0

Cover Design: Taylor Dawn, Sweet15 Designs, LLC

Copperheads and Fireflies Playlist

1. "Tuesday's Gone" Lynard Skynyrd

2. "Wagon Wheel" Old Crow Medicine Show

3. "Was I Right or Wrong?" Lynard Skynyrd

4. "Safe in the Arms of Love" Martina McBride

5. "Wild Angels" Martina McBride

6. "Mamas Don't Let Your Babies Grow Up to be Cowboys" Willie Nelson and Waylon Jennings

7. "Lithium" Nirvana

8. "Family Tradition" Hank Williams Jr.

9. "Copperhead Road" Steve Earle

10. "You May Be Right" Billy Joel

Other Titles by Courtnee

PARANORMAL MYSTERY

My Brother's Keeper

Pinky Swear

Rose Colored Glasses

ROMANCE

FINDING EMMA

FINDING DAVID

FINDING MRS. WINSOME

PARANORMAL SUSPENSE

Solomon's Tears

THRILLER

Hollis's Hobby

FANTASY

Cascade

Under Archard's Dome

MIDDLE-GRADE MYSTERY AND SUSPENSE

Rasputin's Scorn

COLORING BOOK

Pale Woods Haunted Houses

JOURNAL

Anxiety/Religious Journal

Chapter 1

My fondest memories involved lying in the outdoor hammock with my father. His hand, darkened and calloused by outdoor work, traced the lifelines on my delicate palm.

"I can't wait to see where you'll go," my father said, remarking on his dreams for me to own a business. "A man—or woman—" he amended, "can be free to make their own choices when they're their own boss."

We'd lie in the shade of maple trees, often napping away the heat of the early afternoon. Sometimes, he'd sneak out one of his favorite chocolate bars and share it with me. I loved the feeling of the silky layers of chocolate as they slid over my tongue. I treasured my moments with my father, and even though I was almost an adult, I held him like I was still a child when we heard the familiar crunch of gravel in our driveway.

The vehicles that belonged on our tree-lined road made loud grumblings before they jumped over the bridge and pulled their way up the hill to our little cluster of houses. We were so used to the sounds of farm trucks and my cousin's "souped-up" Honda that we didn't hear the police cruiser soundlessly glide into our driveway.

Daddy's family were the Tiptons, and they had owned the property on a hill at the foot of the Southern Appalachian Mountains since the conception of our small town. After a few generations, the land was parceled off to my cousins and my other kinfolk. The only neighbor we had who wasn't blood-related was Widow Silvers, and she had been married to my cousin before he died in the war.

"Ace," Sheriff Watts said soberly as he rounded his cruiser.

"Danny," my father returned by way of a greeting.

I found it odd that Sheriff Watts was so formal with my father, since he spent most of his Friday nights at the table in my dining room, losing terribly at poker. My father must have sensed something, too, for he sat up in our hammock and stood.

"I think it's best I talk to you at the station," Sheriff Watts said, shifting his eyes to me and back to my father.

My father's mouth formed a thin line, and he nodded to the sheriff. "I'll be along in just a minute."

When the sheriff retreated to his car, my dad bent down to meet my eyes. I sat up in our hammock, and I met his brown eyes with my blue ones.

"What's going on, Daddy?"

Even though I was seventeen, I called him *Daddy*. He didn't seem to mind that I never moved to call him the more mature form of the title, and Mama held her tongue about it, too.

"I don't know, Meg, but I'm gonna find out."

"Will you be home for dinner?"

He glanced at the waiting vehicle. "Yeah. You can count on it."

He grinned, showing his tobacco-stained teeth, and I hugged him. He pulled me to my feet, and he held me there for a moment, swaying gently like the wind blowing through the dogwoods in early spring.

My daddy left me with my arms wrapped around my middle as if consoling myself with a hug. My hand went to my mouth automatically, and I chewed the nails I'd been trying to grow out.

I tried to tell myself my daddy would be home soon. He'd only gotten into a little fight we hadn't known about, or he'd messed with the wrong man's wife. But the reason Sheriff Watts picked up my daddy that day was worse. Much worse. And he wasn't home by dinner.

Chapter 2

We didn't hear more about my father until the next morning.

My mother stayed up most of the night. She alternated from wringing her hands in front of the picture window in our living room to uselessly checking on my younger brothers as they slept. I tried to stay up with her, but my lids dropped over my eyes even when I tried to lift them.

I woke in the early morning hours as my mother sipped coffee on the couch. She stared at a book she'd been reading, but she didn't see more than the letters on the page.

I gained my love of reading from my mother. She devoured books, keeping her library card and a stack of her most beloved novels by her bed. Because of my choices in literature and my precise pronunciation, most of my family considered me a genius, though they ignored my mathematical abilities. My father was the only exception. He encouraged my skill with numbers but wanted me to apply it in a business sense.

I tossed aside the quilt my mother had placed over me. "I'll make breakfast," I offered.

"I whipped up some blueberry muffins," she told me. "They're in the stove so the ants don't get them."

Since I could remember, we'd had an ant problem. My mother wouldn't kill anything, even the bugs that threatened to carry her baked goods away in tiny pieces, but she devised ways to work around them, like placing food in sealed containers and wiping dish soap across the counters. Even though she assured my father that we only had an ant problem from late spring to early fall, he took it seriously. He sprayed the area around the house, and the only way my mother kept him from fumigating indoors was to tell him it would harm his young sons who were touching every surface.

I put a muffin on one of my grandmother's glass plates for each of us. My mother accepted my gesture, but her muffin sat beside her, completely untouched.

Pickles was next to rise, padding into the room and climbing onto our mother's lap. Instead of asking him how he slept, she stayed silent, running her fingers through his long, blond hair.

Pickles was as brazen as any five-year-old boy, but he could feel the atmosphere wasn't right for mischief. He laid his head on our mother's chest and wrapped his sun-kissed arms around her neck.

"Where's Daddy?" he spoke, and the still morning sprang to life around his voice.

Until then, the day had been muted, but Pickles's voice woke up everything from the birds in their nests to the toddler in his bed. Si gasped and ran down the hall. He stood in the hallway, scowling at us as if we'd intentionally planned to keep him out of our morning party. Most offensive to him was the sight of Pickles in our mother's arms. He stomped over to her chair, climbing into it while trying to push Pickles out.

"She's my mommy, too," Pickles declared, but he climbed down and grabbed one of his trucks from in front of the television.

Even though they were three years apart, Pickles and Si looked alike, but it was mostly because Si had the same honey-blond hair, periwinkle eyes, and easily tanned skin as his brother. He'd picked up Pickles's cocky smile, too, even though he didn't use it as often.

"Should I wake up Barton?" I asked my mother.

She gave me a gentle nod. Si was wriggling around in her lap, feeding on one breast and moving to another, but she said nothing to him. I doubted she even registered it.

Pickles heard me ask about Barton, and he jumped up with a truck in his hand. "I'll wake him up!"

Before I could stop him, Pickles ran down the hall and yelled, "Wake up, Barton!" He'd just learned to annunciate Barton's name after years of calling him something that sounded nothing like it.

I walked into the room as Barton pushed himself up on the bed and rubbed his eyes. His brown eyes cleared in the morning sun as Pickles climbed into bed with him, showing him the truck in his hand.

"That's cool," Barton commented. "Is that the one your dad got you for Christmas?"

My mother was married to Barton's father when she met my dad. They'd had an affair while her first husband was in jail, but it wasn't something we discussed. It didn't keep me from wondering if she'd gotten pregnant with me during the affair and if I was the reason she divorced her husband and married my father. It would certainly explain why Barton never fully accepted him.

"Yep!" Pickles responded, hopping off the bed. "Mama made muffins, so you better hurry before Si eats them all!"

There was no chance the smallest member of our family would eat the rest of the breakfast our mother had prepared. It was more likely Pickles would stuff his mouth with as many muffins as possible before his stomach started hurting.

"Make sure you save me one," Barton said seriously. "In case Si is really hungry." He threw me a wink.

I helped Pickles put two muffins on a plate for our brother. Barton couldn't miss a meal. He and I were both too thin, like our mother.

Barton ate quickly and whispered, "How's Mama doin'?"

I shrugged.

"It's about what I expected," he said.

"Do you think you could stay home from work today?" I asked.

He lifted back in the chair. Mama always barked at him when he balanced it on the hind legs, but I held my tongue.

"Some of us aren't as privileged as you, Meg," he said. "Mr. Rosen would flip out if I asked for personal time." He ran a hand through his hair, and I noticed how long it had gotten over the winter. "Besides, Ace is not my father."

Blood rushed to my face, but three sharp knocks at the door interrupted whatever I was going to say. I settled for narrowing my eyes at my older brother as I walked swiftly to answer it.

Our mother had heard it, too, and she balanced Si in her arms as she ran to open the door. I let her breeze past me, as I knew the person on the other side would want to speak to her first.

The door caught, and she couldn't open it the first time she tried. My dad had promised to fix it, claiming it was only a slip on the latch, but he had been too busy sowing seeds in the garden to get around to it.

The sheriff stood on the other side of the door. Dressed in his navy blue police uniform, he held his dark hair in place with a healthy dose of gel.

"Sara Beth?"

I took a deep breath. Even though he'd called her by her first and middle name when they were in school, he'd only used both names around me when he was serious.

My mother stared at him expectantly.

"Could Meg take the kids into another room?" he asked, motioning to Si and Pickles.

"No," I said.

They both looked at me strangely. My mother opened her mouth, but Barton spoke before her.

"I'll take them," he volunteered.

After we were alone with the sheriff, my mother asked him to sit down. He stood in the doorway, shifting from one foot to the other.

"It's best I get out what I have to say." He almost choked out the last word.

I panicked. "Where's Daddy? Is he okay?" I had to hold myself back from grabbing and shaking him. I wouldn't have done a lot of damage to his six-foot tree trunk frame.

"Your daddy's fine," he told me quickly, wiping a thin layer of morning perspiration from his forehead. "He's still at the station."

"What in the world is it, then?" my mother asked.

"It's your sister," the sheriff replied, looking at my mother. "Mary Beth is dead."

Chapter 3

My mother and her sister, Mary Beth, hadn't been close for almost two decades, but it was a long story. The damage was as deep as the well outside my Aunt Tonya and Uncle Catfish's house.

Mama and her sister grew up on the other end of town. Their mother had been a homemaker, and their father had sold insurance for a lucrative company.

The girls enjoyed fine schools and attended nice parties, but Mary Beth was a bit of a rebel. Most whisperers thought she'd become pregnant at a young age, and when Mary Beth caught wind of the gossip, she'd smile knowingly and say aloud, "I am quite the fan of birth control."

Whatever her faults, my mother adored her, and Mary Beth dragged her sister all over the county, sometimes sneaking out their window at night to go to parties with people who did not gain their parents' favor. During one such party, my mother met her first husband.

Dandy Hughes pulled up on an older model Harley Davidson after he'd let his blond hair fly in the wind. According to the stories I'd heard, he'd held my mother's attention with his creamy skin and cerulean eyes, but it shocked everyone when she left the party with him. It surprised Mary Beth, too, as she had to go home without her sister in tow.

The next morning, when their mother asked her about her sister's absence, Mary Beth lied and said that she had gotten up early to complete a class project. As it was summer, and the school hadn't provided the students with work during the break, the lie fell flat.

Her parents summoned the police, and they coerced Mary Beth into telling them about the party and the man who had taken her sister away on his motorcycle. The authorities ran a check on his name and informed the family that Dandy Hughes was six years older than their teenage daughter. Upon hearing their daughter was with a twenty-three-year-old man, my grandmother had fainted, and my grandfather called his oldest child, Barton, to begin legal proceedings.

Fearing the worst, my Uncle Barton, twelve years older than his siblings and terribly protective of them, organized a search party. Everyone he knew covered ground from Dandy's last known address to the edge of town.

Three days later, my grandparents received a call from Uncle Barton's assistant. He told them that a private investigator had spotted my mother and Dandy in Dandy's trailer.

Mary Beth had ridden with her parents as they drove to the address. She watched her father climb the steps and pull Dandy out the door when he answered it. He threw the man on the ground and dragged Sara Beth, who was only half-dressed in the clothes she'd worn to the party.

"I love him!" Sara Beth had shouted.

Her father threw her into the car next to her sister. "You don't know what love is," he growled. "You hardly know him."

"We're married!" she'd shot back.

My grandmother had turned on her daughter. "Married? How? You're not old enough to be married!"

"We went to North Carolina," she'd answered.

My grandfather had sped away from Dandy's trailer, and he'd called Uncle Barton when he'd gotten home. Dandy produced a marriage certificate dated the day after he'd met my mother, and Barton confirmed its validity. Through a loop in the law that no longer exists, Sara Beth was a married woman.

My grandparents allowed her to take her clothes and a few possessions, and they drove her to her husband's trailer. She cried with her sister in the back of the car, promising to call her every day.

"You will have nothing more to do with Sara Beth," her father had commanded Mary Beth from the front seat. "She's made her bed in the gutter and now she can lie in it on her own."

Mary Beth had to watch as her father stacked her sister's suitcases on Dandy's dilapidated deck. She held onto Sara Beth, crying in anguish for her sister to stay, and regretting her idea of attending the party that had led to the situation. Dandy came to the car, and Sara Beth pushed her sister gently away, rushing back to her new husband.

Mary Beth saw the way Dandy held her as if he were protecting her from the hostility of her parents. Part of her envied her sister's freedom and happiness, the other part hated her for leaving her alone.

That was the moment the divide formed, and no matter how many times the sisters came together and broke apart, they never really bridged the gap. Mary Beth always remembered the way it felt when her sister pulled away from her and ran willingly into Dandy's arms.

My mother had never breathed a word of the story to me, and Barton hardly spoke about his father. I'd heard everything from my Aunt Mary Beth. She'd told me the truth, plainly and simply, and now she was dead.

Chapter 4

My mother's legs gave way, and she fell onto the floor. The sheriff and I rushed to help her, but she held up her hand. "I just need a minute."

I relieved Barton so he could be with our mother. He was better at consoling her than me. I tended to use humor to lighten a situation, and it was not the time for my type of comfort. Barton was better at soothing our mother by reminding her of all the beautiful things around her. I knew I'd made the right decision when I heard my mother crying. It was best for her to get her emotions out; it was always worse when she held them in.

Si yelled for her, but I bounced him until he fell asleep. He had woken up early, so it was more of an extension of his sleep than a nap. I doubted my mother would mind the mild shift in his schedule.

Pickles kept making excuses to go to the door that blocked the kitchen and dining rooms from the rest of the house. At first, I lured him away with the promise to play with him, but after he heard our mother crying, he stood by the door, caressing the knob.

I wanted to be irritated with him, but I couldn't find the energy. Besides, he wasn't doing anything wrong, and I was glad he showed empathy. Sometimes I wondered if he had any, but that was usually after I'd been hit in the head with a toy truck or he'd peed on my foot when we were outside. In the world of little brothers, he certainly lived up to the stereotype.

"Egg," he whispered.

Because it was the way he'd first said my name or he knew it irritated me, Pickles left off the *m* in my name. He was usually proud of himself when he said it, too, but now he just seemed scared.

I held my arms out for him to run into them. He didn't cry, but his concern looked foreign on his face. I wanted to do anything to return him to the carefree boy he had been the previous day.

"What's wrong with Mama?" he asked, looking up at me.

I could have lied. I could have told him everything was fine, and he didn't need to worry, but I was unwilling to damage his trust.

"Something has happened," I said. "It's not my place to tell you about it, so can you wait for Mama to talk to you?"

He nodded, but then crossed his arms. "I'm five. I'm big enough to take care of you, Mama, Si, and Barton."

I smiled at his faux courage and realized he was more concerned about our father. "Daddy will be home soon."

No sooner had the words left my mouth than a wail sounded from the kitchen. Barton's voice filtered through the door in hushed whispers as he tried unsuccessfully to calm our mother.

Pickles bolted to the door, opening it before I reached him. He ran to our mother, who was on her knees, her blue and white checkered dress spilling out like an umbrella from her waist.

Barton scooped up Pickles and hurried back into the living room, closing the door behind them and leaving me with the mess in front of me. I couldn't keep Pickles at bay, so now he'd condemned me to handle our crying mother. I didn't know what else had caused her to become an emotional wreck.

I looked at the sheriff for clarity, but he seemed as lost as me. I don't think I had seen my mother weep openly, so the scene was foreign. She covered her face with her hands and shook with sobs, showing no signs of stopping.

I crept over to her like I was approaching a wild animal. Extending my hand, I rested it firmly on her shoulder. I almost expected her to jump at my touch, but she didn't seem to register it.

"Mama."

Her crying stopped like I had shut off the flow myself. As abruptly as it ended, she needed a moment to compose herself. Once she had dabbed at her blue eyes and taken a few steadying breaths, she rose. My hand fell from her shoulder as she stood, and when she looked at me, dewdrops of tears dotted her fair lashes.

No one spoke, and I wondered if it was as uncomfortable for them as it was for me. The sheriff shifted his feet, but my mother stood proudly.

The need to fill the silence finally won over. "What happened, Mama?"

Her hands moved to her waist, and her fingers danced across one another. She looked down at them and then at the sheriff. He seemed to take his cue from her, but he didn't look happy about repeating whatever he had told my mother.

"Meg," he started. His voice wavered, and he coughed. "I'm gonna be keepin' your daddy for a while."

I was instantly defensive. "Why?"

The early morning sun reflected my image in his gold-rimmed glasses. I crossed my arms over my small chest and noticed my long, flaxen hair was sticking up in several places. My almond eyes were smudged with mascara and glitter, extending from my button nose to one temple. I wouldn't have taken me seriously if I had been on the receiving end of my glare, and the sheriff didn't falter.

"It's not official yet, but your daddy's been charged with Mary Beth's murder."

Chapter 5

My grandparents unofficially gave the house we lived in to my parents as a wedding present. My daddy had lived with his aging parents until he married my mother, helping them with their garden and two horses. After he moved out, Aunt Tonya assisted her parents daily. She had lived in a house next to them, and she was more than capable of lifting her fair share.

My grandparents loved my mother, and they seemed to be unaware of the scandal surrounding her relationship with my father. They held a wedding reception for the couple on their farm and gave them the keys to the house two blocks away.

Even though my mother must have only been in the early stages of her pregnancy with me, I imagine my father carrying her over the threshold and talking about the type of home they planned to make for Barton and me. My parents brought me home from the hospital to the house, and I'd rarely slept outside its walls in almost eighteen years.

The home was red brick, set in the shape of a cracker box. It boasted three bedrooms, even though my father had to convert the laundry room into a bedroom for Barton by moving the washer and dryer to the basement. My daddy and Mama slept in a bedroom beside the living room, and the boys and I shared a room on the other side of the house.

I wondered why my brothers had to be placed in my room. After all, weren't teenage girls supposed to have some privacy?

"You're more maternal than Barton," my father had responded when I'd asked about moving my roommates. "He's a boy, so he won't wake up if they cry or start choking in their sleep."

My budding feminism wanted to argue several points, but I stayed silent. My father hadn't put my brothers in my room to ruin my life. He hadn't been able to establish a good relationship with Barton, and he trusted me.

He'd told me he and my mother might move the boys into their room when they got older, but I knew it wouldn't happen. Daddy knew I was on my way to college soon, and he liked to sleep alone with my mother. The second part I understood a little more as I matured.

We had shared holidays and family nights in our home, and our house had served as a beacon to poker players in and around Tipton Hill. The sheriff had even played cards at our house every Friday night and usually lost miserably.

As I stood grinding my teeth in the same dining room where I'd learned the value of a royal flush, a thousand thoughts rushed through my mind. I flipped from one to another, never settling on something to say. The sheriff saved me from speaking.

"I know it's a shock."

"That's an understatement," my mother commented. She was more composed, and a fierceness shone out of her ice-blue eyes.

"Sara Beth," the sheriff started, attempting to placate my mother. He stopped when her silvery eyebrows rose.

"You won't tell me why you think my husband murdered Mary Beth, and you haven't officially charged him with anything, so I think it's time for you to go."

I mirrored my mother's thin-lipped expression, in hopes I stood as solid for my father as her.

The sheriff stared at her for a long moment before he looked at his feet. "Sara—"

My mother was firm. "It's time for you to leave, Sheriff Watts."

Upon hearing his title, the sheriff's eyes popped up. They'd been friends, so my mother had always called him by his first name, but an invisible line had been drawn, even if he didn't understand it.

Without another word, he put on his wide-brimmed hat and made his way out the door. My mother's posture deflated when it closed.

She flew into action, issuing commands as she prepared our family for several outcomes. "Meg, Barton needs to get ready for work, so watch over your brothers while I call the funeral home."

"I'm going to see Sanders," I said defiantly.

She glared at me with one hand on her phone. "This is no time—"

"His mother died."

"And she was my sister," she shot back. "I need you here to support your family."

"But he's family, too." My defense was weak, but I held my ground.

My mother's shoulders sagged. "Look, I can't fight everyone. I need to tell the rest of the family and see if they've heard anything more about her murder. Then I need to call your Uncle Barton. Your father's going to need some good legal representation."

"I heard my name," Barton said as he came into the dining room. He glided over to the kitchen counter and finished his juice in one long drink.

"She was talking about *Uncle* Barton," I told him.

Barton nodded. "Do you need me to take anything to his office on my way to work?"

My mother hugged him. "No. And for the record, I think it's a bad idea for you to go to work today."

"Noted," he responded, ending their hug prematurely. "But we're gonna need money now that your husband is in jail, and I don't want to explain to Mr. Rosen why I need the day off."

Our mother let out a long sigh. "I guess you're right. Just be sure to text me when you get there."

My brother laughed at her sudden overprotectiveness. "Sure, Mom. I'll text you, even though I'm less than two miles away."

Barton adopted a lighter approach than I'd seen from him in the past. Usually, he would go along with whatever my mother said, but he had a sarcastic air that was uncommon for him. It left me in a position to be more sentimental.

"Take it easy on her," I said. "Aunt Mary Beth is dead, and Daddy is in jail."

They both shot me daggered looks. Mama didn't like for her children to think of her sister as our aunt, and my brother was unwilling to be lumped into my father's children.

Barton checked his phone, noticed the time, and looked at our mother apologetically. "I'll be home right after work."

I heard his rattling truck burst with life and rumble down the road next to our house. I missed him as soon as he left, as my brother had been a buffer against my mother's ever-changing moods.

Chapter 6

My mother went through the motions of her day, and I tried to help her until it was time for me to go to school. When I slung my bag over my shoulder, my mother put her hands on her hips.

"Where are you going?"

"To school," I answered.

"And how are you going to get there?"

"I can walk a block and a half," I told her.

"No," she said resolutely. "Barton has already left for work, and I have a lot to do today. With everything going on, you really need to stay home."

"Barton didn't."

My mother's jaw clenched. "Fine! Do whatever you want; you're going to anyway." She threw up her hands and walked out of the room.

It wasn't the end of the argument, but I let the screen door slam on anything my mother might have added. I thought I heard her say that I only cared about my father, but I wasn't sure.

I had only given myself twenty minutes to walk to school, and it took a little longer. I supposed the time it had taken to argue with my mother hadn't helped. I couldn't go to my locker before the final sound to signal the start of classes echoed across the loudspeakers.

Imani poked me with her pencil. "Why are you so sweaty?" she whispered.

I shifted in my seat to face my friend. Her raven hair puffed out around her chocolate features, completing a fullness that made her look both innocent and breathtaking. The yellow top she wore reflected against her skin, giving her a buttery glow.

"My aunt is dead and Daddy's in jail," I told her in one breath.

She purposely allowed her mouth to drop open. "Why are you here?"

I shook my head. "I needed to get out of the house. My mama's trying to manage and micromanage, so it's best if I'm out of the way."

"She didn't want you to go, did she?' Imani said. "Girl, you are gonna get the silent treatment when you get home."

Imani had visited my house when her father played cards at our table, and we'd become fast friends. She knew my mother's moods were like a whirlwind, as she'd witnessed them most of her life.

The teacher called our attention to the topic on the board, and we started writing. He didn't reprimand us for talking, as we were graduating in less than a month, and most teachers gave up on punishments for minor offenses when students were in their senior year.

After class, Imani walked with me to my locker. "I've got culinary class in five minutes, so I can't really talk now, but will you ride the bus with me so we can talk?"

The bus took fifteen minutes to reach the high school from the middle school, and twenty more minutes to drop me off at my road, so I declined. "I have something I need to do after school, but I'll call you later."

"Sanders," she guessed.

I nodded. "I haven't seen him, and I need to know what happened."

Tipton Hill had three parts: lower, middle, and upper.

The lower part had a couple of trailers where some of my older relatives lived. They were next to the creek, so they could fish and enjoy the sound of the water, but they didn't have a lot of land or big houses to maintain. My Uncle Catfish mowed their lawns on the weekends and attended to minor repairs.

I lived in the middle of Tipton Hill. It was far enough up the one-lane road to keep Sunday drivers away, but it was close enough to other people to be part of a clustered subdivision.

I skirted the edge of one of my neighbors' properties to keep out of my mother's sight. I knew she'd be expecting me anytime, but I hoped I could buy half an hour by telling her I had ridden the bus.

My Aunt Mary Beth lived in upper Tipton Hill. She was an experienced gardener, and her pansies were already popping up. Her house had recently been pressure washed, an experience that had taken Sanders almost an entire Saturday afternoon.

I rapped on the door, using a special knock I'd learned from my daddy. He called it our "shave and a haircut" knock.

I heard movement right away, and I braced myself for whatever might follow. Sanders wasn't good at controlling his emotions, and I was clueless about his current stage of grief.

The wooden door swooshed open, and Sanders held the screen door for me. He hadn't showered, and his dark hair clung to his scalp in several places while it stuck straight up in others. His green eyes were rimmed in pink and swollen, and his already small frame had lost the few pounds he had gained over the winter.

No sooner had I stepped inside the house than he swallowed me in his arms. "Meg." He said my name several times, like he couldn't believe it was really me.

"I just found out this morning," I told him. "I'm so sorry."

He lifted his face from my hair. "You've known since this morning?"

I couldn't deny the hurt I saw in his eyes. He would have run straight over to my house if he had learned either of my parents had died.

"I had to go to school to throw my mother off. She wasn't going to let me see you until she was finished with everything she had to do."

We both knew she was still busy, and she wouldn't have let me leave until the next day, if then. Barton may have been able to soften her heart, but I hadn't been willing to take that chance.

Sanders's coal-black eyebrows met. "Why didn't you come here instead of going to school?"

I let my bag slip off my shoulder and land on the carpeted hallway. "The school calls your parents and lets them know you missed."

He looked away. "Yeah, they called this morning. I didn't have anyone to give the phone to."

Sanders had celebrated his eighteenth birthday the month before, so he was technically an adult. The school, however, only saw a senior was missing in the attendance ranks, so they checked on him.

I followed him to the living room and allowed him to settle on the couch before I joined him. I laid my head on his shoulder and waited for him to speak. We stared at a silent television, and I felt minutes pass away. I needed to know what had happened, but I didn't want to push him.

"I'll have to go soon," I said, hoping he'd talk about my aunt's death. "Mama may not let me leave tonight, but I'll come by after school again tomorrow. She should let me stay for the afternoon."

"I doubt it."

His lack of faith in my mother struck me. She'd probably insist on coming with me to check on her niece and nephew. She may not have favored Sanders, but she adored Crystal.

Crystal glided in from the other room. Her tanned limbs had soaked up the early spring sunshine, and her chestnut hair shimmered in the afternoon light.

Crystal had been born early, and her body never seemed to catch up to its full potential. She walked late and never mirrored the expressions most children learned at an early age. She was a few months older than Pickles, and he knew his name and nickname, but Crystal never responded when she was called.

She hardly acknowledged me as she sat down on her blue and yellow rug. She surrounded herself with toy rockets, sending each one up with noises that closely matched a true take-off.

"How is she?" I asked Sanders.

He took a deep breath that didn't inflate his flat stomach. "Part of her knows Mom isn't coming back, but she hasn't asked about it. I don't know if I should talk to her or let the therapist do it."

I nodded sympathetically. "You're her brother, and normally, I'd say you should have already sat her down and talked to her." I looked over at Crystal as she launched another one of her rockets. "But this is a different situation."

"She sees her therapist tomorrow," he said. "I think I'm going to let her talk to Crystal." He looked over at me. "This is gonna sound horrible, but I can't handle one of Crystal's outbursts right now."

I leaned back onto his shoulder. "That's not terrible. You've been through a lot, and you may not be a kid, but you need to think about how you feel, too."

I stayed with him for a few more minutes. I tuned out Crystal's sounds and listened to the faucet drip in the kitchen. It was a familiar sound that reminded me of afternoons with my Aunt Mary Beth as Sanders and I raced around the house with a cookie in one hand and a squirt bottle in the other.

My eyes misted over, and tears fell before I could stop them. Sanders sat up, concern etching his features, and held me in his arms. Sitting up fully, Sanders's height was more noticeable, and he rested his chin on my head.

"I'm so sorry," he whispered.

"Why are you sorry?" I said between my sobs, trying to keep Crystal from hearing me. "Your mom died, and I'm crying when I should be comforting you."

"She was your aunt," he replied. "Besides, she was only my step-mother."

I was a little irritated by his casual dismissal of the woman who had raised him. My aunt had her faults, but she had loved Sanders and had legally adopted him after it was clear his mother had abandoned him.

Sanders loved her, too, and they worked well together as a team when fulfilling Crystal's needs. He had confided in me he felt like an imposter, though. After his father had died in service to our country, Sanders had told me he'd never felt like he was part of the family, even though he loved it so much. He joked that marrying me would give him a stronger place in our lives, and realizing he was half serious, I told him that anyone who had seen me in my candy corn bathing suit when I was seven years old wasn't in the running for my future husband.

"Don't say that, Sanders," I scolded him. "You don't get to deny your grief. You loved her."

Tears glazed his eyes, and even though he tried not to let them fall, he lost his battle, and they spilled over. Instead of letting me comfort him, though, he ran from the room.

After a few minutes, I got up and looked for him. He was in the hallway with his head down and his hands against the wall. I slipped under him and hugged him.

"I have to go."

"I know." His voice was still husky with emotion. "Will you come back when you can?"

His emerald eyes pleaded with me, and I didn't want to disappoint him. I knew my mother wouldn't want me to leave the house when I got home, and I'd be there all night.

"Mama and I will be by tomorrow."

His eyebrows drew together sharply. "You don't know, do you?"

I don't know if I answered him, as his question deeply bewildered me. *What didn't I know?*

"Of course she didn't tell you," he huffed, running a hand through his hair and causing more of it to stick up. "Why would she tell you?"

"What is it, Sanders?" I said firmly. I had to get home, but I didn't want to leave before he told me whatever my mother had neglected to say before I left for school.

He set his jaw before he spoke, letting me know he was serious. "Your mother isn't going to come see me, and I don't think she's going to let you around me. I'm the one who had your father arrested. I'm the one who found him after he killed my mother."

Chapter 7

I walked home in disbelief. The afternoon sun seemed like such a contradiction to the events of the day, as its warmth pushed at my back and shoulders, trying to slip past the defense of my black and white flannel shirt and freckle my moon-kissed skin.

I had known Sanders for the biggest portion of my life, and he had never lied to me. He had been brutally honest with me about certain life decisions and their outcomes.

But my daddy was my daddy. He couldn't be a murderer. I tried to imagine him with his hands around my aunt's long neck or with a hammer in his hand as she slowly bled out on her kitchen floor, but the images didn't make sense. I'd seen him kill spiders and put out traps for animals, but he'd never been homicidal.

I searched my brain for the events of the night in question. It had been a Tuesday, and Barton had been working late, so Mama had put his dinner in the microwave. We'd had corned beef and cabbage, and my dad had talked about the cabbage he planned to plant for the fall. There were no arguments or hasty exits. As far as I knew, my father and mother had gone to sleep in their bed and woken up together the next morning.

My house came into view, and I tried to wipe the thoughts from my mind. Hopefully, the funeral arrangements and my daddy's legal defense would distract my mother, and she wouldn't notice my lateness or preoccupation. My hope was dashed as soon as I walked through the back door.

"Where have you been?" she demanded.

"At school," I answered, hoping the conversation would end. I stepped out of my shoes and headed to my room as my mother chased me with her hands on her hips.

"You weren't at school," she accused.

"Did they call you to report my absence?" I turned around and faced her with my hands up. "I rode the bus home."

That seemed to stop her in her tracks until she thought it through. "Then you would have been here ten minutes ago," she countered. "Where did you go after school?"

I dropped my arms to my sides, unwilling to argue. "I went to check on Sanders. He and Crystal are fine, by the way. Not that you'd want to check on your niece and nephew."

She straightened and crossed her arms. "Megara, if you knew—"

"I already know," I informed her. "Sanders told me."

"So, you know your cousin is a liar."

I tried to think of a way to defend Sanders that wouldn't betray my father, but I came up short. "Don't talk about him like that."

Her eyebrows shot up. "Why? It's true. Why else would he have accused your father of killing Mary Beth?"

I couldn't answer her. I turned on my heel and made a big production of stomping into my room.

"Hey, Egg," Pickles said from his toddler bed. He rolled out, wrapped in his monster truck blanket, and landed on the floor.

I laughed at the production. "Aren't you supposed to be napping?"

He made the blanket into a burrito around his body before he answered me. "I'm not tired."

"Well, that makes one of us."

I suddenly thought of something, and a question popped out of my mouth before I thought about it. "Did Daddy leave the other night?"

I felt guilty for asking my little brother about my father's whereabouts on the night our aunt died, but Pickles could be pretty observant, even when I thought he wasn't paying attention.

He moved his head up and down until the blanket fell from his face. He blinked his long eyelashes as he pulled his thoughts from the ceiling.

"He went outside to turn on the radio."

Our father planted a garden every year, and he had gotten an early start in the growing season. Many of the neighbors scoffed at his attempt to sow beans, lettuce, and broccoli so early, but they agreed on his expert gardening skills when his efforts flourished in vibrant greens. The weather had been pleasant, and the rain was plentiful, helping my father deliver produce to our table much sooner than usual. I doubted he'd try it every year, but I was glad he had been successful.

In the past, deer had been a big problem for him. After my father threatened to shoot them several times, our mother suggested putting out a clock radio. The sound of people talking on the frequency would make deer think humans were in the area, and they'd avoid the garden. My father had heard of the tactic, so he tried it. Once the radio was on, my father had no trouble keeping deer away from his garden.

"I didn't think about the radio," I admitted, more to myself than to Pickles. I was reluctant to ask him anything more, so I laid down, turning my back to him.

Several minutes later, I felt a nudge. I could hear Si's steady breaths from his bed; any upset would jar him awake. Still, I couldn't resist the urge to pounce on my little brother and tickle him.

Si shot up in his bed, and he laughed at our display. When our mother rushed in to chastise us, she could only stand with her arms crossed, a large smile spreading across her face.

"I needed them to get a good nap," she said. "Your Uncle Barton is coming by for dinner, and I don't know how long I'll be awake."

Promising to help with the housework and children, I joined my mother in the kitchen. She had chopped carrots and onions, and I added celery to the mix. After she added the ingredients to the beef stew, she sat at the dining room table. I pulled out one of the remaining five chairs and held her hand.

"They won't let me talk to him," she confided. "They said I had to wait until he was officially booked and placed in his cell. Then he has to get a calling card, and we don't have the money—"

"Mama." I squeezed her hand to show my support. "We'll figure it out. We always do."

She smiled sadly. I echoed words my father had spoken many times when finances were low or troubled times visited our home.

"I'm just tired," she admitted. "I'm emotionally exhausted, and I think I have been for a long time." She rubbed her temples with her thumb and forefinger. "I don't know how he's going to get out of this one."

I pulled away, and my heartbeat pounded in my ears. I had to focus on my mother's face to keep my breaths steady. I found new lines around her eyes and mouth, and sunken cheeks that used to bring out her full smile. I didn't trust my voice for a long time, but when I spoke, it sounded like someone else was talking.

"You think he did it, don't you?"

Chapter 8

Dandy and my mother celebrated their marital bliss until Barton was born. As it often does, having a child put pressure on their romance, and Dandy started spending evenings away at a local bar. It wasn't long before my mother started hearing rumors about other women on the back of his bike as he cruised through town.

Instead of being pleased with her efforts to raise their son, Dandy complained about the baby's crying and clinginess. My mother left Barton with a neighbor to take day trips with her first husband, and they had romantic adventures, but they came home to the reality of life with a baby.

Dandy got a job in another state, and he happily sent money home to my mother and Barton. Dandy needed the time away from a howling infant, and even though my mother was resentful, she liked the large sums of cash she retrieved from her mailbox weekly. On most weekends over the next year and a half, Dandy drove the twelve-hour round trip to spend time with his wife and child, but their visits were strained.

My mother found out she was pregnant again, and she dreaded telling her husband. She believed he would leave her before he endured the demands of another baby.

She told him when he took her out for one of their rides together. Dandy had found a hiking trail in the mountains, and he had pulled my mother along as he climbed. Halfway up the mountain, my mother fainted, and he flagged down a trucker on a nearby road who drove them to the local hospital.

While there, she miscarried the baby. She begged the doctor to keep her miscarriage a secret from her husband and he agreed.

The police arrested Dandy three weeks later. He had been working in another town, but it hadn't been legal. He had been transporting cocaine and heroin across state lines.

My mother begged my Uncle Barton to help her husband, but he refused. He was uncomfortable with the number of drugs and guns in his possession when the investigators arrested Dandy, and he knew he couldn't argue his case.

My mother stayed in contact with her husband, visiting him at the local jail and accepting his collect calls. Soon, the phone company disconnected her service because she couldn't afford the bill.

When he couldn't call her, Dandy's irritation grew, and their visits became screaming matches. My brother talked about sitting in the chair beside his mother and holding his ears as Dandy accused her of cheating on him. Sadly, it was his first memory.

After one of those visits, my mother bumped into my father. Literally.

She walked out of the small jail's visitation booth, muttering something about her husband angrily, and bumped into a man going in the opposite direction.

She fell, and the man helped her up. "I'm not used to women falling for me so soon," he had said, showing her the only positive male attention she'd received since she'd met her husband.

My mother took one look at his raven black hair and tanned skin, and she lost her breath. Satisfied he had her attention, my father asked her to dinner, inviting Barton, too.

His interest in her flattered my mother, but she told him she was married. They parted ways that day, but she saw him again the following week. He had waited for her on a bench, and when she walked out of the visitation booth, he waited for her to notice him.

He introduced himself as "Ace," and he explained he couldn't stop thinking about her. He told my mother he'd looked up her husband and his charges, and he knew Dandy would be in jail for a long time.

"Don't waste your life waiting on him," he'd said.

Flattered by his motives, my mother asked him to come to dinner at her house. He was still there the next morning. Two weeks later, she was late for her period.

Once she started seeing my father, my mother asked her brother to prepare divorce papers. Her attorney's fees were free, and my father paid for the court costs. Within three months, my mother was divorced. One day after, she married my father.

Dandy was sentenced to twenty years in prison, and he was moved to a facility in Georgia. After she moved away from the trailer she'd shared with her first husband, she no longer received his letters begging her to stay with him.

Everything seemed to be going well. But crimes of passion had been committed, and more people had been hurt than my parents realized.

Chapter 9

We politely conversed with Uncle Barton while he and the boys ate their stew. My mother and I were too anxious to eat.

My uncle was clean-cut and distinguished in his gray suit and polished shoes. He had several wrinkles, but his trim features made him appear younger than his fifty-eight years. He'd managed to keep a full head of silvery hair, and he only needed glasses for reading. He wasn't married, but there were tales of failed romances, following him like the scent of withered flowers.

Pickles seemed to take longer to chew his food, and Si wanted extra attention after he ate. My mother held him at her breast and asked Pickles to watch television in the living room. He cheered at the uncommon occurrence and leaped over his brother's chair on his way out. Satisfied that the most impressionable ears weren't listening or aware of what they heard, my Uncle Barton folded his napkin and told us what he knew.

"As of five o'clock today, Ace was officially charged with Mary Beth's murder."

We waited for him to speak again, but when he didn't, my mother cried, "You have to help him, Barton!"

He shook his head once. "It's a conflict of interest. I cannot defend the man who murdered my sister." He looked away and inhaled deeply. "And I don't want to."

"You can't possibly think he's guilty," I said.

He looked at my mother for support, and receiving none, he addressed me. "I think you're too young to be part of this conversation, but your mother insisted I tell you, too. You are only here to listen."

It was like a verbal slap. I looked down at my lap and willed the tears back that were glazing my eyes.

My mother had steeled herself. "What do I need to do?" she asked her brother in a deadpan.

He may not have been able to help us directly, but my uncle was glad to give his sister the advice she requested. He wrote down the name of an attorney in Johnson City and advised my mother to make the twenty-five-minute drive instead of requesting a video conference call.

"This is a lawyer you want to deal with face-to-face."

"What about Pickles and Si?" my mother asked him. "Megara is in school and Barton has to work, so who will watch them?"

"What about Aunt Tonya?" I suggested.

My mother put her head in her hands. "I guess I could ask her, but what if she thinks I'm the reason her brother is in trouble?"

"Why would she think that?" I asked.

A look passed between my mother and Uncle Barton. I couldn't read it, and I hated being on the outside. My mother didn't answer my question.

"What else can I do?" she said. "Can I bring him some clothes from home?"

My uncle's mouth turned up in the corners. "He'll be wearing Tennessee orange for a while, and they'll give him a couple of pairs of underwear and socks. You can send him some money, and he'll be able to spend it at the commissary."

"What's a commissary?" I asked.

"It's like a store in the jail," my mother said. "They sell food and underwear to the inmates."

"At highly inflated prices," my uncle added. "But it helps them eat better if they have a little money in their account."

"I still have the money from my last babysitting job," I volunteered. "How much will twenty-five dollars get him?"

Tears rolled off my mother's cheeks, and she patted my hand. "It's a good start, honey."

Uncle Barton softened when my mother cried. His chair scraped against the hardwood as he stood. He embraced us and whispered to my mother. I heard him say something about love and justice.

When he broke away, his eyes were just as misty as ours. "Don't worry about the money for the commissary. I'll put one hundred dollars into his account. After that, he'll have enough to enter the jailhouse poker games, and we know Ace will wipe the floor with all those boys." He winked at us.

It was true. My father was the best card player in the county. I had watched him win almost every card game since I was old enough to climb into his lap and watch the men gathered around our dining room table trying to beat him.

The only man who had bested him at any card game was Imani's father. They had played gin rummy, and my father claimed he was sick when Dr. John laid down his last cards. The money pot in the center of our table had grown sizably, and my father lost the money for our electric bill. Amazingly, when our mother requested an extension, the customer service representative explained our bill had been settled anonymously.

Dr. John was a good man who played cards at our table for fun. He didn't need the money, but he liked the atmosphere at our house, and his daughter and I were best friends. He understood Ace Tipton had started the game to supplement his income, and one hundred dollars was the difference between my father's family eating with the lights on or bathing with cold creek water.

In jail, my father wouldn't play poker with long-time friends, but it might be for the best. He could hustle the other inmates until they realized he was good at the game or reign in his skills to make a steady income.

"Can I bail him out?" my mother choked out.

"Bail money will be determined at his arraignment on Monday morning," Uncle Barton told her. "But you won't be able to afford it." He read my mother's face. "Don't put up the house as collateral."

My mother rubbed her temples. "I couldn't do it. The house is in Aunt Margaret's name."

My father's Aunt Margaret had been his father's sister. In my grandfather's will, drafted before his children were born, he'd left his three properties to his siblings. Aunt Jo had already signed over the property on which my Aunt Tonya lived to her and her husband. Uncle Sidney alternated between his trailer and the home my grandparents had shared, but Aunt Margaret refused to sign over the house to us.

Aunt Margaret had worked painting Blue Ridge Pottery with my maternal grandmother when my mother had run away with Dandy Hughes. The scandal resonated deeply with her, and it horrified Aunt Margaret when my mother married my daddy.

She refused to sign over the property to my parents. Even though they had been married for seventeen years, Aunt Margaret insisted she was afraid my mother would run off, and then my father would have to sell the house and give her half the money.

As she inched closer to her hundred-year mark, my parents grew nervous. They feared she'd die without a will and the government would seize our home. My father had appealed to her several times on behalf of my siblings and me, but she only sucked in her thin bottom lip and shook her aged head.

"I could try to talk to her," I piped up.

My mother's mouth formed a grim line. "It's no use."

"I don't think it's a good idea," my uncle agreed gruffly.

Uncle Barton was careful not to speak against my father in front of his children, but his feelings were well known. Any time he had been around my father, his demeanor had changed. His openness would revert to something just shy of hostility, even though my father continued to speak to him as if they were old friends. My uncle may not have wanted my father in jail, but it was only because it upset his little sister.

I filtered out of the room, as I felt the bulk of the information had been shared. I drifted into the living room and sat down with Pickles, wrapping my arms around him. He shoved my arms away but leaned against me.

"What were you guys talking about?" he asked.

"Just grownup stuff," I replied.

"I know it's about Daddy."

I sighed, realizing my little brother would learn about our circumstances eventually. "Yeah, it was about Daddy."

"He's in jail."

It wasn't a question, but I nodded. "He may be there for a while."

"We need to take care of the garden while he's gone."

I looked at his sweet face and blond curls, and I hated whatever situation had caused my brother to feel like he needed to assume any adult responsibilities, but like my mother, he needed direction. I didn't want him to go outside at night to turn on the radio, so I thought of the best task to give him to set his mind at ease.

"Could you help me with Si?"

He narrowed his eyes. "Why would I want to take care of a baby?"

"That's just it," I explained. "He's only a baby, and he needs extra attention." I wasn't winning over my brother's allegiance, so I persisted. "And he'll forget Daddy if he doesn't see him. You can remind him what Daddy looks like, and when he does something wrong, you can tell him what Daddy would say about it."

Pickles nodded. "Like when he told me I couldn't pee in the rosebush and switched my legs after I tried to jump off the roof?"

"That's it!" I remarked, smiling. "Except you should let Mama handle the punishment." I tried to be serious, but I burst out laughing. "You peed in Mama's rosebush?"

"Yeah."' He smiled, revealing one front tooth barely hanging onto his gums. "It's the one that won first place at the Apple Festival." His face lost its mirth. "Don't tell her!"

I mimicked locking my lips and throwing away the key. "You can tell me anything."

It almost looked like my brother wanted to say something, but he turned away. When I pushed the subject, he wouldn't answer me and stared at the colored pictures on the television.

I let the matter drop, but my curiosity was eating at me. *What had Pickles wanted to tell me, and did it have anything to do with the night our aunt was murdered?*

Chapter 10

The school day flew by, and I successfully avoided a landslide of questions from Imani about what had happened in my family. She'd chastised me for standing her up at the bus stop, and I'd received ten text messages from her before I'd gotten home. Later that evening, she'd contracted food poisoning, and it had dampened her fire. She had stayed home to recuperate, only texting me a green emoji every time I checked on her.

On my way out, someone called my name. I turned around just as Garrett and his friend, Owen, jogged up to me.

Garrett's freckled face was slick with perspiration. Even though he was thin, Garrett didn't get a lot of exercise. His thumbs did, though. He only played one online military game, but he had nearly mastered the newest version that had dropped only two weeks prior.

Owen was a little heavier than his friend, but his shoulders were firm. Honeyed-brown eyes stood out over a Roman nose and small mouth. His perfect smile added to his look, and he never lacked a date, even though he stayed away from the potential of a steady girlfriend.

Garrett was going out with Imani, and he asked me about her. I didn't have a class with him, so it was the only time he'd seen me at school that day.

"What did she eat?" he asked.

"I think it was a chicken sandwich she picked up in the store's deli."

My friend had a job in the bakery at the same grocery store as my brother. It belonged to a small chain of slowly dying stores, but Imani didn't plan to work there after she graduated. Hoping to secure a good future reference for future business connections, she was determined to be a good employee during her final months at the store.

Both boys made sympathetic faces. They'd heard the stories about the woman who managed the deli and her reluctance to throw out food.

"I think they put too much mayonnaise on them," Owen said and winked at me.

My stomach took a nosedive, and it wasn't because of the thought of too much mayonnaise. I opened my mouth, but Owen's wink had tied my tongue. I'd talked to Owen a couple of times since Imani and Garrett had started dating, but he'd never flirted with me. I mean, there was that one time he'd tried to kiss me after a football game, but it didn't really mean anything. He'd had his arm around another girl the next time I had seen him.

Garrett picked up on my awkwardness and offered me an easy way out of the situation. "Well, I didn't mean to hold you up. I know you gotta get home."

Garrett's father was a police officer, and he'd accompanied the sheriff to our family's poker games a couple of times on Friday nights. His father had probably told Garrett about my family's mess.

I waved at the boys and practically jogged up the hill. Our conversation had taken precious time away that I should have been spending with Sanders.

Once I arrived at his house, part of me relaxed. I was supposed to be there, so I wasn't worried about the need to be anywhere else, even though the minutes before I needed to be home seemed to fall off the clock like the leaves on the maple trees in October.

I accepted the glass of iced tea Crystal brought to me. She was hyper-focused on placing the glass on the coaster in front of me, so I waited until she seemed to be satisfied. My aunt had expressed the need to make their guests comfortable, and she had involved Crystal in making several batches of tea when she was a toddler. The experience had resonated with Crystal, so no one visited their home without a tall glass of sweet tea, whether they wanted it or not.

During my last visit, Crystal had been preoccupied with her mother's sudden absence. She relied heavily upon her routine, and I didn't want to ask my cousin how many of her fits he'd had to endure from the upset in his sister's cycle.

Crystal looked freshly showered, and her brown hair had been brushed and fixed into two Dutch plaits that ran behind each of her ears. Mary Beth had insisted that her hair was properly maintained, and it seemed Sanders had continued the tradition, or Crystal had demanded it.

Sanders was still unshowered, and a raw onion smell escaped his armpits when he wrapped his arms around me. His hair was oily, and it stuck up in the back like he'd been lying on it before I arrived.

"Go take a quick shower," I ordered. "I'll hang out with Crystal."

At first, he seemed wounded, but then he looked down at his stained white shirt and rumpled flannel. He darted up the steps, and the water ran through the pipes.

Crystal wandered over to her rug where her rockets waited for her. Meticulously arranged, they had been placed in order from smallest to largest. She picked up one at a time and initiated a countdown. I wasn't sure who had taught her to count backward from thirty instead of ten, but I guessed she was better at counting backward than she was at counting forward.

Pickles could read short sentences and add and subtract small numbers. He was ahead of some of his classmates, but he wasn't the best student in his grade. Crystal attended the same school, but she stayed in another room with teachers who were aware of her unique needs.

Sanders reappeared, scrubbing his hair with a towel. "Did I take too long?"

I shook my head. "You were in desperate need of that shower, so I'm surprised you're finished so quickly."

"He smelled like a bum," Crystal commented without looking up.

Sanders's mouth raised to one side, and I laughed. I didn't think Crystal had been close enough to smell a bum, but I agreed with her.

"How long can you stay?" he asked.

"Mama knew I was here yesterday, and she could probably guess I'd come here after school today, so I'll stay as long as you need me."

He brightened as I spoke. "Then you probably should have packed a bag, because I need one of our up-all-night scary movie-thons."

"I doubt I can stay that late, but maybe I can help you with dinner."

The cupboards were full of noodles and rice, two things Crystal would eat in any form. I took down a packet of white rice and paired it with American cheese and baked chicken. The aroma made my stomach rumble, but I didn't fix a plate for myself, as I wanted Sanders and Crystal to have the leftovers.

As he ate, Sanders asked me about the classes we shared. I wasn't in his advanced biology class, but I told him about the work our other teachers had assigned.

He pulled the gristle from the chicken out of his mouth and placed it on his plate. "That's not too bad. I'm going to try to go back on Monday."

I couldn't hide my shock. "Monday? Don't you think that's a little soon? I mean, you've not even" —I softened my voice— *"buried her yet."*

"Crystal needs to get back to school," he answered. "And, honestly, I need to get out of here." He motioned to the surrounding walls. "It's a constant reminder of" —it was his turn to soften his tone— *"the way she died."*

"What happened?" The words were out of my mouth before I'd thought about them, and I regretted my question.

Sanders's face fell, and he put his plate of half-eaten food on the coffee table beside him. He tried and failed to speak several times, shaking his head after each attempt.

Sharp knocks sounded at the door. It was a recognizable pattern, and I ran to the door.

"Daddy!" I said out loud before I saw the person on the other side.

It never occurred to me that other members of our family could have adopted the knock that almost sounded like a code, so my face fell when I saw my mother on the other side.

She didn't look around me to see the other occupants in the house or try to step inside. She held Si on one hip and grabbed Pickles firmly by his hand.

"It's time to go," she announced. "They're going to let us see your father."

Chapter 11

Pickles wriggled in my lap, and Si played with the phone cord as we waited for my father to join us. In the past, inmates were ushered into a room on the other side of a partition, but after several violent outbursts, family members could only see their loved ones on a television screen as they spoke through a landline phone.

It was my brothers' first time in what my mother and I referred to as the "visitation shed," but I'd been there several times. My father had served some time for minor offenses, like when he got into fights in bars, but my mother stopped his fits of rage after the tumultuous early years of their marriage. When it wasn't a fight she initiated, my mother seemed to soothe my father when his fire ignited, putting out the flames before they raged.

We were encased in a six-by-nine wooden room with two metal folding chairs. A television had been placed behind a sheet of plexiglass, and the floor was littered with gum wrappers and napkins. An identical booth was on our left, and we could hear the mutterings of visitation in progress.

The dismal room reflected on the television screen was an area in the jail, and for all I knew, it could have once been a broom closet. The walls were concrete, and the floor had chips in the tile. A hard, plastic chair sat empty, but I couldn't note its color, as the screen projected only black and white images.

My mother sat beside the receiver, her leg bouncing more in her anxiousness than in an attempt to soothe Si. Her eyes were trained on the screen, staring at a sliver of a widow on the door. She'd squint as lines moved across the screen, but the interference she noticed wasn't the shadows of deputies escorting her husband down the hall.

The door on our television opened, and my father pushed back the only chair in the small room, grabbing the receiver from the cradle in one swift motion. He paced back and forth, unwilling to stay stationary. He reminded me of a caged bird, and I hoped he'd fly free before the claws of the justice system robbed him of his wings.

"Hey," my mother said into the receiver.

He glanced up at the monitor and waved. His smile was indulgent as he saw Pickles and Si staring back at him.

I was privy to only one side of the conversation, as the receiver wasn't loud enough for me to overhear my father's words. At first, my mother's tone was clipped, and I worried about my brothers overhearing a one-sided argument.

"Tonya couldn't watch them," my mother informed him. "I took the first opportunity Sheriff Watts gave me to see you."

She rolled her eyes in response to whatever my father said. "Because we need to formulate a plan for your defense, and I missed you, Ace." Her voice broke on his name.

My father seemed to soften, and he stopped pacing to look at my mother. His mouth spoke words I couldn't hear, but they stopped my mother's tears, and a small smile tugged at the corners of her mouth.

Si reached for the phone, and she allowed it. He jabbered some words and nonwords before Pickles grabbed the phone.

"Hey, Dad. Why are you in jail?"

He waited for our father's reply. "Well, I don't like it. Tell the sheriff I said to send you home."

I could hear my father's laugh. I relished it, as it was the first sound I'd heard from him since he'd left our home with the sheriff.

Pickles sulked when he handed the receiver to me, but I clutched it greedily. "Hey, Daddy!"

"Meg!"

I could finally put words with the face on the screen. "You didn't come home for dinner." It was the only thing I could think to say, but it put a damper on our conversation when he apologized for something he couldn't control. I followed it with, "How are you?"

He looked at his feet before he glanced back up. "To tell the truth, I'm not that great, but it's only because I'm worried about you guys. I don't know what your mother plans to do for money, and Barton's car is on its last legs."

"We'll be fine," I assured him, even though I was concerned about the same things. "Mama is pretty resourceful, and Barton doesn't go too far in his car."

Upon hearing her title, my mother wound her hand, indicating that I should finish my conversation with my father. I resented her for giving me less than five minutes to talk with him. I wrapped up my part of the visit, but I was sulky when I handed the receiver to her.

My father had told me he loved me, to do well in school, to care for the garden, and to be good to my mother. He usually told me most of those things, but they seemed to mean more to him now that he wasn't there to enforce his wishes.

Pickles turned around in my lap and pushed my nose. I let him look through my phone, but he grew disinterested when the building prevented him from connecting to the internet.

Si crawled over to my mother, wrapping her long hair around her face as she attempted to speak with my father about her conversation with my Uncle Barton. My father resumed pacing, twirling the phone cord in his irritation.

"They'll set your bail on Monday, and I thought we could put up the house—"

My father barked something and shook his head. The tone of his voice caused Si to bury his head in my mother's neck, even though he could hardly hear it.

Sensing an argument, my mother looked at me and nodded to the door behind us. I was unwilling to wait outside, but my brothers didn't need to witness a screaming match between our parents.

It was a little easier to keep my brothers entertained outside. I gave Pickles a smooth rock from the landscaping, and he played his version of hopscotch with it. Si pulled up the grass and stuffed it down the front of his shirt.

I stared at the building that had become my father's home. Constructed with dark brick, it sat next to the county's courthouse. The location was convenient, as inmates were only walked from one building to the next for their arraignments or trials.

Just beyond the shed that had been converted into a visiting room, a carport opened, and officers pulled in and out of it. I imagined what it must have been like for my father to have stepped out of one of those vehicles and into the jail, knowing he had lost his freedom.

What would it be like to eat whatever sad meal the government served me? What would I do if I couldn't see my family unless it was for a predetermined time over a television screen?

Sheriff Watts slung open the courthouse door and strode across the street to the parking lot. He noticed me before he made it to his cruiser, partly because Pickles was swinging wildly around the pole that held the deposit box for commissary money. He seemed to consider it before he crossed the street and approached us.

Sheriff Watts bumped fists with Pickles and Si, and he put a consoling hand on my shoulder and shook it before he released me. There was an awkward moment of silence that I had no intention of helping him fill.

"Is your mother visiting with your father?" he asked me.

I nodded in answer to his obvious question.

"They're havin' *words*," Pickles emphasized, putting up air quotes.

"I imagine they are." Sheriff Watts glanced at the building where an older woman was stepping out of the other visitation room. "They're two hard-headed people."

Realizing he had said something inconsiderate about our parents, the sheriff cleared his throat. "Did you get to talk to your dad?"

"Not long enough."

He glanced up at the sky and back at me. "I might be able to fit you in for a thirty-minute visit this Tuesday. The rooms are usually cleaned during that time, but our custodian has the week off, so one of the deputies volunteered to clean it. After he finishes with it, you can talk to your dad."

"Really?" I tried not to jump out of my skin or hug him.

"Come by around four-thirty, and ring the bell in the carport," he told me. "If you ask for me, I'll take care of the particulars."

The sheriff didn't stay to chat as he sensed my mother's visit was ending. He hurried to his car and was gone before the door creaked open.

"Let's go," my mother commanded.

Twelve blocks isn't a lot for some people, but I hadn't eaten. By the time we were halfway home, I lagged. My mother had placed Pickles and Si into a double stroller, and Si slept soundly, but Pickles kept easing over his side to grab a rock or rub the back wheel of the stroller.

My mother was tight-lipped about the conversation she'd had with my father, but I thought I could figure out most of it. She'd wanted to bail him out, and he refused to use the house as collateral for his bond.

"I could talk to Aunt Margaret," I suggested.

My mother shook her head. "I already visited her. She won't budge. She insists I'm trying to sell the house while my husband is indisposed."

"You took the boys?" I asked.

She didn't confirm or deny it, so I assumed she had taken them with her. "You know how she hates children!"

Si stirred, and my mother threw me a look. I rolled my eyes, but I spoke in a lower tone.

"She doesn't *hate* children," my mother argued. "She just can't handle it when they move the things in her house."

My great-aunt had scores of trinkets, and they adorned the cabinets and walls. They were meticulously arranged and were very dear to her.

My brothers were young and didn't understand they should leave the trinkets alone. Thinking they were more like action figures, Pickles and Si tried to pick them up and play with them, causing the vein to pop out in the middle of my great-aunt's forehead.

"Pickles cracked one of her ceramic unicorns," my mother admitted.

"Why did you take the boys?" I asked. "You knew they'd irritate her."

"I had to do something," my mother bit back. "I can't stand to sit in the house and do nothing."

"You saw the lawyer today."

She sighed. "I did get that done, but he's going to charge us ten thousand dollars, and that price goes up if your father doesn't accept a plea bargain."

"What!"

My mother's stern gaze reminded me to keep my voice low. "He's a good lawyer. To him, the fee is reasonable."

"It's not the fee, Mama." I ran a hand through my sweaty hair. "I don't think Daddy should go to trial. He didn't kill Aunt Mary Beth, so they need to be looking for her murderer."

My mother was silent for a few steps. Her tone was softer when she spoke again. "I envy the faith you have in the ones you love. It's one of your most admirable qualities, but it will end up hurting you in the long run."

Before I could explore my mother's statement, a truck idled next to us. Uncle Catfish yelled over the motor of his aging farm truck.

"You guys want a ride?"

My uncle was driving home from his job at the tire factory, and his dark hair was greasy. A fine sheen of sweat covered his jovial face and beaded over his heavy eyebrows. His thin mustache twitched when he smiled. It was the feature that had earned him his nickname.

"We don't have car seats for the boys," my mother called back.

"Just toss 'em in the back and let 'em roll around," my uncle joked, laughing at his suggestion.

My mother smiled, clearly unamused, but willing to placate him. She'd still need his wife to babysit at times. "We only have a little way to go, so it's not a problem."

"What about Meg?" he asked. "She looks a little weak-kneed, and she doesn't need a car seat." Another good-natured laugh followed.

My feet ached, and I wanted to climb into my uncle's truck, but I didn't want to leave my family behind. "I'll be okay," I assured him.

As my uncle drove away, the sun eased behind the mountains. The trees cast shadows, and the road blurred into black and dark shades of gray.

We crossed the bridge that ran over the creek, and the crickets chirped their evening serenade as we climbed the last hill before our house. A couple of sticks were still in the road from a short thunderstorm that morning, and they crunched under the stroller. As I looked up the road, one stick lifted, and my heart stopped.

"What's that?" I whispered, pointing to the moving branch.

My mother squinted her eyes, and to my horror, continued walking toward it. I had a good idea what it was before she confirmed my suspicion.

"It's a snake," she announced, moving closer for a better look.

"Get away from it, Mama," I begged.

She shooed away my concern and crept around the reptile. "Not all of us share your fears, Megara."

I'd developed an early fear of snakes when I'd been playing hide-and-seek with Sanders in the woods. I'd hidden next to a nest of copperheads, but I hadn't been frightened until my cousin dragged me away. He told me about their venom, and since I was already scared of needles, I was horrified that a snake could bite me and inject a deadly poison into my body.

As if sensing my mother, the snake twisted in the road. I was glad when my mother backed away quickly.

"It's a copperhead," my mother confirmed.

Most of the time we saw black snakes, but occasionally, we'd run across a rattlesnake or a copperhead. They were very good at camouflaging themselves, but we could usually spot them before we were within striking range.

"We have to go around it," my mother said, grabbing the stroller handles.

"Nope!" I returned emphatically. "It's in the middle of the road, so this is *its* road. We can turn around and go up another road."

My mother let out an irritated breath. "That doesn't make sense. We have to get home, and this is the only road to our house."

"We can go through Widow Silvers's yard," I said.

My mother put her hand on her hip. "Do you know how hard it'll be to climb the grass in her yard with this stroller?"

"I'll push it," I offered hastily as I watched the snake lift its head again.

"That's ridiculous." My mother pushed the stroller until I stuck my foot under one of the wheels."

"Stop it. I'm going around the snake."

I tried another angle. "You shouldn't endanger the boys. You may not be afraid of snakes, but we don't have your bravado."

That wasn't necessarily true. Si wouldn't even notice the snake unless it bit him, and Pickles would throw rocks at it to see if it moved. My mother considered my cautions, though, and she pushed the stroller into Widow Silvers's grass.

We rounded her vinyl cottage, and our home came into view. I saw a figure by our maple tree and wondered if Barton had gotten off work early. As we neared, the figure dashed away.

"Hey!" my mom called. She ran after the man—for with his boots, haircut, and physique, he resembled that sex the most, but I stopped her.

"Don't leave me alone with the boys," I pleaded. "He could be dangerous."

"You're scared of your own shadow!" she barked, getting angry as her fear mounted. "That guy was probably casing the house or stealing your father's vegetables. He would have stood his ground if he were dangerous."

I tried to rationalize his presence to comfort myself. "Maybe he was here for the poker game. It's Friday night, and not everyone knows Daddy's in jail."

She paused as she considered it. "Maybe. But I called all the usual players to let them know we wouldn't be having poker nights for a while. If he had been here to play cards, why didn't he just ask me if the game had been canceled?"

I couldn't stop thinking about the man for the rest of the night. I'd left the radio next to the garden on all day, but I had to water it, and I kept glancing over my shoulder the entire time I held the hose. Afterward, I huddled in the house, but every time one of my brothers made a loud noise, I jumped, adding to my anxiety.

The dawn brought imagined security, but my dreams were plagued by shadowy men running between our maple trees. Was the man trying to sneak around and steal my daddy's vegetables, or was he like the copperhead in the road, waiting for us to get close enough to his unnoticed position so he could strike us?

Chapter 12

In my eyes, my father was everything. He was the man who held me up until my head touched the ceiling, and dropped me, securely catching me every time, and he worked hard to take care of our family. But, like any other person, he had his faults. His imperfections never troubled my mind, though, as I was his daughter, one of the most special people in his life.

My father worked at a tire shop in the middle of town. I don't know exactly what he did, but he consistently arrived on time every morning. The owner promoted him as high as he could go before he was thirty, but over the next eight years, my father was content to stay while earning an hourly wage that only increased to adjust for inflation.

I didn't know about my father's infidelities until I was in school. I was called out of class one day by Sheriff Watts. I gathered my things from my second-grade classroom, and he drove me to the hospital.

My father held my mother's hand as she lay in a hospital bed. Barton sat in a chair in the far corner of the room, glaring at the wall. I looked at my unconscious mother and begged for an explanation.

"Your mama was shot," my father said. His voice was gravelly and choked.

Barton's head whipped toward him. "By one of your girlfriends."

"Bart, your—"

"Don't call me that," he spat. My brother jumped up, ready to fight.

"Barton, " my father corrected himself. "Your mother is what's important right now."

Barton sat back down, but his jaw clenched. "Yeah. She should have been important enough for you not to cheat on her."

My father sighed. "You're too young to understand—"

"That you don't cheat on your wife!" Barton barked at him. "I think I'm old enough to get the idea."

After their outburst, my father and brother seemed content to sit silently. I sat on the edge of the bed and flipped between old cartoons and newer sitcoms. That night, as I lay across the bottom of the bed, I heard my parents whispering. They must have thought Barton and I were sleeping, but once I'd heard them, I tuned my ears to their voices.

"Are they okay?" my mother croaked.

"Meg's fine," my father answered, "but Barton's mad at me. That boy has a bite harder than a cornered snake. And he's just as mean."

"He loves his mother."

"I'm not disputin' that," my father said. "But he doesn't know the full story."

Medication coated my mother's words, and they came out slowly. "What? That one of your little floozies shot me?"

My father breathed deeply a couple of times to keep his temper in check. "You were on her property, Sara."

"I wouldn't have been on her property if you weren't in her house," my mother countered. Even though arguing with my father should have kept her awake, my mother's words slurred her into sleep.

I heard my father kiss her, and he got up and left the room. He was gone for almost half an hour, and I was worried he wasn't coming back, but the door opened, and the smell of dark coffee wafted through the room.

Our insurance wasn't the best, so the hospital discharged my mother the next day. The nurses told her how to care for her wounded arm, and the doctor prescribed painkillers that my mother never took. My father offered to get the prescription, but she declined, citing the need to "keep her wits about her."

It was the first time I had proof my father cheated on my mother, but it didn't change how I felt about him. I noticed when he was absent overnight, and I heard my mother crying when I was supposed to be asleep, but my father's presence at the breakfast table on the following mornings made me feel better. I couldn't understand why my mother wasn't happy he was home. He may have spent the night with another woman, but he came home to us.

In middle school, I started to understand the problem. Imani's boyfriend, Robert, asked her to the Halloween dance. She was excited and tried on every dress at a local shop while I watched her model them. On the day of the dance, Robert said he had to help his parents with something, and he couldn't go to the dance.

It disappointed Imani, but she told him she'd be okay. She told him she planned to spend the night watching scary movies with me.

That evening, we settled onto her couch with a movie in mind, but I could tell she was upset. I suggested we go to the dance, and Imani lit up at the opportunity to wear the dress she'd purchased.

When we got there, we received a few awkward stares but brushed it off. We went out on the dance floor and noticed Robert with his arms around another girl.

Imani was furious! I used every ounce of strength in my tiny body, but I couldn't tug her off the dance floor. After she'd called Robert some things I'd never repeat, it took three teachers to drag her outside.

They called our parents, and my father rode with Dr. John to pick us up. They listened to the teachers, assuring the outraged women they would deal harshly with us. Once in the car, though, Imani gave them our side of the story, and they laughed. They had no plans to punish us. Imani's father seemed pleased with her.

"That boy deserved everything he got," he'd said.

My father had nodded along, and the irony struck me like a foul ball. *Why was it okay for him to cheat on my mother, but he didn't want anyone to cheat on my friend or me?*

I debated it loosely in my mind over the next few weeks as my father's overnight adventures grew more frequent. He'd always say he was playing poker in a bar, and then he'd stay gone all night. When I'd heard them argue about his absences, my father blamed his cheating on getting too drunk to remember anything.

Over the years, we'd had poker games at our house when we needed a little extra money. My father loved the game and thrived in the atmosphere, often winning every match he played. I formed a plan, and one evening after my parents had fought until they had no energy left, I proposed my idea.

I suggested making our sporadic poker nights at the house a weekly event. My father gathered the players, my mother threw together the food, and Barton and I ran out for anything they needed, except alcoholic beverages, of course.

It was a great idea, and it would keep my father out of bars. My parents agreed to try it and were pleased with the way it took shape. The extra money didn't hurt either.

My parent's relationship improved, and there was less fighting. My father may have cheated on my mother a few times after our family's poker nights started, but I never heard about it.

Like any other child, I wanted my family to stay together, and I would have done anything to make that happen. Even at seventeen, I still tried to hold on to a family that had fallen apart long before I knew it.

Chapter 13

"No, you're the cutest," Imani told Garrett as he hugged her before class.

I steadied my laptop under my arm and tried not to roll my eyes or throw up in my mouth. Owen grinned at me, but I pretended to drop my pencil.

"I think they're sweet," he commented, making me face my friends' public display of affection. "It would be nice to have someone who liked you."

I startled. *Did he mean no one liked me?*

Owen saw my expression and colored. "I mean, I'd like to have someone feel that way about me. I'm sure lots of people feel that way about you."

He was tripping over his words, and it entertained me. I let him keep talking, restraining myself from saying anything to ease his discomfort.

"Maybe lots of people don't like you, or maybe they do, but if the right one likes you—"

Garrett and Imani had been staring at us since Owen had started his doomed dialogue. Garrett and I seemed equally amused by it.

"Just ask her out already!" Imani said.

I saved Owen the trouble by muttering something about getting to class and walking away. I was happy to escape the embarrassment, but I wondered what I'd say if Owen had asked me out.

He was marginally attractive, and kind of nice, but he went through girlfriends like water through his hands. I wasn't willing to be heartbroken just to say I'd had a boyfriend for a week.

As expected, Imani accosted me when she got to class. "Why did you run away? Owen's been trying to ask you out forever."

I raised my eyebrows. "Really? Because we've basically been alone together every time you and Garrett run off into the woods after school."

She blushed. "Anyway, you could at least give him a chance."

"I don't want to be dumped when a pretty blonde flashes him a smile," I answered.

"He's not really like that," Imani defended. "He only acts that way because—" She pressed her lips together. "Never mind. How's Sanders doin'?"

"About as well as you can expect," I told her. "I managed to get him to take a shower before the weekend, but my mother made me help her the last couple of days, so I didn't make it back to see him. I thought he'd be at school today, but he's not here."

"That explains why you ran off so fast," Imani said.

Catching her insinuation, I replied, "He's my cousin."

She raised her prettily penciled brows. "All I'm sayin' is that you have a weird relationship."

"He's my cousin," I repeated.

"Not by blood," she said. "Your aunt married his dad. She didn't adopt him until she had to."

I was in no mood to explain my family's dynamics or feelings about them, so I turned around and paid attention to the lecture. The material was dry, but it was better than Imani's attempts at matchmaking.

At lunch, I was left alone with Owen while Garrett took an extra-long time helping Imani pick out ice cream from the deep freezer. They peered through the clear glass as if she was going to select something that wasn't a strawberry shortcake ice cream.

Owen stared at me the entire time they were gone. I people-watched, looking at a boy sitting next to the trash can and shifting my gaze to a group of girls taking selfies with their food.

After a deep sigh, Owen moved onto the seat next to me. "Will you be my girlfriend?"

I swallowed a bunch of air and tried not to choke on it. No one asked another person out that way. It was old-fashioned and endearing, and I couldn't think of an answer. It caught me off-guard because even though I thought he might ask me out, I didn't think Owen would be so direct.

The air I'd swallowed filled my lungs, and saliva tickled down the wrong pipe. I started coughing and ran out of the lunchroom to the nearest bathroom. Imani joined me as soon as I got my coughing fit under control.

She put her arm around me. "Do you need me to do anything? I could get you some water."

"I'm okay."

She hadn't witnessed the situation, so she was skeptical about my motives. "Was it an excuse to get away from Owen?"

"Not really," I said. "It was a happy accident, though."

She pressed her lips. "Do you like him?"

I pretended to think about it. "Maybe. I told you, remember? I don't want to be his flavor of the week."

"You really are blind, aren't you?"

The buzzer sounded over the intercom, indicating our lunch period was over, so I didn't have the chance to ask my friend what she meant. I followed her out of the bathroom.

Garrett was waiting for us, and he wrapped his arms around Imani before a passing teacher threatened them with detention. Thankfully, Owen had gone to his next class.

I didn't know what I'd say to him the next time we were alone, but I hoped he'd move on and forget about me, just like he did after the football game when I'd almost let him kiss me.

Sanders didn't answer the door when I went to his house after school, and I was worried. Once I was home, I texted him, and he sent back a message right away. He told me he hadn't heard me when I'd knocked, and he asked me to walk to school with him the next morning.

My mother kept steady tabs on me, so I left for school early, walking in the direction of the school. After she could no longer see me out of the windows, I turned through my great-aunt's yard and hiked up the hill.

Sanders and Crystal were arguing, and the door was ajar, so I walked inside. Crystal stood on her rug, her rockets in a circle around her. Sanders waved his finger at her, but his tone was defeated.

"Can't you just choose one to take with you?"

Crystal crossed her arms. "No."

I rushed in to help. I made sure I had Crystal's attention before I addressed her, so as soon as her brown eyes met mine, I appealed to her.

"I love all your rockets. Can you tell me about them?"

She discussed each of them with technicalities I only pretended to understand. I urged her to tell me if her mother had purchased any of them for her.

She held up an American rocket with the country's flag on the side. "This one."

I waited for a story to follow, but Crystal didn't elaborate. She clutched it to her chest, hugging it fiercely.

"Do you think you could take that rocket today?" I asked.

She nodded. "And the rest of them."

Sanders let out a frustrated sigh behind me. "And here we go again."

I reached inside for the patience I usually reserved for Pickles's tantrums. "If you bring all the rockets, the other children will want to play with them."

Her eyebrows went up. "Only three people touch my rockets."

I guessed that those three people weren't her classmates. I kept urging her.

"If you brought one rocket like you usually do, the other kids would know it was your special toy."

She nodded. "And Lucy Havenshaw will keep her hands off it?"

"Yes," I told her, hoping little Lucy wouldn't prove me wrong.

Crystal stepped out of her circle of rockets and allowed Sanders to slip her backpack onto her shoulders. It was warm enough to go outside without a jacket, and the dogwood blooms were full. Crystal's school was right below ours, so we walked her to the front door.

Crystal needed a routine to function well. Otherwise, she would get upset and lash out at anyone who tried to help her. Thankfully, Sanders and I usually walked her to school, so her morning wasn't disrupted. Sanders had called ahead, and the school had sent an aide to watch Crystal as she walked to her classroom.

Sanders kissed his sister once on her head and told her, "Have a good day."

Crystal was expressionless as she slumped into the school. The aide waved at us and followed her without letting Crystal know he was there. I was grateful for his discretion. Crystal could probably make her way to class like she did every day, but it gave Sanders peace of mind to know she had arrived in her classroom safely on the first day she had gone back to school. The people who worked in special education understood the value of little things, and a child's perceived independence was one of them.

"Egg!"

I turned quickly and saw Pickles waving his arm at me as he jumped down the bus steps. There was a section of grass separating the unloading zones for bus and car riders, but my brother was ready to speed across it. I held up my hand to stop him and signaled I would go to him.

"Sand Man!" Pickles said, curling his fingers and bumping them against Sanders's fist.

"Hey, Pickles," Sanders returned. "Are you ready for school?"

Pickles bobbed his head. "I guess so. Margie Willis gets to bring her pet frog to class today."

"That'll be fun," Sanders said.

"Hey, Pickles," I interjected. "Please don't tell Mama that you saw me with Sanders. She's kind of weird when it comes to me hanging out with him right now."

"Because Sanders told the police that Daddy killed her sister."

Sanders wasn't fazed by my brother's boldness. "Yeah."

"Okay," Pickles responded, shifting the weight of his backpack from one shoulder to the other. "I'm good at keeping secrets. I keep them all the time."

I tried not to think about my brother's words when Sanders and I hurried to our school, but they itched my brain in a place I couldn't scratch. *Were they just an embellishment of a boy who was told not to tell our father when our mother burned the biscuits, or was he keeping a more coveted secret?*

School dragged by, especially my third-period class, as Sanders and I had different math classes. I was doing well in my third-level algebra class, but he was the best student in trigonometry.

Sanders could see figures in his head, and he had notebooks full of numbers. He'd come up with math problems and solve them for fun. His excellence in math had earned him a spot at the University of Tennessee, or UT to the people who followed the athletes more than the achievements of the university.

I had always loved math, but my cousin's achievements in the subject overshadowed mine. I wanted to get a mathematics degree, but Sanders was already considered the math genius in the family, and my father expected me to own a business one day, so I didn't argue when my father told me to pursue a business degree when I went to college. I still longed for days surrounded by numbers, though, as sometimes, they seemed to be the only constants.

Imani was across the room from me, as the teacher had arranged our seats at the beginning of the term, and she had known we were friends. Garrett took the seat at the front of the room, but Owen sat at the desk beside me.

He kept flipping glances at me, and I successfully avoided them until he put a note on my desk. It was impossible to ignore, so I opened it and read the only two lines he'd written: *I'm sorry for making you choke when I asked you out. I won't do it again.*

He stared at me until I acknowledged him. I nodded once, as it was the only reaction I could give him.

When class was over, Owen drifted out before Garrett caught up to him. He shot me an accusatory look.

"Why'd you break his heart?"

I matched his pace into the hall and Imani joined us. She tapped her laptop, waiting for my answer.

"I didn't break his heart," I defended. "I didn't respond to him, and he took it back."

Imani narrowed her eyes. "He took it back?"

"Yeah. He said he wouldn't ask me out again." I held up the note for proof.

Imani snatched it out of my hand. Garrett smiled as he read it.

"You know," he said, "the way I see it, he only said he promised he won't make you choke again."

I rolled my eyes. "I think we both know what he meant."

Garret rubbed his smooth chin. "Nope. I know my boy, Owen, and he's not gonna let you get away."

Chapter 14

My father was already in the visitation room waiting for me. I was relieved when I saw him on the screen, and I grabbed the receiver off the wall.

"Sheriff Watts told me I could have an extra visitation with you," I told him. "I don't know if I believed him before I saw you on the screen."

"Danny's a good man," my father said. "I trust him to keep his word."

"Did Uncle Barton's money come through?"

My father looked away. "Yeah. I've got a good card game goin' here, so I should be able to pay him back soon."

"I don't think he expects you to pay him back, Daddy."

My father leaned over in his chair. "A man is only as good as his word and the debts he leaves behind."

"What about a woman?" I chided.

"It's the same," he returned, spitting into a white styrofoam cup.

"They let you have tobacco in there?" I asked.

"Yeah," he said. "We can't tell nobody about it, but the sheriff lets us dip 'baccer if we don't make a mess."

"Then you must be doing better than I thought you were."

He smiled and extended his arms. "I can't complain about these five-star accommodations."

"Do you need anything?"

"Not that you can get me, sweetheart." He rubbed his jaw. "I got a tooth that's been botherin' me. You know, the one that kicks up about every couple of months."

I nodded. I remembered him talking about it, but my mother gave him peppermint tea and a saltwater rinse to help ease the pain.

"Do you want me to see if Mama can send in some of the tea?"

"No," he replied. "They won't let it through. And I'm not hurtin' too bad yet." He chuckled. "Who knows, maybe I'll be home soon."

"What did they say in court yesterday?"

My mother had been tight-lipped about the arraignment. She had been able to go, as Tonya had watched Si for her, and Pickles had been in school, but when I asked her what had happened, she'd ignored me.

"I have a bail." His laugh was dry and forced. "It's $500,000."

"What?"

He nodded along with my realization. "The judge thought he was doin' me a favor since I'm not a flight risk, but a bail bondsman will want ten percent of that figure. It looks like I'm stuck here until my trial."

"They don't have enough evidence to take your case to trial," I said, even though I didn't know what the district attorney had gathered against my father.

"They have plenty enough," he said, scrubbing his face with his hands.

"Look, Meg, you need to be ready to help your Mama when they send me down the river."

I understood the reference, but I was unwilling to accept it. "You're not going anywhere."

He leaned forward, attempting to stare into my eyes. "It's okay, sweetheart. Everything is going to be okay."

I shook my head. "No. Daddy. You sound like you've already given up, and you haven't been in jail for a week. Fight, and we'll fight with you. I'll fight with you."

He reached out and touched the glass in front of his screen. It was the closest he could get to me.

The door opened, signaling the end of our visit. I wished for more time, but all the seconds in the world wouldn't be enough.

"I love you, Meg," my father said as I protested the end of our visit. "I have to go back to my cell, but I'll see you on Friday when you visit me with your Mama. Take care of her and be a good example to your brothers."

He kissed two fingers and touched them to the glass. I cried, and the receiver fell from my hand as I watched him go.

Chapter 15

Even though they punished her every time her parents found out she'd seen Sara Beth, Mary Beth didn't give up on her sister. Her parents had told her to stay away from her sister, and they threatened to take away the new convertible they'd gotten for her, but my aunt didn't listen. She drove her shiny red car over to Dandy's trailer every day after school.

My mother was pregnant with Barton early in her marriage to Dandy, and Mary Beth took her to appointments. Dandy worked until well into the evening, so my aunt was present when the obstetrician detected my brother's heartbeat, and she held my mother's hand during the ultrasound that confirmed she was having a boy.

My aunt was overjoyed for my mother. She learned to sew and crafted my brother's first baby blanket. Barton still had the blue blanket with yellow bears folded in his closet.

Dandy wanted the baby to be named Daniel, after him, but my aunt disagreed. They argued, and Dandy threw Mary Beth out of his house. She returned the next day, though, with a box of glazed doughnuts for my mother's increased cravings, and she left before he got home.

When my mother started having labor pains, she couldn't find her husband. He wasn't at work or the bar. She called Mary Beth, but she couldn't reach her either. Finally, Uncle Barton answered her call and drove her to the hospital just in time to have the baby. He held her hand as my brother was born. My mother thought it was fitting to name him after my uncle, as he had been present at her son's birth, but she gave my brother his father's middle name.

Mary Beth showed up within minutes, dressed in her cheer uniform. My mother had forgotten her sister was at a game in a nearby county.

Mary Beth doted on my brother and didn't want to leave him. Uncle Barton promised to give their parents an excuse for Mary Beth's whereabouts, so she wouldn't be punished for seeing her nephew in the hospital.

Dandy came to the hospital that night, smelling like strong drink and women's perfume. My mother wouldn't let him hold the baby, but Dandy cried when he saw Barton. He promised to stop running around, and my mother did her best to believe him.

At first, Dandy was a doting father. He changed the baby's diapers and got up at night to pace the house when the baby needed gentle motions to stay asleep. But the baby needed more than a month or two of attention, and when my brother slept less and cried more, Dandy took longer to get home from work, often leaving my mother at home alone all weekend.

During the weekends when her sister was alone, Mary Beth lied to her parents and claimed she was staying with a friend. She helped my mother take care of the baby's needs and formed a strong bond with him.

Later, there was a great deal of distance between Mary Beth and my mother, but my mother never threw out the pictures she took of her sister playing with Barton. She stuffed the photos into the back of an old album, but they showed moments like when Mary Beth was at the hospital in a cheer uniform with red lipstick and teal eyeshadow holding a screaming infant, and her surprised face when my brother took his first steps. Among the pictures was one of my mother and aunt that Uncle Barton must have taken. In it, my mother looked tired and worn next to her sister's lively face. Both girls looked happy to be together, and there was an energy between them. Sadly, I'd never witnessed the spark.

One weekend, after working in another state, Dandy came home when my mother thought he'd stay away, and Mary Beth was on the couch. Thinking she was my mother, he lay down next to her. My aunt screamed, and my mother ran into the room with the handgun my uncle had given her for protection. Upon realizing his mistake, Dandy started laughing. He fell on the floor in his state, and the girls joined in on his mirth. After that instance, Mary Beth was welcome at his house. Dandy knew he couldn't keep the sisters apart.

One night, when he got home late, Mary Beth caught Dandy chopping a white substance onto a plate. Realizing it was a drug, she launched into him for doing drugs while his wife and child slept on the other end of the house. He offered her the plate and told her to try it. She hesitated, but my aunt finally gave in to the pressure.

Mary Beth's life changed. She dropped out of cheerleading, but she didn't tell her parents. She snuck money from them and gave it to Dandy so he could buy more drugs for her. They wrecked her car on the way back from a drug run, but my aunt could drive the car back home. Her parents paid to have the car fixed, but they grounded her. She sweated at night, and her moods were worse than usual. Her parents attributed it to teenage hormonal changes, but Mary Beth was experiencing the first signs of withdrawal.

She was supposed to go to school and stay home for three weeks, but after four days, my aunt called Dandy to pick her up. Late in the night, she climbed out her window and ran to the corner where he waited on his motorcycle. She took all the money she could find in the house, and no one saw them for a week.

My mother was spared from the gossip, as my grandparents covered their daughter's disappearance by claiming she was sick. Her car stayed in the driveway, so no one questioned them. Dandy was known to leave for long periods, so my mother had no idea her sister had run away with her husband until my grandparents showed up at her door.

Mary Beth had left them a note explaining that she was with Dandy, so they wouldn't call the police. My grandparents were concerned about their moral standing in the community, especially after one of their teenage daughters had gotten married and had a baby before she finished high school, so they were willing to search for Mary Beth privately.

My mother's parents blamed my mother, who was unaware Dandy was supplying her sister with drugs, for Mary Beth's new habit. She tried to appeal to my grandparents, but they rejected her attempts to reconcile with them.

A week later, my grandfather climbed the steps to my mother's door triumphantly. She was still moving slowly, as she was recovering from a miscarriage. When she opened it, he thrust pictures at her chest and walked away, chuckling.

When my mother called after him, he said, "We have our daughter back. You need to keep your husband away from her." More seriously, he added, "I hope he hasn't gotten her pregnant, too."

My mother stood at the door, holding the pictures to her chest, and stared as her father's Lincoln pulled out of her driveway. He had been long gone before she jolted back to reality and examined the pictures in her hand.

The first showed a seedy motel with busted doors and cracked windows. She recognized Dandy's motorcycle parked in front of one of the rooms. From an open door, a photograph had been snapped of Mary Beth and Dandy lying in bed together. Mercifully, the blanket covered any skin that might have been exposed, but my mother could only imagine what had taken place.

She thought about the drugs Mary Beth and Dandy had taken, and she concluded that her sister and husband had betrayed her. It was one thing for Dandy to be unfaithful to her with other women, but it was unforgivable for him to sleep with her sister.

When Dandy came home, he talked about quitting his job and looking for work closer to home, as if he thought my mother would never find out about his indiscretions. She listened to him speak about a new future they could share, but she hardened her heart against him.

She cooked his favorite meal, country-fried ham and grits, and drew a bath. After he had pushed his plate away and was settled on the couch, she laid out each picture her father had given her on the table, flipping each one against the wooden surface.

"It's over," she told him.

Dandy begged my mother not to leave him. He promised he had never cheated on her, and he said he'd come home every night from that point on.

"You won't have a choice," my mother had responded. "I poisoned your ham and grits."

Uncle Barton had told me the story, and I'd had him repeat it a couple of times. My mother never spoke about her first husband, and my brother was too young to remember a time when his father was in his life, so my uncle was the only one who'd freely discussed Dandy Hughes with me.

My uncle would laugh when he'd tell that part of the story, and the first time he'd relayed it, he'd made an excuse to get a soda, so I'd have to wait for the conclusion. Back then, I didn't know Barton's father was in federal prison, so I'd imagined a body buried in the backyard or thrown into the Nolichucky River before my uncle finally resumed his story.

My mother didn't poison her husband's food, but she scared him into thinking she had done it. She stood stone-faced as he tried to get her to admit she was joking. He felt sleepy, either from the suggestion he had been poisoned or the effects of his week-long drug binge with Mary Beth. He was so scared that he jumped on his bike and raced to the emergency room.

Dandy waited for several hours before he was seen by the doctor. He demanded that they pump his stomach because his wife had poisoned him, but the doctor assured him he would have already felt the effects of the poison within the five-hour time frame since he had eaten.

Dandy confronted my mother, but he did it carefully. She admitted to lying about the poison, and they seemed to make up. He thought his wife had gotten back at him and they could move on. Dandy believed he had his family back, so he resumed his usual activities.

The police arrested him within three days, and I know who called them.

Chapter 16

I was extra snappy with my mother that night. My father had wanted me to be good to her and look out for my brothers, but who looked out for me?

I stewed on my feelings until Sanders messaged me. He wanted me to go with him to drop off Crystal at school the next morning. I didn't know why he kept asking me, as I'd done it every day, but I replied that I'd be at his house at the same time the next morning.

Crystal had been easier to manage after the first morning, simply taking the same rocket to school every day. I was glad I'd helped establish a comfortable routine for her and given Sanders some peace on school mornings.

I was about to fall asleep when my phone vibrated. I had to look twice before I realized it was a video call from Owen.

My brothers were already snoring in the dark room, so I hurried into Barton's room and shut the door, leaning against it. I accepted Owen's call, and his face filled my screen.

"Did I wake you up?" he asked, his eyebrows meeting.

"Uh, no." It was only nine o'clock, so I didn't want him to think I had no social life. "I was just reading."

"Oh." He looked away, and I hoped he wouldn't ask me out again.

"Do you need something?" I tried to smile, but it felt forced.

That seemed to inspire him. "Yeah! I need some help with algebra. Could I pay you to tutor me?"

Normally, I would have rejected the offer. It would be hard to balance my studies at the end of the term and be responsible for someone else's learning, but my family needed money, and my father had asked me to take care of them.

"Sure. When do you need me to tutor you?"

His mouth formed a line as he thought about his answer. "I could probably use the help any time you're free."

"Things are a little weird right now," I said, seeing understanding in his eyes when I'd expected bewilderment.

"Don't be mad," he hedged.

"You already know," I guessed.

He nodded.

"Did you find out from Garrett's dad?"

"Well, Garrett told me, so I guess his dad told him."

I couldn't hide my irritation and hated we were on a video call. My silence would have been telling enough, but I wasn't good at camouflaging my reactions.

"People will find out anyway," he said, and I narrowed my eyes before he added, "But I didn't want to hide it from you that I knew."

I thought about what he'd said. He could have acted like Garrett and kept silent while secretly spreading my family's business to others, but he had taken a risk and explained how he knew about my difficulties.

"I'm here if you want to talk about it," he continued, "but it's cool if you want to avoid it."

Barton barged through the door, knocking me over. I spilled onto the floor and barely caught my phone as it slipped from my fingers.

"What are you doing in here?" he demanded.

"The boys are in bed. I came in here for some privacy."

"Privacy," he remarked slowly, stroking his stubbly chin. "Why would you need privacy?"

He lunged to look at the face on the phone and I turned the screen over. He grabbed my arms and wrestled the phone away.

"Who is little Meg's boyfriend?" he sing-songed as he pried the phone out of my hand.

I don't think Owen could see my horror as I tried to grab my phone. Barton extended it, raising it just beyond my reach. I wasn't much shorter than him, but he'd stretched another inch or so over the winter months.

"So, who do we have here?" he asked Owen.

Owen told my brother his name and explained that he was my friend. For his part, Owen was casually cool about Barton's interference.

Barton almost cackled. "You're Meg's *friend*, huh? I'd only want to be her friend, too, after I found out she used to suck her big toe while she watched cartoons."

"Barton!" I yelled at him.

My brother held a finger to his lips. "Now, hush. You don't want to wake up the kids."

I used his arm as leverage and climbed up his other arm far enough to knock my phone out of his hand. It fell on his bed, and I snatched it before he could pick it up.

I ran out of the room. "I'll talk to you tomorrow," I said quickly before ending the call.

Barton chased me into the living room, where our mother sat with a pen and notebook. She wrote letters to my father in the evenings and mailed them the following morning. It was her way of keeping him up to date with the family's progress.

"Barton took my phone," I told her.

"I did not," Barton defended. "She's holding it."

Having an uncle and namesake for a lawyer had helped him develop his defenses. Leave it to him to focus on the technicalities.

I glared at my brother. "I have it now, but I had to wrestle it away from you while I was trying to talk to..."

I didn't finish my sentence, and my mother understood the reason. "If Meg has a boyfriend, you shouldn't make fun of her for it. Don't you have a girlfriend?"

"Well, yeah," he responded. "But I'm not a little girl."

"Neither is your sister."

He laughed as if he didn't believe her and backed into his room. He forced a haughty chuckle before he shut the door.

"Brothers," I said, shaking my head.

"Don't I know it," my mother returned.

"You and Uncle Barton have a great relationship. I'll bet you guys never fought like that."

"Only because he didn't live with our parents for long after I was born. He still tried to control my life, though."

I motioned to the notebook in her lap. "Can I add a letter to it?"

"Sure," she said, closing the notebook. "Just put it on the counter tomorrow, and I'll send it.

"Mama?"

She raised her eyebrows. It was my chance to have a serious conversation with her, but I was emotionally exhausted.

"Is it about the boy on the phone?" she tried.

I wanted to talk about so much more. I wished she would share her secrets with me, the ones people had already told me and the ones no one knew. But I understood my mother, and she had her boundaries. They were like thick walls of cement block that surrounded her.

"Yeah." I looked at the floor and moved my toe across it. "He wants me to tutor him."

She smiled indulgently. "Isn't that the way it always starts?"

"He's offered to pay me."

Her smile vanished. "Oh."

"I want to help out."

She pulled at her shirt, straightening the wrinkles. "I wish I could tell you we didn't need it, but—"

"I know, Mama."

She closed her eyes for a few seconds before she spoke. "You can use the dining room after school. I'll keep the boys in another part of the house or take them outside."

I thanked her and hurried back to my room. I typed a message to Owen, asking if we could start the next day. His reply was instant.

"I guess I have a job," I said in the dark. And then, for no particular reason, I rolled onto my side and cried myself to sleep.

Chapter 17

The cry I'd had the previous night had helped clear some emotional stress for me. I felt a little lighter as I grabbed Crystal's hand and walked her to school. Sanders popped his gum until I threatened to rip his tongue out, and I thought I saw Crystal smile when he spit it out.

The aide had stopped following her to class, and Sanders didn't seem to worry about his sister's emotional state. He waved at her until she went through the double doors, but his face fell as soon as she was out of sight.

He put his arm around me as we walked up the hill to our school. I waited for him to speak, but he stayed silent. I tried to think about how I'd feel if my mother had been killed. *Would I want to talk about it, or would I stay in my thoughts where I could remember her without people pushing their condolences on me?*

Before letting go of me, Sanders whispered, "Mom had her faults, but she loved you."

We sat down at our desks. I positioned myself near the back of the room where I wasn't right under the teacher's nose, and Sanders liked to sit next to me. Owen was behind me, but he didn't offer morning salutations. I was ultra-aware of him, though, as I knew we'd spend the afternoon together.

Imani talked to Sanders about Crystal and asked if there was anything she could do to help him. She had said the same thing to Sanders every morning he'd been at school, but it didn't seem as strange as it would if I had said it. Sanders and I were so close that I was expected to know what he needed and do it.

"Your family has done so much already," he replied. "My mother's casket is beautiful, and Crystal could have finished your father's meatloaf by herself." He rubbed his stomach. "It was so good!"

Imani smiled benignly. She didn't mind receiving accolades for her father when it came to his cooking, but she tried to humble herself when people mentioned her family's money.

Imani could have worn designer clothes, but she preferred shopping at thrift stores and celebrated with me when I found a deal online. She understated her beauty with neutral prints and muted colors. The only feature she exemplified was her full lips. She lined them in plum and moistened them frequently with lip gloss.

Imani's father was a surgeon. They lived in a five-bedroom log cabin near the woods on the other side of Tipton Hill. It was easy for them to walk to my house every Friday night for my father's poker nights.

Even though it was a light class day, Owen didn't talk to me until third period. I had been especially hungry, so I thought eating had loosened our tongues and improved our moods.

"Are you walking or riding the bus back?" Owen asked.

"I thought I'd walk back home with Sanders and wait for Crystal at the bus stop."

"Oh," he replied, losing the momentum of his mood for a moment and then picking it back up. "I could drive you home."

I admitted that Owen's plan made better sense, as he would either be waiting for me at my house or killing time until I got home if I walked home with Sanders. I agreed to meet him in the senior's parking lot after school.

"I hope it'll be okay with Sanders," he mentioned.

Imani threw him a look I couldn't read. *What was I missing?*

I decided Owen was referencing Sanders's need for extra attention since his mother's passing. "He can probably do without me for one afternoon," I returned, expecting everyone to smile and nod. Instead, Imani raised her eyebrows at Owen and sighed.

After class, I asked Imani what I had missed. She waited until we were surrounded by people who weren't trying to listen to our conversation.

"Girl, you miss everything. Owen likes you!"

"I know. But why was everyone acting so weird about Sanders?"

She put her arm around me, and we walked toward our last class. "You may not see it, but for cousins, you and Sanders have a weird relationship."

"I treat him like any other friend," I defended.

Her curls bobbed as she agreed with me. "Yeah, you do. But Sanders acts like you're his girlfriend. He walked into class this morning with his arm around you. He's just really possessive."

There were times when I'd felt the same way. I laughed and brushed off her comment.

"You have your arm around me now. Does that mean I'm your girlfriend?" I batted my eyes playfully.

Imani nudged me into a locker. "You're cute, but you have too many mommy issues for me."

We laughed at our inside joke. I knew it was Imani's way of deflecting her situation. Sure, my mother and I had our differences, but Imani's mother left her family when Imani was a toddler, opting for a life of drugs over spending time with her husband and daughter.

Imani and I parted ways at our lockers, and Sanders joined me. He had chosen the locker above mine and helped me to my feet after I'd gathered my notebook and pen for my last class.

"I think I'm going to try my hand at lasagna today," he mused. "At some point, I'm going to have to start cooking something besides macaroni and cheese for Crystal."

He put his arm around my shoulder, and I remembered what Imani had said about our closeness. I pretended to drop my pencil, and when I picked it up, I moved a little farther away from him. I tried to measure my cousin's reaction, and he seemed unaffected by my maneuver.

"I have plans after school," I told him. "I've started tutoring for extra money."

Sanders seemed crestfallen. "Could you come over after you're finished? You could help us eat the lasagna."

"I doubt my mama will let me out the door to go to your house, but I'll try."

His chest puffed up, and he imitated an Italian accent, but his country twang made the result rise and fall. "I will attempt to make it a culinary treat, but it may be a delicious disaster."

Our laughter was louder than we'd intended, and it echoed down the almost empty hall. It was the first time we'd shared a joke since Mary Beth's death, but it felt right.

Chapter 18

"My parents made me buy my car," Owen said as an apology. His passenger side door creaked when he opened it for me, and his door joined the chorus when he climbed inside.

The car was a silver, mid-sized box shape, with a cracked taillight and a missing bumper. When Owen started it, the smell of oil covered the staleness of the interior.

My feet were the only way I went anywhere, so I shrugged. "It's a better car than I have."

I pointed down the roads that led to my house, and we were there within minutes. On the way, we passed Sanders as he walked next to the ballfield, and I felt a pain in my heart. He'd just lost his mother. *Shouldn't I be spending as much time as possible with him?*

"This is a nice place," Owen said when he opened my door.

My mother was staring at us from the kitchen window, and Si waved his entire arm in greeting. I felt like I should warn Owen before he met my family.

"Watch out for Pickles."

His eyebrows drew together. "Pickles?"

"His name is Archimedes, but my father started calling him Pickles when he found him in the pantry drinking pickle juice."

He held out an arm for me to link mine around. "Okay, Meg. I'll watch out for Pickles."

"And my real name is Megara," I went on. "My mother won't call me anything other than my full name."

Owen seemed skeptical. "But she calls your brother Pickles?"

"It started as a joke and kind of stuck," I explained.

"Is Pickles the one in the window?"

I shook my head. "He's Poseidon, but we call him Si. Mama will walk down to the bus stop to get Pickles soon. The bus can't come up here." I motioned to the road we'd just traveled. "It's a little too narrow."

Just before he opened the screen door for me, he whispered, "And I knew your name was Megara. The teachers say it every year before you tell them to shorten it."

Owen had been in school with me since my early elementary years. Of course he'd heard my full name mentioned.

My mother's good Southern manners took over when she met Owen, and within less than five minutes, he had a piece of pound cake and a glass of sweet tea in front of him. Once we sat at the table, my mother asked Owen about his family, attempting to make connections.

"I think I went to school with your mother."

"It's possible," Owen said, forking a piece of pound cake. "This is really good, Mrs. Tipton."

"Mrs. Tipton was my mother-in-law. You can call me Sara." She nodded to the cake he had almost finished. "And the secret to my pound cake is sour cream."

"How much do you use?"

"That's the secret," she replied, pushing her nose like a button. "You'll have to be family before I'll tell you."

Owen looked over at me as if it could be a possibility in the future, and my stomach did a nosedive. I was glad my mother hadn't given me a piece of cake, or it would have rolled over in my belly.

After watching our exchange, my mother said, "I'm going to the bus stop to get Pickles. We'll go into the living room when we get back. Hopefully, that'll be the only distraction you'll have while you're here."

We opened our laptops, and I helped Owen with the most current assignment. He listened to me attentively, and we were most of the way through our homework when Pickles charged through the door.

He dropped his bag and stared at Owen before saluting him. "Who are you, soldier?"

My mother walked in behind him and put Si on the floor. "I told you, son. Megara is doing business with one of her classmates. He's paying her to help him with his work."

Owen returned my brother's salute. "I'm Owen, sir."

Pickles made a show of walking around his chair. "You like my sister."

I tried to say something to counteract my brother's assessment, but my lips were locked. I thought I might pass out from embarrassment and hoped my mother would rescue me.

"I do," Owen admitted. "But she won't let me date her, so this is the only way I can spend time with her."

My mother blushed. I don't know what color I turned, but I'm sure it was somewhere between crimson and purple.

"We need to let Megara and Owen finish their schoolwork, so we're going to do your homework in the living room," my mother instructed Pickles.

"I don't have homework," Pickles told her. "I want to stay and talk to Owen."

"I'm sure you do, but I promised your sister we'd leave her alone, so we're going into the living room."

When her back was turned, Pickles snaked his tongue out at her. She glanced over her shoulder, and he shrugged as if he'd done nothing.

Owen and I finished the assignment within an hour. He wasn't a hopeless student, but it seemed he hadn't picked up some foundational concepts on which the class was built. When I asked him about it, he nodded along.

"I played basketball this season, and I was busy. Usually, after football is over, I can relax and spend more time on my homework." He rubbed his arms. "I didn't expect to have to practice all the time."

"I heard Coach Williams is brutal," I said.

"Yeah. She made us do layups until Joey passed out."

I opened my mouth a little to show I was shocked but wasn't surprised. Joey weighed less than everyone on the team and needed to eat more often. Any extended practice could have caused his blood sugar to plummet.

"You're caught up for now," I said, motioning to his completed work. "We can probably wait to meet again until a couple of days before the end-of-term tests."

He grinned at me sheepishly. "Actually, I'm not caught up."

I raised one of my eyebrows, a trick I'd learned from my mother.

"I'm behind on a couple of assignments," he admitted.

"How many?"

"Five or six."

"You haven't done over a week's worth of assignments!" I'd been louder than I'd intended.

Owen hung his head. "Am I a lost cause?"

I looked at the situation practically. "Did the teacher give you an extension?"

He grimaced. "Yeah."

"For how long?"

"I have until next week."

I put my head on the table and wrapped my arms around it. Sighing deeply, I realized Owen required my help. He may have wanted a way to spend more time with me, but he truly needed me to tutor him.

I lifted my head and met his eyes. "We'll have to meet over the weekend."

"That's okay with me." A smile spread across his face and revealed a hardly noticeable dimple. He dropped his smile when I didn't return it. "I don't have anything to do, so I can come over anytime."

"Okay," I said. I uncrossed my arms and wondered when I had crossed them. It was something I'd seen my mother do when she talked to my father after one of his wilder poker nights.

"Do you want to start one of the lessons now?" he asked.

As if on cue, my mother opened the door to the den and Si and Pickles ran after her. She dropped to the floor to put on my youngest brother's shoes, and Pickles leaned on her back.

"We have a visitation scheduled with my dad," I told him.

"Oh, okay." Owen grabbed his laptop and notebook in one swift movement. Before he left, he carried his glass and plate to the sink.

"I like your manners, Owen," my mother remarked. "Please give my best to your mother."

I walked Owen to his car, and my brothers dancing around my legs made it less awkward to tell him goodbye. He waved at us as he backed out of the driveway.

I made a conscious effort not to look in the direction his car had gone, and I denied the flutter I felt in my stomach when I thought about spending the weekend helping him.

Chapter 19

My brothers and I were sent out of the visitation booth after only ten minutes. It would have been less if Pickles hadn't regaled our father with the story of a chicken that chased him at the bus stop.

My mother had spent some time acquainting herself with my father's charges. After his arraignment, they were publicly recorded, and our neighbors would know about them as early as the following week when our town's newspaper was printed.

Even though I knew my father had been charged with her murder, it was still unclear how my aunt had died. The charges didn't specify a murder weapon, so I'd have to look for a way to ask Sanders or my Uncle Barton about it. Both had been close to my aunt, but they were my best chance of gaining information without a guilt trip or damaged feelings.

Each of the children had spoken with our father, starting with Si and ending with me. My mother had taken the phone from me gently, and I thought we were going to have a pleasant visit. However, I knew any chance of salvaging our family time was gone when she spoke.

"Why did you do this to your family?"

My father had been staring at his shoes, but upon hearing my mother's words, he stood swiftly. The chair slid out from behind him with such force that it toppled over.

I braced myself to witness more physical reactions, but he noticed the eyes of his children on him, and my father's muscles relaxed. He said seven words, picked up his chair, and sat on it with his arms crossed.

"Take your brothers to play," my mother told me.

"I don't like it out there," Pickles whined.

My mother picked him up with the arm that wasn't holding Si and placed both boys outside. She held the door open for me to follow them.

I wasn't worried about missing their conversation. It had more to do with my mother's emotions than real information. I sat down on the sidewalk, still warm from the springtime rays, and watched Pickles catch ants and Si study small rocks in the landscaping.

"Kicked out again?"

I looked up from my place on the sidewalk and met Sheriff Watts's eyes. He was tired, but it seemed like he was more overstressed than overworked. Maybe they were the same, though.

"I think they needed some privacy."

I could tell he'd misread my meaning by the way his eyes widened. "Oh."

"No," I said hurriedly. "Mama got Daddy started, and he didn't want us to see them fight."

"Say no more." He spit tobacco juice into a white cup. "Your Mama could always push his buttons."

I remembered some of their arguments from my youth. Over the years, they had gotten better at hiding their disagreements from us, going out in the garage or garden to raise their voices.

My mother came out of the room and slammed the door. She'd been crying, but when she saw Sheriff Watts, she raised her head.

"Hello, Sara Beth."

"I think he wants to go back now," she said without returning his greeting.

"But there's fifteen minutes left," I protested.

"Why don't you go talk to him?" Sheriff Watts suggested. "It might calm him down before I have to deal with him." He looked back at my mother. "Besides, I need to talk to your mama."

I jumped up and bolted into the visitation room. I didn't want my father to get the attention of one of the deputies and leave the visitation room before I could see him.

My father lifted his head when he saw movement on the screen. He unclenched his fists and picked up the receiver.

"Hey, Meg."

I tried to think of something to cheer him up, but I drew a blank. We'd spend hours together without talking, but in our new situation, the conversation was necessary.

"I didn't want to lose any time with you."

I tried to force my tears back, but they slipped down my cheeks. The screen became a blurry black-and-white image, but I saw my father put his hand on the glass in front of the screen.

"I'm sorry it's been so hard on you, sweetheart."

"I'm okay," I choked out. "I just miss you so much."

"I know, but you have to stay strong for your mama and brothers. Your mama's a firecracker and her fuse is short. I don't want you guys to get burned."

My father was a simple man who had barely completed high school. He was a hard worker and placed more value on physical achievements than mental accomplishments. He still had a way with words, though, and I loved when he used metaphors. He had a shelf of poetry books at home, and my mother claimed he had a notebook of his own poetic verses, too.

"I think I might be fizzled out," I said, extending the metaphor.

He acknowledged my admission with a nod and changed the subject. "Has anyone checked on Crystal and Sanders?"

"I've been helping Sanders with Crystal, and Imani's dad sent some food."

I left out the part about the casket. I didn't want to upset him when we had only a few minutes together.

"That's good," he answered. "There's some money in a jar behind the wood pile. You'll need to watch for snakes but get the jar out and give it to them."

I was confused. "Shouldn't I give it to Mama?"

He looked at me as though I should be able to answer my question. "Your mama is a capable woman. Sanders and Crystal are children, and they need our help."

"But Sanders is eighteen, and he has a—"

"When did you get so greedy, Meg?"

His soft-spoken words were like a slap. I tried to recover from it, but I had to forget he had said it before I could talk again.

"Okay."

I reached for another topic of conversation. I could only think of the most basic subjects.

"How are your teeth?"

He sucked his tongue through his mouth like he did when he was bluffing in poker. "Most of my teeth are okay, but one of 'ums givin' me the devil."

"Can they take you to the dentist?"

"I think they made an appointment for next week," he answered, smiling. "At least I'll get my tooth fixed on Uncle Sam's dime!"

I laughed along with him. I was glad his mood had seemed to lift a little.

The same tooth had bothered my father for a little over a year. He had ignored the pain, as it cost too much for him to visit the dentist.

Fifteen minutes passed faster when I was with my father. Sheriff Watts collected him and waved at me through the screen. I had conflicting feelings about the sheriff, but I waved back. It was better to make him think I still liked him.

My mother was waiting for me with the boys strapped into the stroller. When I stepped out, she started walking. I caught up to her easily, but she didn't speak. I waited a couple of blocks before I asked her why Sheriff Watts had wanted to talk to her.

"He offered me a job," she responded briskly.

"At the jail?"

The side of my mother's mouth went up in irritation. "Not at that jail," she answered. "At the women's correctional facility on the other side of town."

My mother had been looking for jobs online, but even with her precise pronunciation and good phone skills, she couldn't find work. She obtained her GED when I was a young girl, but she didn't have work experience.

"What did you tell him?"

My mother's hands tightened around the stroller's handle. "I told him I would take the job."

"But you'd have to walk there, and who would watch the kids?"

She stopped the stroller. "I'll ask Tonya to watch Si until school is out, but I'll need you to look after your brothers when you get out of school."

I wondered if my mother had made plans for my brothers' care beyond the end of summer, but I decided it didn't matter. Surely, my father would be out of jail before Labor Day.

She took my silence as acceptance. Another thought sprang to my mind.

"What will you be doing?"

Her voice was lighter as she explained that Sheriff Watts wanted her to be a cook. "There's a more technical term for it, but I forgot what he called it."

"It's probably a food technician," I remarked.

I meant to simply pass on the information but was caught by the humor of the phrase. "It's not like you're working on the mechanics of the food."

"That's a lot like what I'm going to be doing," came her curt reply.

I was instantly chastised. I had belittled my mother's first work opportunity to lighten the mood and had offended her. I quickly thought of a way to help ease the tension and repeated one of my father's favorite phrases.

"You're right."

We walked on in silence. Cars zoomed past us, some yelling comments at us that the wind whipped away before they met our ears.

"How are you going to get to work?" I asked.

My mother looked at her feet. "I will walk there."

My father would have worked twelve jobs before he would have let my mother walk to work. Not only was the road between our house and the correctional facility dangerous, but she'd have to endure the extreme heat and unpredictable rains of summer.

"Couldn't Barton take you?"

She shook her head. "My shift is a little later, and I'm not going to bother him with it."

"How would it bother him? He lives in the house with us."

My mother set her jaw. "Your brother helps pay the bills, and I'm not going to ask for anything more from him."

The subject was closed as far as she was concerned. I wondered why she was so upset with my suggestion, and I decided it was because she had a closer relationship with Barton. She wouldn't want to risk him moving out by placing another burden on him.

My mother couldn't take Barton to work and drive to her job, as his shift sometimes ended before she'd leave. She didn't have a license, so she didn't get behind the wheel often.

My father had wanted to teach her more about the road, but she'd always declined. They'd only had a car for about eight years of my life, and my father drove to work in it, so there was never really a need for my mother to learn to obtain a license.

"We should be able to pay the light bill with the money Owen is giving me."

I had hoped to restore my mother's spirits or make her proud of me, but she rolled her eyes. "And this will be the only month you can do it. You graduate in two weeks, and no one will need to be tutored over the summer."

"I could get a job," I suggested.

"You have one," my mother returned. "You're watching your brothers over the summer, and in the fall, you can arrange your school classes around my work schedule."

I didn't respond. I hadn't planned to live at home while I went to college, but my mother assumed I was going to the local university. Sanders and I wanted to attend college in Knoxville. It was two hours away, and I'd have to live on campus.

I had applied to four colleges. In my eagerness to please my mother, I filled out the application for East Tennessee State University, or ETSU, but also applied for the University of Tennessee and two other colleges. One of them was well-known for its business school, and even though ETSU had an accredited business college, the other college specialized in finance.

As we neared the house, I scanned the road for snakes. I thought I saw the shadow of a man dart behind Widow Silvers's house, but I decided it was a product of my tired mind and the experience we'd had the last time we'd visited my father together.

Besides, who would watch us, and why would they want to?

Chapter 20

I was asleep before Barton came home from work, but I was glad to see the marshmallow cereal he'd brought home with him when I woke up the next morning. I poured a bowl of it and soaked in the rare silence.

The cupboards had been pretty bare over the past couple of months. Barton usually brought home bags full of groceries, but he'd only been grabbing cooking and cleaning essentials. I'd heard him talking to Mama about a few of the bills, too, and it didn't seem like he could help out as much.

Owen was supposed to come over around four o'clock in the afternoon. I thought the time he had chosen was a premeditated excuse to take me out when most people were eating dinner, but my mother would probably thwart his plans by preparing food for us.

I thought I might sneak over to see Sanders. He planned to go back to work on Monday, and I'd have fewer chances to see him before we graduated.

I heard voices outside, but they didn't get my attention until I could make out the words and who was speaking them. I crouched low and looked out the picture window in the dining room. From it, I had a clear view of my mother and her brother.

My mother crossed her arms, and her fingers almost dug into her skin. Uncle Barton looked defeated. He'd wave his hand and say something, but my mother wouldn't give in. I caught snatches of the conversation that I could turn into full sentences in my mind by inferring from the context of their conversation.

"Why didn't you leave him years ago?"

"You know why," my mother responded.

"But it wasn't the first time," he pointed out. "You've put up with it for too long, and now you need to get you and the kids out."

"Listen to yourself." My mother's hands went to her hips. "My husband is in jail, and you think it's a good time for me to leave him? He needs me."

"Did he need you when he asked Milton Banks to help him file for a divorce?"

I felt my cereal churn uncomfortably in my stomach. Milton Banks was a family lawyer in town.

"That's not true," my mother said through clenched teeth.

"He has the papers in his office, Sara Beth," my uncle insisted. "He wouldn't lie to me."

"Isn't it against attorney-client privilege?"

Uncle Barton looked at his feet and stuttered, "Y-Yeah, but he told me as a favor."

My mother rolled her eyes. "I can only guess what he wants in return."

Uncle Barton looked up, and his eyebrows drew together. "I know you've had a hard life, but sometimes you're a real—"

I purposely didn't hear his last word.

Crystal never told him when she was hungry, so Sanders kept her on a routine. He'd feed her breakfast when she woke up, and he spaced her meals four hours apart. I arrived at lunch, and I tried to help by finding suitable leftovers in the refrigerator.

Imani's father wasn't the only one who had brought food to the house. There were stacks of meals that could have been frozen, but Sanders had piled them on top of each other on the refrigerator shelves.

I pulled out one of the lasagnas on top. "How long has this been in there?"

A smile touched his lips. "That's the one I made last night. It probably needs to go into the trash. Get the casserole beside it."

I raised an eyebrow. "You didn't make it?"

"No. Tonya brought that one over."

I lifted the aluminum foil and placed it on the table. As I waited for the casserole to heat in the oven, I asked Sanders simple questions in hopes he'd tell me how he felt. I selfishly hoped he'd explain more about his mother's death, but I didn't want to push the issue.

"How are things going with Crystal?"

He bobbed his head from side to side. "As well as they can be, I guess." He dropped into a chair and put his head in his hands. "Pretty awful, actually."

I put my hand on his shoulder and leaned in to hug him from behind. When I pulled away, I asked, "What can I do to help?"

He touched my hand and pulled his fingers around it. "You being here is enough."

When he squeezed my hand, I moved away with the excuse that I needed to check on the casserole. He collected Crystal while I dished out the food.

Crystal took one look at her plate and announced, "It has squiggly pasta. I don't eat squiggly pasta."

"Pick it out," Sanders said before he stuffed a forkful into his mouth.

"No," she said and walked out of the room.

"We have siblings on opposite ends," Sanders remarked.

"What?"

"You know," he amended, "in activity. Pickles is all over the place, and Crystal would stand there staring straight ahead with her hand on a hot stove."

"The doctor told you and your mom—"

"I know. Let's just change the subject."

"Are you caught up on your homework?" I tried.

"Yeah. It wasn't that hard." He nodded at me. "When we get to UT, it'll be a little harder, but you'll have me there to help you."

I punched him in the arm playfully. "I make good grades."

"They could always be better," he joked.

"Actually, I'm getting paid to tutor someone."

He slid his plate into the water I'd set dishes in to soak and flicked me with the moisture on his hands. "What poor soul is wasting her money?"

"His, actually."

The humor evaporated and Sanders grew serious. "Who is it?"

I raised my eyebrow, unamused by his jealousy. "I'm tutoring Owen, but it's really none of your business."

He held up his hands. "Sure. But don't come cryin' to me when he uses you and moves on to another girl."

"I'm not dating him." I spoke a little louder than I intended.

"I know how he is," Sanders said. "He bet the guys on the football team that he'd date all the single girls in the senior class before graduation."

I shot up out of my chair. "How do you know that? You aren't friends with him."

He advanced a step. "That's *why* I'm not friends with him. And isn't it obvious? He's dated a girl a week since we started high school!"

Crystal walked into the kitchen. "You're fighting," she observed.

I ran a hand through my hair and lowered my tone. "I'm sorry, Crystal. We'll stop."

"I don't like fighting," she commented in a deadpan. "It reminds me of..."

She trailed off, leaving me to wonder when she'd heard fighting. My curiosity got the best of me, and I asked her for clarification before I thought better of it.

"They always fought," she said.

"Who did?"

Sanders made a move to quieten her, but he was too late. She spoke quickly, fully aware that her brother didn't want her to answer me.

"Mommy and Daddy."

I was confused. Crystal's father was in the military, and he died when my aunt was pregnant with her. I remembered my father had to drive Aunt Mary Beth to the hospital to deliver Crystal because she couldn't drive herself.

"But your Daddy died before you were—"

"Not *that* Daddy," she said simply. "My other Daddy."

Sanders took her out of the room, but not before I realized who she meant.

Chapter 21

Mary Beth insisted she did not have sex with Dandy.

She begged her sister to listen to her side of the story, and after several months, my mother let her tell it. Unimpressed by her lack of proof, she still forgave her for running away with her husband.

Mary Beth came over every day and helped with Barton. When Dandy went to jail, she drove my mother to visit him.

To prove she was uninterested in her sister's husband, Mary Beth latched onto an older guy she met at a party. He took her on long drives and shared milkshakes with her, and she asked her sister to meet him.

The trio spent many nights playing cards and watching television while Barton slept, and Mary Beth imagined her beaux would try to propose. She worried about gaining her parents' approval, as her boyfriend worked a blue-collar job, and she asked her sister if she should break up with him.

My mother encouraged Mary Beth to continue her relationship, but Mary Beth broke up with him before he had the chance to ask her to marry him. She disappeared for a while, and when she resurfaced, I was almost five years old.

There was some tension between my aunt and mother, but they worked it out. Soon, Mary Beth was coming to my father's poker games with his cousin, Tom.

Tom was known for his brash actions. They either gave him giant wins or terrible losses in poker. No matter the outcome, Tom kept a positive attitude, laughing with equal measure at the end of every Friday night.

Tom had enlisted in the Air Force when he was eighteen, and during one of his military leaves, he'd impregnated his high school sweetheart. They married quickly, and he left for his next assignment. When he'd returned, his son, Sanders, had been left with his mother, and the baby's mother was gone.

Tom's mother kept his son, but when the boy was six years old, her health declined. The military placed him in a desk job after a work-related injury, so he could spend more time with Sanders. In time, Tom healed, and the Air Force had another assignment for him.

Mary Beth was in the right place at the right time. Seeing his girlfriend's kindness to his son, Tom proposed to Mary Beth, and they married within two days. He started the adoption process, and Mary Beth became Sanders's legal mother before Tom left.

Tom Tipton lived at the end of the street that ran perpendicular to mine. His house had three bedrooms, but to my knowledge, Mary Beth and Tom never talked about filling the third room with another child. Sanders seemed to be enough for both of them, and Sanders never expressed the desire for a sibling.

During Tom's absences, my mother was cordial to Mary Beth, often sending me to her house with baked goods. Mary Beth didn't come to poker nights without her husband, and the relationship between the sisters seemed to be on the mend.

Mary Beth spoke highly of her husband, but at times, I thought she pitied him. When he was home, he'd slick his long, dark hair into a bun and throw his lengthy legs onto the coffee table. Sanders and I would run under them as we played, and Mary Beth would sing an old song about a bridge falling.

Tom was present for his family, but he seemed detached, like a leaf hardly hanging on a tree branch. He only seemed to be passionate about the military, and he spoke about it frequently. He encouraged my father to join while he was a younger man, and he told my mother to prep my brother for service in hopes it would better Barton's prospects.

Tom wasn't around enough for me to really think of him as my uncle, but I was happy when he was home. His father's presence always made the light in Sanders's eyes a little brighter and Mary Beth's burdens lighter.

One day, right before our sixth-grade year, Sanders and I were running through the lawn sprinkler when we heard an ear-splitting scream. We ran into the house and found Mary Beth on the floor with the phone in her hand.

Sanders held her as she cried, and I dripped water onto the wooden boards in their hallway. She cupped Sanders's face and told him his father was dead. His features crumpled, and he slapped her.

Mary Beth grabbed her cheek, and I ran out the door. I burst into our house and told my mother what had happened. My father stood up quickly from his chair, but she glared at him.

"I'll take care of this myself!" she had barked at him.

I wanted to run back to my aunt's house, but my mother would only walk briskly, following the roads instead of cutting through yards. It seemed like so much time had passed, but it was less than fifteen minutes between the time I left and when I returned with my mother.

The water was still on, and my mother stopped to turn it off before we entered the open door. She called for her sister, and a weak sound came from the living room.

My anxiety almost spilled over. *Had Sanders hurt Mary Beth in his grief? Should I have stayed and tried to stop him from harming my aunt?* My seventy-five-pound frame was no match for my cousin, who'd had a growth spurt over the summer. I'd only thought of getting an adult to neutralize the situation.

I was relieved when we entered the living room and Sanders sat on the floor next to Mary Beth. She was curled into a fetal position, and he held a rag loosely against her cheek. My mother spotted the offensive mark right away. She'd been holding my hand, but she dropped it sharply and advanced on Sanders. Upon her approach, Sanders jumped up and started backing away.

"WHAT DID YOU DO TO MY SISTER?" my mother bellowed.

"Sara Beth," my aunt squeaked out. "It was a knee-jerk reaction. I had just told him his father had—"

My mother turned away from her sister and pointed at Sanders. "Did your father hit women?"

He shook his head. I'd never seen his eyes so wide.

"Do you think he'd want you hitting his wife, the same woman who has been your mother?"

Sanders tried to speak, but nothing came out. He shook his head again.

My mother's finger was inches from his nose, and she spoke with murderous clarity. "Then I don't want to ever hear about you hurting my sister again, or I will cut you up and put you in a box, and I'll bury it where no one will ever find you!"

She turned and rushed to her sister, embracing her fully. "What do you need?" Mary Beth held her arms and shook her head. "I just can't believe he's gone."

The following days blurred with people clad in black and blank stares. Sanders and I took long walks around the neighborhood. We didn't talk a lot, but I could tell he was more relaxed when he was with me.

The funeral was a formal event, and we traveled to the nearby city of Kingsport for it. Mary Beth and Sanders held hands as twenty-one gunshots sounded over the crowd. Tom's mother had died the previous year, and he'd never mentioned his father, so most of the people who gathered at his coffin were friends he'd picked up in his thirty-four years.

On the way home, Uncle Barton, Barton, and my parents were silent. I tried to make light conversation a couple times, but my thoughts drew back to Sanders.

Mary Beth's car sputtered down the road in front of us. Ten minutes after we'd left the funeral, she lost power and moved to the side of the road. My father got out to help her, and they stood in the sun while Sanders laid back in the front seat.

Thirty minutes later, my father had the car started, and he insisted he should drive Mary Beth and Sanders home. My mother almost came out of the car when he told her his intentions.

"You most certainly will not!" she had yelled at him.

It was an odd reaction, but I dismissed it. Everything my mother did was strange.

As always, when my father was adamant about something, there was no way to talk him out of it. He got into Mary Beth's car, and almost immediately, Sanders jumped out of the passenger seat. Instead of hopping into the backseat of Mary Beth's car, though, he joined me in the backseat of our vehicle. Barton moved into the passenger seat, and Sanders laid his head in my lap for the thirty-minute drive home.

Uncle Barton pulled into our driveway, and my mother opened the house for us. She paced in the driveway for a long time and stayed at the window when she came inside.

Uncle Barton stayed until the early evening hours. He played cards with my brother and me, attempting to deflect the mood that had settled over the house.

At dark, my mother called my father, but he didn't answer. She stalked out the door, leaving Sanders, Barton, and me alone.

I fixed spaghetti for us, and we ate it automatically. Barton washed the dishes, and Sanders curled up with me on the couch.

We selected a movie, but I didn't pay attention to it until Sanders cried. Only then did I realize the story was about a man who had lost his father when he was a boy.

His tears didn't last long, and Sanders dried his eyes before Barton came into the room. My brother asked us if he could watch something else, and I was secretly relieved.

My mother burst through the door an hour later and went straight to the bathroom. I thought I heard her crying, but I didn't pay attention to it.

My father closed the door and drifted to his room. He didn't come out until the next morning.

Barton offered to walk Sanders home, and they left. I tried to talk to my mother through the bathroom door, but she wouldn't respond to me. When Barton came home, he knocked on the door, and she fell into his arms, crying a fresh wave of tears.

I thought about knocking on my father's door, but I decided I'd had enough rejection for one night. I crawled into my bed and fell asleep.

Chapter 22

"When were you going to tell me that Crystal is my sister?"

My mother breathed deeply. She walked out of the room, placed Si on the couch next to Pickles, and closed the door to the dining room.

"I thought that might come out."

"Might come out?" I repeated. "How did it happen?"

My mother's jaw clenched, but she closed her eyes to keep her reaction even. When she opened them, she spoke with a strange calmness.

"I've had many years of dealing with your father's infidelities, but you've only recently learned about his betrayal. It makes sense that you'd feel frustrated and conflicted."

I hadn't really placed any anger on my father, and I reevaluated my feelings. To my knowledge, my mother had never cheated on my father, but he'd been unfaithful many times. I should be directing my questions at him, and I decided it made more sense to do so.

I stormed out the door as my mother called my name. She had to stay with the boys, so she couldn't run after me, but my phone started ringing almost immediately. At the end of the road, a familiar car pulled up beside me.

"What's wrong?"

I don't know what look was on my face, but Owen slung his car into park and breached the distance between us. I held him just as strongly as he held me, and when he led me to his car, I let him buckle my seatbelt and shut the door.

"Can you take me to the jail?" I asked him.

Owen didn't say anything. We were in town within minutes, though, and I stared up at the brick building as he parked the car.

"I'll wait here as long as you need."

I didn't get nervous until I rang the bell inside the carport. I almost walked away before I heard keys rattling in the interior door. An officer stepped out, but there was still a sheet of coated chain link metal between us.

"Can I speak to Sheriff Watts?"

The deputy collected him, and I was glad when the sheriff opened the outer door and stepped into the carport with me.

The smell of motor oil and leather polish drifted through the air. I tried to remember that Sheriff Watts was a friend of our family, and I spoke with confidence.

"I found out something today, and I need to speak with my daddy."

The sheriff met my eyes. "There's no tellin' what you've learned, Meg, but I don't have the time for you to see your daddy. It's Saturday, and the visitation schedule is full."

I held my head up. "When can I see him?"

He smiled apologetically. "I really don't have time until your regularly scheduled visitation."

I could feel the tears burning my eyes as I thought of some way to work around the sheriff's schedule. Finally, I broke down, letting the tears roll down my cheeks like snow from an avalanche.

"I-I have to t-talk to him," I blubbered. "Please let me see him!"

The sheriff put a comforting hand on my shoulder. "I know it's hard, and I wish I could help you, but my hands are tied. I can't imagine what you've learned, but I encourage you to keep it to yourself. The DA has enough to convict him without adding anything more."

"It's not about the case!"

My reaction startled him, and he took a step back. "I'm sorry, Meg. You can't see your father today."

I ran out of the carport and past Owen's car. When Owen caught up with me, he wrapped his arms around me, whispering comforting words I didn't hear through my cries.

After I calmed down, I realized Sheriff Watts was standing next to us. He said something to Owen, and Owen nodded. I felt his mouth move on my head.

I allowed myself to be led to the car, and Owen buckled me again. We drove until the sun had set, and only then did he speak directly to me.

"I'm hungry. Do you have a favorite restaurant in town?"

We lived in a small town, and our choices were limited to fast-food places, two mom-and-pop-styled diners, and a couple of authentic Mexican restaurants. I said the name of the first restaurant that came to mind.

"I didn't even think of that place," he said. "Do you want to try to eat inside or in the car?"

"Can I stay in the car?" I motioned to my tear-streaked face. "I don't want to scare anyone."

"You look beautiful," he said without taking his eyes off the road. "Just like you always do."

He ordered my sub and brought it to me with a bag of chips and a soda. I wasn't fond of brown drinks, but the crisp effervescence was refreshing.

"I can pay you back for dinner," I told him.

"You can take it off my tab," he said with a wink.

My hand went to my mouth. "I didn't even think about your assignments. I'm so sorry."

He waved away my apology, chewing the last pieces of his first bite. "It's okay. You're in no condition to help me tonight, and it gives me an excuse to see you tomorrow."

"I promise nothing life-altering will keep me from helping you tomorrow, and you can deduct any amount you want from what you were going to pay me."

He opened the bag of chips for me, and I took one. He motioned to my food, and I unrolled my Italian sub.

The smell of ham and salami filled the car, and my mouth watered when I tasted the pickles. I took a bite while Owen talked.

"I wouldn't dream of making you pay me for dinner, but it was free."

I arched an eyebrow.

"Yeah. They asked me about the other sub, since my family is vegetarian, and I told them it was for my damsel in distress."

I was glad my mouth was full so it wouldn't drop open. I chewed the bite and wiped my mouth with the back of my hand.

"Don't worry," he added quickly. "I didn't tell them who was in the car. They're just nice people."

"I know them," I said. "They are always really nice when Sanders and I go in."

Owen's eyes clouded over for a moment, and he looked away. "Anyway, the food was free, so you don't owe me anything."

The emotional temperature in the car cooled. We ate the rest of our dinner in silence, and Owen collected the trash.

When he got back to the car, he seemed resolved to speak to me. "I like you, Meg, but I don't understand what Sanders is to you. Is he your cousin or a boyfriend or—"

"He's my cousin," I said solidly. "We're close, and he's pretty affectionate, but that's all."

I thought I'd summed up my relationship with Sanders very well. I waited for Owen to respond, but he drove me home in silence.

I hurried to open my door when we pulled into my driveway. I hopped out, and he was in front of me in seconds.

"Who left the radio on?" he asked.

I laughed. "My father keeps it on to scare the deer away from our garden. I think it makes it grow better, too, because his plants are the strongest and healthiest in the neighborhood."

Owen put one arm around my waist and pulled me to him. "You have a beautiful laugh."

I imagined I felt his heartbeat through his shirt. He brought his lips within inches of mine before I pulled away, telling him I'd see him the next morning to complete his lessons.

I didn't wait for him to respond. Once in my room, though, I watched his brake lights as he drove away.

<h1 style="text-align:center">Chapter 23</h1>

Owen and I worked on his past assignments until almost noon before we took a break. We didn't talk about the previous night, and he seemed to be content with it.

My mother was angry when I woke up. Thankfully, Barton had upset her, so she only lightly discussed her feelings about my outburst.

I told her I'd gone out with Owen, and we had ridden around for a while. She seemed satisfied with my responses, and she had gone over her expectations of me for the summer. I responded with gentle head nods as she kept glancing at the driveway for Barton's car.

"Do you want to go out for lunch?" Owen asked.

"I'll make lunch," my mother interjected as she breezed through the room.

It helped her to stay busy while Barton was gone, so I agreed to eat lunch at home. I helped her prepare the tacos, and we all sat down at the dining room table.

Si wiggled into his place on my mother's lap, sampling food from her plate. When he was full, he climbed onto the table and sat down in front of Owen. My mother and I pulled him away several times until Owen waved away our efforts and invited my youngest brother to sit with him.

Pickles got up and dragged his chair to Owen's other side. Both boys chatted with him, even though Owen could hardly understand Si.

My mother collected my brothers, and they reluctantly left the room. I cleared the plates and wiped off the table so we could finish Owen's assignments. He grasped the material, and his improvement impressed me.

"Your family is really great," he remarked.

"You haven't met my dad yet," I told him. "You'd love him."

Owen's eyebrows furrowed. "Your mom's great, too."

"Sure," I said and forced a smile. "What are we working on now?"

Owen only lacked two more assignments, and midway through the second one, I heard Barton's car rattling up the road. I wondered if I should send Owen home before my brother came inside.

Owen sensed my tension. "What's wrong?"

"Barton was out all last night," I whispered out of the side of my mouth. "Mama's been worried about him."

"Hey, Meg," my brother said as he opened the door. He nodded at Owen. "Meg's friend," he said by way of a greeting.

Owen nodded back. "Hey."

Barton stared at him sharply, and my mother rushed into the room.

"I need to talk to you in your room." Her voice was sweet, but her eyebrows climbed high on her forehead.

Barton followed her without looking back at us. Owen and I were quiet, and I imagined he was straining to hear their conversation as well.

"Let's go in the living room," I suggested.

Owen followed me, and we settled on the couch next to Pickles. It was clear we had moved to hear Barton's excuse for staying out all night.

Pickles glanced up at us. "She asked him where he was, and he told her he fell asleep at the store."

I was amused by my younger brother's presumption, but I nodded at his explanation. "She's not going to believe him."

Their voices elevated, and we were able to make out most of the rest of their conversation. Siblings are never more silent than when their parents are disciplining a brother or sister.

"You should have called me," my mother said.

"How could I do that when I'm asleep, Mother?"

My brother only addressed our mother formally when he was irritated with her. However, she had the moral high ground, so I was surprised he was irritated. On the other hand, he was an adult, and he shouldn't have to explain himself. I could see both sides.

"Why didn't you message me this morning?"

"I went to work right away," he replied. "Imani woke me up."

I mentally noted what he'd said. I'd have to talk to my friend about it later.

"You could have sent me a quick message, Barton. I was worried about you."

My brother's voice rose, and his words were clear. "I bring in the money here now, and I pay for the groceries! What more do you want from me?"

I knew my mother was crying without hearing or seeing her. Her silence was enough to tell me.

Although she never said it, Barton was her favorite child. He was with her during the biggest milestones and heartbreaks in her life. Usually, he was on her side, and she confided in him often. They were seldom at odds, and most of the time, she catered to him to prevent ill feelings from forming.

My mother didn't like to cry, especially in front of people. She told me it was a sign of weakness, and the people I loved would use my frailty against me. But out of everyone she knew, she trusted Barton the most. She knew her tears were welcome on his shoulders.

"I'm sorry, Mama," Barton said. "I'll make sure I call you anytime I'm going to be late."

Once the juicy part of the discussion was over, I led Owen back to the dining room. My mother would never have known we had been in there if Pickles hadn't announced our hasty departure when she rejoined him.

"That little rat," I mumbled as my mother breezed into the room.

"Are you two dating now?" she said casually.

"What?" I couldn't hide my shock.

"Well," she continued nonchalantly, "I figured you and Owen must be dating since you've made him privy to family matters."

Color traveled up Owen's neck and blossomed across his face. He wasn't used to my mother's forthright nature.

I groaned and buried my head in my hands. "Stop it, Mama."

"Gladly. And you can stop eavesdropping." She didn't pretend she'd come into the room to do more than confront us. "Have fun *studying*," she said, putting air quotes around the last word and leaving as abruptly as she had entered.

"I think I need to go," Owen said, gathering his things quickly. "Is there any chance you can come to my house to finish this up tomorrow?" He held up his laptop.

"I have to watch my brothers after school," I told him. "Could we do it here?"

His eyes moved in the direction my mother had gone. I knew what he was thinking.

"My mother starts a new job tomorrow. She won't be here until dinner time."

His relief was visible. "Okay. I'll drive you home after school."

After Owen left, I wandered through the house. I played with my brothers, helping them build dinosaur armies and avoided my mother. She seemed to be lost in her own thoughts anyway.

Barton came out of his room, and when he went back, he didn't close his door right away. I drifted into his room and sat on the bed. Alternative rock played low, and a mix of sweat and his heavy body spray lingered in the air.

"Are you going somewhere?" I asked him.

"Yeah." He pulled a belt through the straps of his jeans. "I'm meeting someone tonight."

"A special someone?" I arched my eyebrow.

He closed the door. "Yeah. I don't want Mama to know about it, though."

"Is it the girl she doesn't like?"

He nodded.

Barton worked with a cashier, Cynthia, with shimmering blonde hair and large blue eyes. He told our mother he liked Cynthia, and my mother walked down to the store to meet her. Barton didn't know our mother had dragged the rest of her children a mile across town to see the object of his affection, so my mother couldn't state her business outright. She posed as a regular patron, buying the first thing Pickles grabbed.

When she checked us out, Cynthia dropped the can of pasta on her hand and uttered an expletive under her breath. She looked around at the children and apologized, but her slip astonished my mother. She left the store and vowed her son wouldn't date someone who couldn't control their tongue. I reminded her that my daddy cussed like a sailor, especially on poker nights, but she ignored me.

As a woman and a young mother, the people in town had judged my mother by different rules than the other people in her life. Without realizing it, she measured other people, especially women, in the same way. She characterized Cynthia as low-class, and she had hardly spoken to her. She referred to her as Barton's girlfriend, but she didn't think they were serious.

"Oh. I guess that's who you were with last night."

He stopped buttoning his stark-white shirt for a moment but resumed the motion quickly. Barton grabbed his keys and left me in his room.

I should have left right away, but I fell back on the bed. Metal clanged behind the bed, and I quickly rose. *What had I knocked loose?*

I waded over a sea of balled-up blankets until I could reach the other side of the bed. The side of the bed was pushed against the wall, so I dove my hand down in search of whatever had made the noise. I succeeded in pushing it around a couple of times before I grabbed it.

I knew what I held before I saw it. Luckily, I'd grabbed the handle, as the blade appeared to have recently been sharpened. The tip was covered in a rusty color I could identify without bringing it closer to the light. It was blood.

Chapter 24

I wiped off the handle with a blanket and put the knife back onto the floor, still holding it with the blanket. I could barely see it through the crack between the bed and the wall, but it'd be easy to find if Barton looked for it.

The knife had been a gift to Barton from my father. He had tried many times over the years to connect with his stepson, but Barton had resisted his efforts every time. My father had a matching knife, and he had told Barton they could use them to gut wild game when they hunted. Barton wasn't exactly an animal lover, but he refused to hunt. He didn't want to bond with my father.

I walked out of the room, closing the door tightly behind me. There was a child safety lock on the knob, so there was no risk that my brothers would go through the door and find the open knife on the floor.

Once in my room, I had time to think about the blood. *Where did it come from?*

Barton rarely used the knife, as it was a connection to his stepfather, and he didn't hunt, so how did he get blood on his knife?

He cut himself, I rationalized, but even that explanation didn't feel right.

My mind moved to a possible answer, but I tried not to think it through. *Could my brother have killed our aunt?*

Barton was supposed to be at work that night, but he could have easily left the store early. I thought I'd ask Imani about that, too. She might not remember if my brother left work early over a week ago, but it was worth a try.

Wait a minute! Was I really thinking my brother was a murderer?

Barton was kind and hard-working, and it was out of character for him to raise his voice. I couldn't imagine what would drive him into thinking homicidal thoughts.

Maybe that wasn't true. I had seen him get angry over the treatment of our mother. I had watched him rage through the house when our mother left to find her husband when he'd been out all night. But my father was alive and well in jail. It was Mary Beth who had died.

My brain continued to work, concocting scenarios where my brother had found out about Crystal's true paternity, or he had discovered a rekindled affair between my father and Mary Beth. That might be enough for my mild-mannered brother to kill his aunt. After all, Mary Beth was our mother's sister, and sleeping with her husband was a significant betrayal.

I tried to shake the thoughts out of my head, but the nagging idea my brother had killed our aunt plagued me. He worked long hours, and he could easily have slipped into her house and killed our aunt before Sanders got home from work.

As if he had read my thoughts, my phone buzzed with a message from Sanders. He wanted me to sneak out and meet him at his house.

I'd avoided his messages since I'd learned Crystal was my sister. He hadn't tried to call me, as any verbal conversation might have been awkward, but he had texted me almost nonstop.

I did not commit to him, but I tried to think of the best way to leave without my mother's knowledge. She'd been up the previous night, worried about Barton and her new job, so she could be tired enough to fall asleep immediately. On the other hand, her anxiety might keep her pacing the floors until after midnight. The former was confirmed when she settled onto the couch to sleep.

My mother hadn't slept in her bed since my father was arrested. She curled up with one of my brothers or slept on the couch. Maybe she felt like the back of the couch was similar to sleeping against her husband's back.

After Barton came back home, and the soft snores of my family filled the house, I slipped out of bed. Pickles's finger brushed my leg as I passed his bed.

"Where are you goin'?" he whispered.

I decided to tell him the truth. "I'm going to see Sanders."

His eyes, dark with shadows from the night, looked up at me. "Why won't Mama let you see him?"

"It's just a big misunderstanding," I answered, brushing the hair away from his face. "You won't tell her I snuck out, will you?"

He shook his head. "I can keep secrets. I do it for the rest of them."

"For who?" I questioned automatically.

Pickles shrugged and pulled the blanket over his head. Requiring his silence, I didn't push him for an explanation. I crept past my mother and edged my way out of our back door. Once I was free, I ran across the dark yards until my feet padded up my aunt's porch steps.

Sanders was sitting on the porch swing, looking out into the night. "I didn't know if you'd come."

"How long would you have waited for me?"

"Forever," he responded.

The remark was too intimate for our relationship, so I searched for a way to change the subject. "What did you want to talk about?"

He shrugged and stayed slumped against the armrest of the swing. "I'm sorry I never told you about Crystal."

I sat down next to him. "Why didn't you tell me?"

He blinked and shook his head. "At first, I wasn't sure. Mom told me Crystal was my sister, and I thought of her as my father's daughter, but there were things that made her different than—"

"My brothers and I don't have—"

"I know," he spoke over me. "I'm not talking about her condition. I'm talking about how her eyes are brown, but my father's eyes were blue, like mine."

"Genetics can vary in siblings. Pickles and Si have blue eyes, but mine are kind of blue-green, and Barton can tan more easily than me."

"Sure," he said, flicking his finger on the metal chain holding up his side of the swing. "It's just..."

I waited for my cousin to pick back up. It took him a long time, but he completed his thought.

"I saw them together."

I pulled away from him. "You saw Aunt Mary Beth with my dad?"

His head bobbed, and his jaw clenched and unclenched. "And with Crystal."

I took a deep breath that didn't fill my lungs. "He came up here to see her?"

Sanders looked at his lap drawing the fingers of one hand into a fist. "It didn't happen all the time. Sometimes, he wouldn't come to the house for months at a time, but he didn't treat Crystal the same way he treated me. He treated her"—he looked up at me— "like you."

Chapter 25

I could hardly hold up my head at school the next day, and I was glad when Sanders let me lean against him during lunch so I could nap. Twenty minutes of sleep refreshed me, but the day seemed to drag on until school was dismissed for the day.

I declined Owen's offer to drive me home, and I helped Sanders walk with Crystal, but I didn't stay with them. In a lot of ways, I felt guilty about my relationship with Crystal. *Should I be closer to her? Should I be the one raising her since she was my biological sister?*

I wondered if she understood I was her sister. It was an easy connection for me to make, but she was barely six years old.

I called Owen on my way to my Aunt Tonya's house. He was already parked in my driveway, but he promised to wait on me until I picked up my brothers.

My Aunt Tonya didn't stand on ceremony, so I opened her door and stepped into the kitchen. The house smelled like burned beans, but everything was tidy. A horse's saddle hung on the opposing wall, and Si's musical toddler toys were splayed across the floor.

"Good mornin'," Uncle Catfish called to me as he stepped out of the living room.

"Did you work last night?"

"Yep. They got me on swing shift, so I just woke up."

Aunt Tonya breezed into the room. "I swear, I think they did that just in time for me to watch these younguns. I could have really used your help today."

"I have to work tonight, sweetheart."

"Don't 'sweetheart' me," she admonished. "I work, too."

My father's sister was gruff and burly. She could easily out lift most of the men I knew and tell them what they were doing wrong while she was doing it. She had the same dark hair and roughly tanned skin as my father, but she wasn't as quick-tempered. She never drank alcohol, and she wouldn't put up with sideways comments. Early in their marriage, my aunt and uncle had elected to remain childless, as my aunt was nervous around children and my uncle did anything to please her.

Uncle Catfish was kind and gentle. His frail frame and humor gave balance to his relationship with my aunt.

"How're Sanders and Crystal doing?" he asked, taking the focus away from my aunt's troubles.

"They're getting along as best as can be expected," I told him.

"I need to send another casserole," my aunt said to herself, running a hand through her short hair.

Si toddled into the room and held his arms out to me. I picked him up, smelling the grass and sunshine in his hair.

"He wouldn't take a nap for me," my aunt complained. "Maybe you'll have better luck."

I grabbed his bag and waved at my aunt and uncle.

We were just in time to pick up Pickles at the bus stop. He looked both ways before jumping off the steps, as the chicken that liked to chase him might wait for him.

"That chicken is long gone," I told him on the walk home.

"It watches for me," he said seriously. "Daddy called it a Dominicker."

"I think it's called a Dominique."

"Whatever," he said, waving away my words. "It's mean, and I don't like it."

After I'd rocked Si to sleep and given Pickles a snack, I sat down with Owen to complete his assignment. We spent an hour on his work, and his hand purposely brushed mine a few times.

"I guess that's it," he said, leaning back in his chair.

I reached out, putting pressure on him to lean forward. "My mama always says to keep 'all four on the floor.'" I tried to laugh it off.

"Aww. I didn't know you cared." He smiled and wrapped his arm around me.

I wriggled away easily, noticing his wounded look. I pretended to be too busy to see his reaction by cleaning up our pencils and papers.

Owen put his hand over mine to stop me. "Will you be my girlfriend?"

I wanted to accept his offer. I wanted to fall into his arms and let him share the burden I was carrying. I knew it was a bad time to start a relationship, especially if his feelings were as fleeting as they had been with his past girlfriends.

"Owen, I don't think this is a good time."

"That's not a *no*," he said, smiling. "I must be growing on you."

"I like you," I told him, surprised by my confidence, "but I don't want to drag you through the mud. My family is about to go through some difficult times."

"You already are," he remarked.

I realized he was familiar enough with my situation to comment. He had been there for me when I'd found out Crystal was my sister, yet he hadn't blabbed to Garrett because Imani didn't know about it.

He leaned close to me, and I didn't stop him. My first kiss was slow and sweet, with notes of mint and salt. I didn't think about how many girls he'd kissed before me or how many he might kiss after me. I held onto the moment and gave in to it. If I was going on the ride, I'd enjoy it with the windows down and the radio up full blast.

Chapter 26

I didn't tell my mother I was dating Owen until I told my father. I made her stay outside with the boys as I spoke with him. Exhausted after her long week at work and the mile and a half she walked to and from the women's correctional facility, she sat despondently on the sidewalk as Si slept in the stroller and Pickles flipped her hair.

I led with my happy news, so my father's response wouldn't be tainted by what I discussed next. As soon as he opened his mouth to stress that I shouldn't date anyone until I was out of college, I told him I knew Crystal was my sister.

He looked at me for a long moment, his eyes sad and distant. "Who told you?"

"What does it matter?" I yelled. "You lied to me!"

He let out a deep breath through his nose. "I didn't lie to you."

"How did I know you were going to say that?" My legs started shaking, and my arms soon followed. "You weren't honest with me. Is that why you wanted me to give the money in the jar to Sanders?"

He popped out of his chair. "You still haven't done that?"

I shook my head, unmoved by his display.

"They need that money, Meg."

I coughed out a laugh as a tear traced its way down my cheek. "*We* need that money, Dad. Mama is working almost every day, and she walks miles to and from the jail. Barton works double shifts so he can bring home groceries, and I've been tutoring Owen for extra cash."

He chose to focus on my mother. "It's a good job," he commented. "She'll have decent benefits, and they'll treat her well. She'll be able to buy a clunker soon."

My father had owned several *clunkers*. They lasted a year or two before a gasket blew or the transmission fell out.

"She doesn't need a cheap car, Dad. She needs you to come home."

He waved his hand dismissively without looking at me. "That's not gonna happen."

"Did you kill Mary Beth?"

He glared at me. I had never been the recipient of one of my father's hard stares, but I returned it.

"Go get your mama and the boys," he ordered. "Why did you bother me with all this?"

"Why did you sleep with my aunt?" I shot back. "Why did you hide Crystal's paternity from me? Why are you in jail?" I spat out the words with as much venom as I could muster.

"GET YOUR MAMA!"

I didn't bother hanging up the receiver. I slung it down and walked outside without a backward glance.

I messaged Owen while I was waiting for my mother to finish her visit. She stepped to the door to tell me my father wanted to speak to me again, but I shook my head.

"He wants to apologize," she said. "His tooth has been hurting, and it's made him more irritable."

I rolled my eyes. "I thought he was getting it fixed this week?"

"They had to put it off for a week or two."

"I really don't care, Mama. He was ill with me, and I have more self-respect than to go in there and let him do it again."

"You're being a brat," she said before she closed the door.

Owen was at the house when we got there. My mother went inside with the boys, and I was glad the evening was warm enough for me to lie in the hammock. Owen tried to get into it with me, but I made the excuse that it was unstable, and I walked him to our gazebo.

"We're graduating next week," he commented. "What are you going to do after?"

"Sanders and I are going to UT," I answered automatically.

He'd been holding my hand, but he dropped it. "Is there anything going on between the two of you?"

My anger bubbled up, but I reminded myself that Owen was my boyfriend, so I should be a little more patient with him. "Sanders and Imani are my best friends, and Sanders is also my cousin." When he didn't seem convinced, I added, "We wouldn't even be having this conversation if I was going to UT with Imani."

Owen seemed to roll that around in his mind. "You're right. I don't know what I was thinking."

Our conversation flowed more easily around our adult prospects. Owen was going to stay and attend ETSU, but he planned to move after he earned a history degree.

"I'm going into business."

He put his arm around me. "That's great. What part?"

His interest in me boosted my self-confidence, and I told him about my father's dream for me. "I know it seems small, but he's wanted me to do it since I was a kid."

He shook his head. "Not everyone wants to be a lawyer or a doctor one day. I think you have a solid plan for the future, and if you're excited about it, that's all that really matters." He leaned back against the picnic table. "You hear about these students who change their minds or drop out of college. I think for some of them it's because their dream was too big, or it was forced on them."

"That makes sense."

"Do you want to own your own business?"

My head dropped, and I focused on an ant crawling across my foot. I settled on a diplomatic answer. "It's what's best for me."

He rubbed my shoulders, and the movement of his fingers sent tiny pricks of electricity through my back. Before I knew it, my arms broke out in gooseflesh.

"You should pick what you want." His mouth was inches from my ear, and he sent warm puffs of air across my skin when he spoke. "What do *you* want, Meg?"

My sudden rush of hormones jumbled my nerves, but I squeaked out a response. To my surprise, I told him the truth. "I want to teach math to little kids."

He chuckled. "I feel like you've already started doing that."

I playfully smacked his arm. "You were a great student and a little older than the kids I'd want to teach."

"I think you should go for it," he commented, moving my hair across my shoulder. "You know, ETSU has great math and education programs."

Owen had left a subtle hint. Whether he thought Sanders was his competition or he didn't think our relationship would survive the distance, he wanted me to stay in the area.

He went on. "I just want a simple life. To have what I want, I'll need a good wife who wants the same thing." He moved a strand of my hair and looked at me. "Have you thought about a family, Meg?"

It may have been his way of creating a balance in the conversation, but it felt like more. Thoughts raced across my mind as I tried to settle on what I wanted.

"I guess I've always pictured my life here" —I motioned around me— "on Tipton Hill. My family is all around me, so I imagined coming back and raising my kids here."

Owen's mouth tugged up at the corners. "It sounds like a simple life I can live with."

I couldn't stand it any longer. "Are you asking me to marry you?"

He startled. "No. I was seein' if we wanted the same things."

My sudden statement horrified me. *Why had I assumed he was proposing?* It had seemed like he was leading up to it, but now that he had explained himself, I understood his intentions more clearly.

"I'm sorry. I—"

Owen cut me off. "I know it may seem like I'm rushing things along by askin' you what you want, but we're about to graduate soon, and it's only reasonable to make sure we're goin' in the same direction, especially if we're gonna have a long-distance relationship."

"I guess I didn't think about it that way."

He took my hand. "I've liked you for a long time, even if you haven't let me show it." He chuckled, and I smiled, dipping my head away shyly before returning to his gaze. "I have dated a lot of girls, and I think we both know that I have a reputation."

I had no choice but to nod along. I couldn't defend his past relationships.

"But have you ever heard any of the girls I've dated complain about me?" he asked.

It was a new spin on the way I saw my boyfriend. "No."

He seemed pleased. "That's because I had the same conversation with them that I'm havin' with you now."

He let his words sink in.

"You see," he went on, "my parents sat me down at the beginning of my freshman year and they told me their story. They fell in love in high school, and they broke up before graduation because they wanted separate things. My dad planned to travel the world, and my mom wanted to stay in her hometown."

"Did your dad get to travel?" I asked.

"Yeah," he answered, "and he hated it."

I arched my eyebrow. I couldn't imagine being disappointed with anything I saw in another place.

"He loved the scenery and the cultures, but he missed my mom. He went back and proposed to her, and they traveled the world together until they settled here. In the end, my dad got to travel, my mom got her small-town residence, and they got each other."

"That's a beautiful story, but wouldn't they want you to stay single until you knew what you wanted?"

He looked at his feet. "No, I think the idea was to get me to think about what I wanted and express it clearly to whoever I was with."

"Oh," I said, disappointed that I hadn't seen the point right away.

"Do you see a future with me?" he asked.

I decided to be as honest with him as he'd been with me.

"I don't know, Owen. I like you, but I just started letting myself like you a week ago. I didn't know you had been talking to your past girlfriends about their hopes and dreams instead of just dumping them, so it makes me think of you in a new light."

"Is it a good one?" he chuckled.

I squeezed his hand. "Yeah. I think so."

Chapter 27

"He's with her all the time," Imani told me.

I had gotten to school a little earlier than usual, hoping I could talk to my friend before classes started. Luckily, she had been at her locker when I retrieved my laptop, and only a few people dotted the other seats when we walked into class.

"So, he's not working double shifts?"

She shrugged. "Yeah. Barton works a lot, but he sneaks off with Cyn all the time."

"What about the night Mary Beth died?" I asked. "Did he go out with Cynthia that night?"

Her face scrunched with irritation. "How am I supposed to remember?"

I fell back into my seat, clearly defeated.

"You don't think your brother helped your dad kill Mary Beth, do you?" Her eyes sparkled with intrigue.

"I don't think my dad did it," I told her. "I don't know why he's still in jail for something he didn't do."

"But Barton?" Imani was as skeptical about my brother's involvement in my aunt's death as I was when I'd first thought about it.

"I found a bloody knife hidden in his room," I revealed.

Her chocolate eyes widened. "The police can test it for Mary Beth's DNA," Imani whispered.

I looked around, and more students were filling the surrounding chairs. Owen had just walked in, and he waved at me. I returned the gesture and went back to my conversation with my friend.

"I'm not going to turn in my brother."

I waited for her response, but her color had gone ashen. She ran out of the room, and I followed her. Retching sounds echoed against the bathroom walls when I opened the door.

After she rinsed her mouth, she looked at me in the mirror. It was then that I noticed the bags forming under her eyes and the sharper ridges in her cheekbones.

"I'm late."

I patted her shoulder. "I'll get us an excuse from—"

"Not like that," she barked at me. She closed her eyes and reopened them. "I'm late for my period."

On the way home from school, Sanders asked me if I'd watch Crystal for him while he was at work. Crystal kicked some fallen dogwood flowers, oblivious to our conversation.

"I guess I should get to know my sister a little better."

Sanders nudged me. "Don't be that way. Besides, she's my sister, too."

"Not technically," I said without thinking.

Sanders moved away from me. "That's not fair, Meg. Blood isn't the only bond."

I closed the distance between us and grabbed his hand. He didn't pull away, but his expression didn't change.

"Of course not. I'm sorry. My head is still spinning from finding out the truth about my father, and I shouldn't have taken it out on you."

He scoffed. "The truth about your father? You haven't even scratched the surface."

It was my turn to be hurt. I dropped his hand and stood still. He walked on a couple of paces before he noticed Crystal and I had stopped.

"C'mon, guys. I don't have time for this."

I narrowed my eyes. "Why? Do you need to go home and wallow in self-pity some more?"

"If you have forgotten, my mom died, and now I don't get to go to college." He threw his backpack on the ground. "You, on the other hand, get to go about your life like nothing happened!"

He struck me speechless. Sanders had never spoken to me that way.

"It would be better if I had never been born," Crystal said. She spoke it matter-of-factly, and no tears followed.

I looked from Sanders to Crystal, unclear about what to say. Finally, it was clear someone needed to reassure Crystal, so I bent down and took her tanned hand.

"I'm glad you were born," I said. "I always wanted a sister, and now I have you. I just wish I would've known about you sooner, and we could have done all kinds of things with our daddy."

"He's going to jail forever," she remarked. "I'll never see him again."

"That's not true," I said. "We'll find out who really killed your mom, and he'll get out of jail."

A look passed between Crystal and Sanders, and she gave him an almost imperceptible nod. "Daddy killed Mama."

I glanced at Sanders. "Did Crystal see it happen?"

He took a couple of steps back. "Let's go. We need to get home."

"Wait just a second," I called after him.

He stopped and turned around slowly. "Did Crystal see who murdered her mother?"

He nodded. "She was there, so she saw him in the house."

Up to that point, I had assumed my father had been wrongly accused and he would be released any day. Sheriff Watts had told me that the case against my father was ironclad, but I hadn't believed him. Now, I was forced to admit that my father may never come home.

"They're going to use her statement against him, aren't they?"

"No," Sanders said, looking anywhere but into my eyes. "I couldn't let her be the reason her father went to prison." His voice broke in places. "I gave them a statement, and I'm going to testify against your father."

Chapter 28

"Absolutely not!" Aunt Margaret said. "Your floozy of a mother will sell the house out from under my nephew and God only knows who will move into our neighborhood."

I ignored the slight against my mother. I needed to be cordial to my great-aunt so she would consider my request.

"But, Aunt Margaret, if he doesn't get out on bail, then we may never see him again."

I thought my plea might work on her, but she buttoned up her slash of a mouth before she rejected me again. "It's his own foolish fault for spreadin' his seed."

I grew even more irritated that she was referencing Crystal's paternity, but I pushed on. "I'm graduating on Saturday, and I want him to be there."

That didn't pull on her heartstrings either. "Why? He can't do anythin' more for you. It's best that you figure out your own way and get away from your free-loadin' relations."

I guessed she meant my mother and Barton. "My brother works to pay the bills and bring in groceries, and my mother's been working and walking back and forth from her job every day."

"For two weeks," she scoffed. "And when has she done anything else to help? Not to mention how she unloads that baby on Tonya so she can run off."

I stood up, jarring a couple of her knick-knacks in their case. "She only has Tonya watch Si when she goes to work."

Her lips tickled up on the sides. "I could build a mountain on the things you *think* you know."

I couldn't take it any longer, so I stormed toward the door. "Don't you care about anyone besides yourself? You're gonna die here with a bunch of useless junk around you, and no one is going to care!"

I slammed the door to her trailer and marched up the road to my house. I thought about telling Sanders about what had happened, but it had been weird between us when we'd last parted. Owen was out with his family, and Imani had decided to tell Garrett about her missed period.

I saw Tonya out in her yard, and I dropped beside her. I matched her gusto for weeding her flower bed, and we worked together in silence for a while.

"What happened?" she asked after it was clear I wasn't speaking voluntarily.

"Your aunt sucks," I said plainly.

She guffawed. "Which one?"

"Aunt Margaret," I answered. "She won't let go of the house so we can do a property bond. Without it, Daddy won't get to see my graduation."

"He has a pretty steep bond," she remarked.

I felt a lump rise in my chest, but I pushed it down. My aunt understood challenges, but she valued proposed solutions over tears.

"I found out about Crystal," I said.

Tonya pulled a weed with such force that I was sure she could have ripped it from the core of the earth. She opened her hands and relaxed them before resuming her task.

"I shouldn't tell you my opinion about it, but that little triangle has done nothin' but tear our family apart."

I decided she wasn't done, so I was silent. I gave her my full attention in case she revealed something.

"I love my brother, but he never really made a choice. He hopped between them, without a thought of what it might do to the kids."

She looked up toward the sun and squinted in its afternoon brilliance. She didn't glance back at me, though, and I wondered if she shouldered the shame for her family.

"And when he'd leave Tom's widow, she'd run through men like water. Good men, who would have been faithful if she hadn't lured them to her house like a spider to its web."

Another weed was jerked and thrown behind her, missing the pile of discarded vegetation. I wanted to stop her, but I was powerless against the scars I hadn't known I was ripping open.

"I didn't know Aunt Mary Beth that way," I told her. "The only man I saw her around was Tom."

She let out a bitter laugh. "That marriage was a scam from the start. She only wanted a way to be closer to my brother. We all knew it, even Tom, but he let it go, 'cause he was usin' her to raise his son." She shrugged her shoulders. "I guess she was good at that, even though she didn't stay true to Tom. Crystal's proof of that."

"But she didn't get pregnant until after he died," I reminded her.

"Oh, honey, I thought you said you knew about Crystal." She wiped the sweat from her brow with the back of her hand. "She was almost in her third trimester when Tom died. She was doin' a good job of hidin' it, too. She learned about hidin' a pregnancy from your mama. Even though they never saw her after they dropped her at Dandy's trailer, Sara couldn't let her parents hear she was pregnant so soon after she got married." She let out a long breath. "Anyway, from what I've been told, your mother's sister was gonna give the baby to an adoption service before Tom took his next leave. It would've been a good idea since Crystal looks so much like Ace."

Her fingers dug into the dirt and squeezed. "I guess that went out the window when Tom died. She found a way to keep her claws in my brother."

"But if she was going to hide the baby from Tom, why didn't she want to hide her from her sister?" I asked.

Tonya looked at me, red veins snaking through the whites of her eyes. "Why should she have hidden it? Your mama knew all along, and the more Sara Beth did to help cover it, the greater her chance that my brother would come home."

Her lip lifted in the corner. "Why do you think Crystal and Pickles are so close in age?"

I ran the idea through my head. When I was young, my mother had seemed content with Barton and me, and there was a large space between my younger brothers and me.

Tonya measured my reaction. "That's right. Once it was clear her sister wasn't going to give up the baby for adoption, your mama had Pickles to keep your father."

Si let out a cry, and we both stood up. Uncle Catfish brought him outside, happily cooing at the baby. He looked from Tonya to me.

"What's wrong?" he asked.

I opened my mouth to mislead him about our conversation, but my aunt took the reins.

"We were just talkin' about Tom's widow and the mess she left behind." She breezed past him, leaving me in an awkward situation.

I watched the color drain from my uncle's face. He stared at me for context or help, his signature mustache twitching.

As she had spoken, Aunt Tonya hadn't mentioned Aunt Mary Beth's name, a practice I was used to associating with a person who was not received fondly. Aunt Tonya stayed on her land, so I never knew she had enemies. Of course, I had never really dissected her relationships with the other people on Tipton Hill, but as I thought back, my memories were full of family get-togethers where either Aunt Tonya *or* Aunt Mary Beth were missing. They were never in the same place together and I was beginning to uncover the reason for it.

At that moment, I knew Aunt Mary Beth hadn't just uprooted the connection between my mother and father, but she'd sabotaged every relationship with a man weak enough to fall into her bed. And my Uncle Catfish had been one of them.

My mother came home early, and I was ready for her.

I had decided that I was going to make her tell me about the sordid history between my father and Mary Beth. I was going to yell at her for not keeping her husband at home, and I was going to accuse her of destroying our family. After all, it was her fault, and she deserved it.

My teenage mind didn't see the true flaw with my father. All I could think was that he would have stayed with her if she hadn't nagged at him all the time. So, by the time she entered the house, I could have recited my case in any court.

I stomped into the kitchen, ready to spit my words like venom, but I stopped short. My mother was holding a paper in her trembling hand.

She pushed it at me, and I took it. "Is this from Great-Aunt Margaret?"

My mother stared at me in disbelief, holding her hands to her chest. "It's an eviction notice. She's asked us to move out."

Chapter 29

Thinking back, I should have seen the signs that my father and mother's relationship wasn't perfect.

After Aunt Mary Beth's marriage to Tom, my mother frequently sent Barton and me to her sister's house to play. When we'd return, we'd find our parents in a despondent state, almost shell-shocked from the war that had raged between them.

I noticed the difference, but I didn't explore it. Barton would help my mother with dinner, and my father would take me outside to lie in our hammock or tend to the garden. All would be forgotten as he showed me how to care for the tommy toes and sweet corn. I learned how to string soda cans on a wire around the perimeter of the garden to keep the deer from walking up and eating our vegetables, and I told him about the games Sanders and I played and shared a few of our secrets with him.

After Tom died, my father was at our house for breakfast and dinner, but I didn't see him much in between. Looking back, I don't know if he was sleeping in his room.

Maybe he was transitioning to Mary Beth's house. On the other hand, he could have been trying to live two lives, one with Mary Beth and the other with my mother.

I remember his presence more after my mother announced her pregnancy with Pickles. He helped her with all the household chores and catered to her needs. After my brother was born, my mother and father seemed happier. My father wasn't just a figure during family meals.

I should have noticed the difference, but I was too wrapped up in my own preteen life. Sanders was on edge, and he was having trouble with some bullies at school, so I felt like I should be there for him. They left him alone after he took off after them in a rage.

I'd never seen my cousin flip out. He'd ripped the hair from the scalp of one boy and had pummeled another one's face until it was purple. As I inched closer to adulthood, I recognized the reason for his anger. He was dealing with grief over his father's death and managing my father's increased presence at his house. It would have been enough to make anyone come undone.

I looked around at the room I had occupied since I'd been born. Sure, I'd planned to leave it in a couple of months, but it had been a safety net, offering me a place if I failed. Now, my mother would be lucky to find a place to live that had more than two bedrooms, and it certainly wouldn't be on Tipton Hill.

My mother and I packed our belongings in boxes Barton brought home from the store. She applied for government housing, but there were no units available, so she turned to her newfound friends for advice. One woman at her job offered her a room in her trailer, but even without Barton and me, my mother had no idea how she'd share the space with two rambunctious boys.

I looked at the documents from ETSU and UT, but both of the universities didn't allow freshmen to move into the dorms until August. Aunt Margaret had filed an eviction notice that had given us until the end of the month to leave.

Even though she could press to keep us there for ninety days, my mother was doing her best to acquiesce. She kept saying she didn't want to leave her long-time residence with hard feelings.

In the middle of it all, I was set to graduate. It wasn't like Barton's experience with a big family party, and it depressed me for most of the day. At five o'clock on my graduation day, though, I grabbed my robe and cap, took the obligatory pictures under the dogwood tree, and rode with Barton, my mother, and my younger brothers to the high school gymnasium.

We'd practiced our walk and been given our places in line. I was toward the end of the procession due to my last name, and Imani was in the front. Sanders was right behind me, but we were in similar moods, so we were mostly silent as we huddled in a room behind the bleachers.

I could hear the proud relatives filling the stands. I lamented my daddy's absence, and even though she was part of the reason for my situation, I wished Mary Beth was alive to see Sanders walk across the stage and hoist his diploma into the air.

The only relative who was there for Sanders was Crystal, and she'd have to sit with the great aunts and uncles. I had a clear understanding of why my mother and Aunt Tonya didn't have my sister around them, but I didn't like their reasons. After all, Crystal was a child, and she had nothing to do with her mother's promiscuousness and the infidelities of the men on Tipton Hill.

The people in front of us moved, and we filed out to the applause of our family members. I sat in my assigned seat and searched for my mother and brothers. When I found them, I almost leaped out of my seat, and Sanders had to pull me down to keep me from running across the gym floor.

My mother held Si in her lap with Barton on one side, and on her other side was my father, holding a wriggling Pickles in his lap. Sheriff Watts was next to him, and I thought he might have winked at me when I waved at my father.

I felt almost electric through the ceremony. Most of the students fell asleep during the valedictorian's speech, but I kept looking at my father in the bleachers. *He was really there!* He'd made it to my graduation.

I'd been upset with him over his affair with my aunt, and for keeping my relation to Crystal a secret, but his presence was enough to make my anger disappear. He'd found a way to be there for me, just like he had my whole life.

I almost bounced to the stage when I received my diploma, and I'm certain I was beaming in my graduation photo immediately after I left the stage. After I sat down, my feet bounced against the floor until Sanders calmed me again.

"He'll still be there after it's over," he assured me. "Sheriff Watts won't take him back before you have the chance to tell him good-bye."

My eyes hardly left my father, dressed in his khaki slacks and white button-up. It was the fanciest outfit he owned, and the sheriff had afforded him the dignity to wear it instead of the sunset orange jumpsuit the inmates wore. He wasn't handcuffed, and I couldn't wait for him to wrap me in a hug.

Finally, the graduates threw up their hats, and we dispersed. I thought I saw Owen in the crowd, but I breezed past him toward my daddy. Sensing my excitement, my father had given Pickles to my mother, and he had danced his dusty boots across her pretty blue dress.

I fell into my father's arms and let him hold me. I had no plan to end the hug, and when he pulled away, I felt warm tears on my face.

"I'm so proud of you!" he said.

I couldn't do anything but sob. He embraced me until I calmed down, and we made our way to the stage to take some pictures. Most everyone had filed out, but there were a few families who wanted the same photo opportunity, so we waited for them and took our pictures last.

After my dad posed awkwardly for a picture with Sanders and me, the sheriff announced it was time to go.

"Can he eat dinner with us?" I begged, new tears forming.

Sheriff Watts shook his head sadly. "I could get in trouble for bringin' him out. Everyone thought he was granted leave by a judge, but the judge denied his request. It'll be my head if they find out I took him here."

I understood the point and the sacrifice he'd made for us. My father hugged each of his children, whispering something to Crystal that made her smile and embraced me last.

"I'm gonna give you some advice," he said. "It's your choice if you listen to it, but I hope you do."

I stared at him as he spoke. He could have told me anything, and it would have resonated in my soul.

"Don't let what everyone expects you to do guide your decisions. You have to live with your accomplishments and your mistakes, so make sure you make the decisions that make you happy."

The sheriff led my father away, and I stared after him. My mother put her hand on my shoulder, but I shrugged her off. I stepped out the other entrance, embracing the warm spring night, and walked back home, climbing into the hammock my father and I had shared.

Thankfully, everyone left me alone. I watched the purple and orange sky transition into navy blue and black, and only the crickets were chirping when I went into the house and fell onto my bed.

Chapter 30

I was sick for three days after my graduation. I don't know if it was because I stayed out in the cold too long, I was around too many people at my graduation, or if I was too burdened by the stress of our family's move and my father's supposed crime.

I stayed away from my other family members. My mother and little brothers kept their distance, and my mother relied more on Barton to help her with them.

My mother walked to and from work, and Barton came home after his first shift to watch the boys. He'd take my mother and brothers to look at apartments, and she tried to rent a trailer on the far side of town before the landlord told her he had rented it to his nephew instead of her.

During one of their outings to look for a house for us, a man came to the door. He seemed official, but I hadn't seen him on Sheriff Watts's force. I opened the door without unchaining it and stared at the man. He didn't seem to expect a greeting and was unaffected by my wariness.

"May I speak with Sara Beth Tipton?" he asked.

It was obvious he didn't know my mother well. She had dropped her middle name when I was in middle school.

"She's not here," I replied.

I thought about my mistake immediately. I was alone in the house, and a total stranger was aware of it. *What if he was the man I'd seen lurking around?* Would I have enough time to grab my phone off the kitchen counter and dial emergency services before he broke through our rusty door chain and attacked me?

I was uncomfortably aware of the long silence since I'd spoken. "She'll be home any minute," I added.

"Thank you," he responded curtly, turning on his heel and leaving as abruptly as he'd arrived.

I tried to get a good look at his car, but I could only see the red color. He'd parked at the side of the house, and I was too slow to look out the far window before he had driven out of sight.

I called Owen, and he pulled into the driveway in less than ten minutes. I opened the door for him, still shaking.

"I'm being ridiculous," I told him.

He shook his head. "My mother was attacked once when a woman asked her to get keys from under her car. She had a cast on each arm, so my mom felt obligated to help. My mom told me she'd had a bad feeling about it because the woman shouldn't have been driving with two broken arms, but she'd assumed the woman's driver was somewhere nearby. To be nice, she'd reached under the car to get the keys, but when she did, a man came out from behind another car and pinned her down. They only took her money, but it could have been way worse."

He caressed the side of my face. "Always trust your feelings."

It wasn't long before Barton's car rattled into the driveway. My mother hurried inside, possibly worried I was trying to make her a grandmother, and relief stamped her face when she saw Owen and me holding hands at the table.

"Boys shouldn't be here when I'm not home," she stated. "You may have graduated, but you still live under my roof."

"A man came to the house, and it scared Meg," Owen explained.

Barton brought in the boys, each one dangling from an arm. As soon as he set them down, Si ran to my boyfriend and sat in his lap as if he were eager for Owen to tell him a story.

"What man?" my mother asked. "What did he look like?"

I tried to describe him, but I could only give them average details. "He was a little taller than me, and he was middle-aged with brown hair and glasses." I was even less help when they asked me about his car.

My mother and Barton ran down a list of everyone they knew, but they had no luck. The sun hadn't set, but I felt just as uncomfortable as if it were the dead of night.

"Do you want to come to my house for dinner?" Owen asked.

I looked at my mother for permission, and she nodded. "I have soup beans in the pot, so you should probably grab something fancier if you can."

Owen's beautiful parents greeted me at the door. His toned father had dark hair and sea-green eyes, and his mother was lean and bubbly, with a straight nose and high cheekbones.

Owen's house was a split-level, and nothing was overly expensive, but his father's easy chair probably cost more than any singular piece of furniture in my house. I tried not to look around in wonder, but it was hard not to gawk at his immaculate home.

The organization of the drawers and bins amazed me. Everything his mother opened lay perfectly in its place. Unlike my house, where items were thrown haphazardly into drawers with child safety locks before little hands grabbed them.

Imani's house was large and beautiful, but even her father's tools were scattered in the garage. Clothes were tossed on Imani's floor, and she didn't bother to put the labels facing forward when she retrieved something from the cabinet, even though it drove her father crazy.

I was instantly insecure about my house. "You must think I live in squalor."

He chuckled at my word usage. "No. I think your house looks like a family lives there. It's just my parents and me, so we each clean up after ourselves."

I still felt self-conscious. I vowed to pick up around my house more before Owen's next visit.

Dinner was a perfectly plated steak and asparagus combination. I felt like I was dining at a fine establishment, and I kept reminding myself to sit straighter and keep my elbows clear of the table. By the time the poppy seed lemon pound cake was served, I was ready to scream from the silent stress.

Owen's parents were delightful hosts, and they seemed genuinely interested in me. After they'd learned a little about my family and my general interests, they told me a few humorous stories about their travels. It shocked me to hear that a police officer had stopped Owen's father as he held a water hose in the rain.

"Apparently, in Nova Scotia, it's against the law to water a lawn when it's raining," he laughed. "It's a good thing I was only carrying the hose to my host's garage, or the officer would've written me a citation!"

Owen's mother flashed a bleached-white smile. "I think the officer was just ribbing you because he could tell you were an American. When I looked out the window, both of you were laughing."

After dinner, Owen led me to his room, and I flipped through comic books while he scrolled down his song list. He finally settled on a Nirvana song and sat beside me on his bed.

It was a little uncomfortable to be so close to my boyfriend while his parents were in the house. I tried to make some small talk, but he lifted my chin and met my lips. I felt gentle pressure from him to lie back on his bed, so I broke our contact.

"Don't your parents check on you or anything?" I asked.

He understood my concern right away. "Not since I turned eighteen." He tried to kiss me again, but I backed away.

"I don't think I'm ready for—"

Owen held up both his hands. "I just wanted to kiss you, Meg. You can decide how far we go."

I was relieved, and we looked at some comic books together. Owen and I spent the next hour talking about retractable claws and the ability to walk through walls. When we left, his parents were sitting on the couch with their arms wrapped around one another.

"Your parents are so perfect for each other," I commented when we were in his car.

He lifted his lip in mock disgust. "They're too perfect. They never seem to disagree about anything."

"I'm so sorry," I joked. "The millions of children with divorced parents feel your pain."

He chuckled. "I know. I should be grateful, and I am, but they stand solidly on everything. That means, when they decide I'm wrong about something, they're both against me."

"They don't want you to go to ETSU, do they?"

He shrugged. "They think I should travel before I go to college."

"Really?"

He expected my surprise. "Yeah. Most parents want their children to go straight to college, but my parents want me to have experiences."

"Once again, boo-hoo for you."

Owen reached out and playfully shoved me. "You shouldn't be so hard on me. Your parents are still together."

I looked out the window into the darkness. "It's not all sunshine and rainbows at my house."

"I guess it's not," he said, turning on the radio to drown out the awkwardness my statement left behind.

We pulled up to the house and Owen walked me to my door. Barton's car was gone, and I could tell by the stillness that something was wrong.

Owen kissed me goodnight, but I didn't let his lips linger. I was too worried about what I might find when I stepped through the door.

Sure enough, my mother was at the dining room table with a letter in front of her. Her head was in her hands, and when she raised it, her eyeliner was smeared down her cheeks.

"What's wrong, Mama?" I cried, rushing to her side.

An official-looking document rested on the table. I tried to read the words, but they were too small for me to make out.

"I solved the mystery of the man at the door." Her voice dripped with sarcasm.

"Who was he, Mama?" I pressed, afraid that I'd be left out if Barton pulled into the driveway before she told me about the letter.

"He's not really anyone important," she clarified. "He was sent here to serve me with papers."

My mind went to my Aunt Margaret. She had given us a handwritten eviction notice, but she could have felt like she needed to make it more legal.

"I'm going to her house right now," I announced, rushing to the door.

"Who?" My mother was clearly confused. "Whose house?"

"Aunt Margaret," I replied. "She has no right to treat our family this way. We'll be out at the end of the month, and she—"

"Megara, enough," my mother said without inflection. "It has nothing to do with your Aunt Margret."

A lump formed in my throat and sat there, making it difficult to swallow. "What's going on, Mama?"

She hung her head back over the pages. "Your father had them served. He's divorcing me." A tear slid off her nose and landed on the papers.

Chapter 31

Crystal sat in the center of her rug, arranging her toy rockets around her. Aside from some rocket-fuel noises, I didn't hear a sound from her. Pickles had asked if he could play with her, but she stared at him until he walked away.

I read Si the same book until he fell asleep on my lap, and I prepared dinner for all of us. I included portions for Sanders and my mother, as they were both at work.

My mother picked up Pickles and Si after dinner, and they walked to our house, with my mother carrying her meal in an old butter container. I stayed with Crystal until Sanders's shift ended. It was the best routine for our family. It kept Crystal in her usual environment, and it was easier for me to watch them all there instead of trying to keep Si and Pickles out of our packed boxes all day.

Sanders came home with a strawberry milkshake for Crystal and me. "I fixed the ice cream machine," he announced.

"It'll be broken again by the time you go back to work tomorrow," I joked. Everyone who frequented the restaurant was aware of their finicky dessert appliance.

He smiled sadly. "Are you really moving away this weekend?"

I stared at my drink cup. "Yeah. Mama found a place in Johnson City."

My mother was sad that she'd have to leave her job and the new friends she'd made, but she'd have to find a job within walking distance of our new apartment. I was going to watch the boys for her, and Barton hadn't committed to going with us.

"I'll need to find someone else to watch Crystal."

"Probably," I agreed. "But you would have had to do that at the end of the summer anyway."

"Yeah." His voice cracked. "While everyone else follows their dreams and I'm left here."

I pulled him out of range of Crystal's ears. "What are you talking about? You have a full scholarship to UT."

"I do, but now I have a six-year-old child to raise."

It hit me. There was no one left to take care of Crystal. Suddenly, it seemed unfair that Sanders was left with her when she wasn't even his biological sister.

"The court granted me temporary custody, and they have no reason to deny full guardianship to me at our next hearing."

I nodded along. I couldn't think of anything else to do.

"I'm so sorry, Sanders."

He let out a long sigh. "Well, when you come back and run a nice business, don't forget to drop by the restaurant for a milkshake."

I thought about his situation on my way home. It made my milkshake taste sour in my mouth.

Once in my yard, I stopped at the woodpile and pulled out the jar of money. I didn't look at it or count it. I walked back up to my aunt's house and knocked on the door. When Sanders answered, I put the jar in his hand and walked away, leaving him staring after me.

My father refused to see my mother. She cried and begged Sheriff Watts, but he told her that my father had the right to deny her visits. The only arrangement that worked for my father was for me to bring Pickles and Si into the visitation booth with me.

Barton refused to take us to see my father, so I asked Owen. He drove us while my brothers tried to talk to him at the same time from their car seats.

"I'm so sorry," I said, putting my head in my hand. "My brothers can be a bit much."

Owen patted my thigh. "I don't mind. I always wanted a younger sibling."

"You can have mine," I offered, only half-joking.

Once we were in the booth, Pickles and Si took half of the visit talking to my father. He seemed pale and much thinner, and I hoped it was because he was having second thoughts about the divorce.

Owen knocked on the door to the visitation booth and offered to take my brothers. I jumped at the chance to speak to my father alone.

"How's my beautiful graduate?" he asked.

I didn't strain our time with forced pleasantries. "Why are you divorcing my mother?"

He recoiled from the suddenness of my statement. "I believe that's between your mama and me."

"It includes all of us."

"Now, Meg, I'm not divorcin' you and your brothers."

"You always told me that family was everything, but you're destroying yours." My tears slid down my cheeks before I could stop them. "Why are you doing this?"

He took a deep breath. "I had it planned for a while. I hired a lawyer after Christmas, but I waited until after your graduation to have the papers served."

I tried to think back to see if I had any clue that my parents were going to divorce, and I remembered the conversation Uncle Barton had with my mother in the driveway. She seemed convinced my uncle's information was false, though.

"Did you tell Mama?"

He gave me a look that I couldn't read. "Your mama knew we hadn't gotten along for some time."

"But you love each other!" I shouted.

He took my words in stride. "Yes. We both love each other, but we weren't meant to be together."

I laughed sarcastically. "I guess you believe in fate the same way Mama describes it when she reads her mythology books."

He shook his head once. "Maybe. My fate was ripped away from me."

"Are you talking about Aunt Mary Beth? She couldn't have been your destiny. She slept with everyone in town, even Uncle Catfish!" I threw the last part at him because I wanted him to hurt as much as he had hurt my mother.

"I left her lonely," he defended. "She looked for attention 'cause I thought I had to honor my vows."

"Well, she's dead," I spat. "What good does it do to divorce Mama now?"

"I told you, it was already put in motion months ago, and I didn't see the need to stop it. Besides, it'll be better for your mama if I divorce her. She can draw money from the state for the boys."

"That's a stupid excuse," I barked. I saw the look on his face, and something inside me wanted to keep hurting him. "Oh, by the way, all the plants in your garden died. No one bothered to take care of it."

He looked away, leaning forward and placing his forearms across his knees. "That's a shame."

"I guess we treated it the same way you treated your family."

"Mary Beth and Crystal are my family, too."

"Crystal might be your daughter, but Mary Beth was a —"

Anticipating my next word, my father jumped out of his seat. "Don't you say one word about your aunt. She loved you!"

I held my posture and tried to make my face as blank as possible. My legs shook, but my father couldn't see them from his vantage point.

He sat down and rubbed his forehead. "I swear, girl. You can push my buttons just like your mother."

My father was right. My aunt had been good to me, and the love triangle between my mother, aunt, and father was none of my business. Still, I couldn't let it go.

The deputy retrieved him, and my father kissed his fingers and blew it at me as he left. I waved and walked out the door, wondering if I should ever come back.

Chapter 32

Mary Beth's funeral was sparsely attended. My mother went out of obligation, but she wouldn't sit in the front row, a section reserved for close family members. Thankfully, one of her new friends from work had offered to watch Pickles and Si, so it kept me from chasing after them during the ceremony.

Sanders sat with his arm around Crystal as she stoically stared at her dead mother. Occasionally, she looked at Sanders, as if asking if he would take her somewhere else, but he ignored her. His eyes were locked on Mary Beth, and one of his fists stayed clenched through the viewing.

Uncle Barton sat with them. He had paid for the funeral, and he'd made certain his sister's service had every enhancement. He'd arranged for peonies, Mary Beth's favorite flowers, to be placed around her. He was clearly reflecting on the memories he had of his sister as soft music played and photographs of her flashed on the screen in front of him.

I was surprised to see Aunt Tonya and Uncle Catfish at my aunt's funeral. Aunt Tonya had avoided my aunt, but now that she was dead, Aunt Tonya seemed to feel more comfortable around her. I supposed it was because Aunt Mary Beth no longer threatened her happiness. A small smile played on Aunt Tonya's mouth, and she tried to cover it. She was at the service to see her long-time nemesis covered by the lid of her casket.

Several men I didn't know breezed in and out. A middle-aged man with a bright blond mullet and a toothy smile waved at my mother as he paid his respects to my aunt. He sat alone, but he kept looking back at my mother. Barton stopped and spoke to him, so when my brother sat down beside me, I asked him about the man's identity.

"He's my father," he informed me, just as the ceremony began.

A preacher who never knew Mary Beth spoke about her kindness and patience. He was right about her emotional attributes, but he failed to move the small audience.

Crystal didn't budge from her spot until Uncle Catfish started closing the coffin. "Don't shut it," she begged, pulling away from Sanders and reaching for her mother. "She doesn't like the dark. Don't put her in the dark!"

I was thankful when my brother got up and helped Sanders lead her out of the room. The coffin was closed, and my mother stifled a sob.

The scene horrified my Uncle Catfish. He was used to making people laugh, and he worried he'd upset Crystal.

"They told me to close it," I heard him say to Aunt Tonya, and she rubbed his shoulder in consolation.

Uncle Catfish was one of eight pallbearers Sanders had selected. He chose four of his friends from school, Uncle Barton, Barton, Uncle Catfish, and me. Since Uncle Catfish was older than most of us, he had elected to close the coffin. As young adults, the rest of us were content to stay away from the dead body, but duty and a sense of guilt moved Uncle Catfish to fully embrace his role.

I was surprised my aunt Tonya allowed him to go to Mary Beth's funeral, and she attended it, too. I understood part of their appearance was meant to heal Aunt Tonya's pride and the other part was to support Sanders and Crystal when I saw her in the row behind them whispering condolences and encouragement throughout the viewing.

Aunt Tonya was especially good with Crystal, and I was glad to see my sister respond to her once. Crystal had hardly acknowledged me when I approached her, but it could have been because my mother was with me.

"It was good to see you," a man's voice said. "I just wish it had been under better circumstances."

I looked up at Dandy Hughes. "Aren't you supposed to be in jail?"

He let out a hearty laugh that shook his muscular frame, oblivious to the people who stared at us. "I served my sentence," he told me. Then to my mother, he remarked, "This one's just like you. She speaks her mind."

"She does," my mother agreed solemnly.

Usually, I would have been offended by his comment, but I felt the need to defend my mother in the presence of her ex-husband. "I have her hair and eyes, too."

There were several other features, like my mother's rounded chin and her skin tone, that I'd obviously inherited, but it was unnecessary to run down the list. He studied me, pinching his clean-shaven chin between his thumb and forefinger before he spoke.

"You know, you're definitely right about the eyes, but the color of your hair—"

"Changed with puberty," my mother finished.

After I had defended her, the way she spoke so casually about an embarrassing topic threw me off. I could have crawled under the pew to hide. Her statement dried up my mouth and turned my eyes away. Thankfully, Dandy had somewhere else to go, and he went there quickly.

After the funeral, we gathered at Aunt Mary Beth's house for light refreshments. I decided I should start thinking of the house as Sanders's house since Mary Beth had left it to him. Her will hadn't officially been read, but Sanders found a copy in their family safe, so he knew Mary Beth had left the house, and Crystal, to him.

In the small house, the mourners seemed more numerous. They milled about between the kitchen and living area, giving a wide berth to Crystal and her rockets.

Imani had sat with her father at the funeral. We'd hugged briefly, but she'd remained with him through the service. After I sat on the couch with Sanders, Imani scooted in on the other side and leaned on me.

We hadn't spoken a lot since she'd told me she might be pregnant, and every day her period was late seemed to be a clear indication that she was carrying a new life. I'd texted her about taking a test, even offering to buy it for her, but she refused. She claimed she could check out a test herself in the store where she worked, but she wasn't ready to face the possibility of a positive result.

The three of us sat silently unless someone offered us expressions of sympathy. Some mourners directed their condolences at Imani, too, and I was glad for it. She'd spent many afternoons at Mary Beth's house with Sanders and me, eating peanut butter pinwheels and dancing through the yard sprinklers.

My mother drifted through the rooms, and no one stopped her. She hadn't had a lot of time with Mary Beth in her adult life, so each porcelain figurine and photograph seemed new to her. It represented the full life of a middle-aged woman who died before her time. I wanted to feel sorry for her, but something held me back.

I overheard someone speaking, and I tuned in to hear it better. I didn't recognize the voice, but she seemed to know a lot about my family.

"It's so sad to see her walkin' around Mary Beth's house," the woman said. "Sara doesn't wear as much makeup as her sister did, but the resemblance is so striking that it's like watching Mary Beth's ghost go from room to room."

The other woman with her must have agreed, as the first woman continued, "It's a shame what happened here, and in the bedroom, too. You know, Sara must have been scandalized when Ace was picked up for the murder."

"They kept their situation out of the public eye for years," the other woman said. "I didn't think it'd come out this way."

The first woman scoffed. "Everyone knew about it. Mary Beth and Sara did everything they could to hurt each other. They let the same man use them like his harem, going from one to the other and getting them pregnant."

"Oh, you're talkin' about the coroner's report," the second woman said.

Sanders jumped off the couch. "Mrs. Nebo, I think you've had too much to drink."

It was a bold statement, as the woman held a cup of coffee in her hand. She expressed her offense, and Uncle Barton rushed to neutralize the situation. He got the woman and her friend to leave without further incident.

"What happened?" he asked Sanders when he returned.

Sanders had resumed his place on the couch next to me, but my uncle's question made him jump to his feet. He leaned in and whispered something to Uncle Barton, and the older man nodded.

"Let me know if anyone else mentions it," he told Sanders.

I wanted to scream at them as another layer of mystery had been thrown over my aunt's death. *What was I missing?*

Then I thought about the woman who had been so kind to me. My father had been right. Aunt Mary Beth had loved me, and all I could think about was satisfying my curiosity. I should have been reflecting on her warm hugs and easy smiles and mourning over the times I'd never share with her again.

At that moment, part of me realized why my father loved her so much. Mary Beth was fun-loving and kind, while the repercussions of her decisions had hardened my mother. Of course my father had wanted to be with the woman who loved freely and embraced forgiveness, but his sense of duty had pulled him back to his wife.

Aunt Margaret approached us, and I braced myself for whatever foul thing escaped her mouth. She leaned on her cherry wood cane and patted my leg, allowing herself a small smile.

"I've given your mother until the end of summer to move out," she said to me. "My nephew finally came to his senses, but there's no reason to rub salt in the wound, so I gave her a rent-free extension. She doesn't have to leave until the divorce is official."

Aunt Margaret thought she was doing me a favor, and maybe she was, but I wanted to knock her yellowing false teeth down her throat. I tried to smile, but I could only squeak out a small appreciation.

"You're welcome, Meg," she said benevolently and crossed the room to talk with my uncle, who looked even less pleased than I had been to deal with her.

I decided to make myself useful. I squeezed Sanders's hand and went to the kitchen. Eyes followed me as if they were judging my movements, and two well-meaning relatives shooed me out of the kitchen when I tried to wash the dishes. I ended up in the laundry room, so I started a load of white clothes, but I couldn't find the bleach. At first, I was going to wash them without it, but I looked harder for the bleach and noticed the grass stain on the elbow of one of Crystal's shirts.

I moved the detergent and several bottles of starch and softener, but my search yielded no results. I stood on the tips of my toes and moved the garments my aunt had put on the top shelf for mending. I didn't feel any bottles, so I withdrew my hand, but when I did, several articles of clothing fell into the washer.

I lifted each piece, folding it and returning it to the top shelf. At the bottom of the pile, I found one of Barton's light blue work shirts. It had been waded up, and when I opened it, blood covered the front of the shirt. It had dried, and flakes of it fell on the white washer.

I didn't have time to process what I'd found as ear-piercing screams echoed through the house. Fully conscious that my brother may have killed our aunt, I took the shirt in my hand and dusted off the flecks of blood on the washer. I carried the shirt with me, concealing it as I hurried down the hall.

I had known my mother's screams since I heard them, and I followed them to Mary Beth's bedroom. Uncle Barton and Barton were already there, and almost everyone else in the house gathered at the door. I pushed past them without caring about the people who almost fell as I parted the crowd. Uncle Barton tried to shut the door, and he gently pushed it against me, but I pushed back, and something in the determination he saw on my face caused him to release enough pressure to let me in.

My mother was on the floor beside where Mary Beth had slept. The nightstand was open, and piles of papers and open books were scattered around her. Barton sat on top of an orange stain, and I wondered if it was the remnants of Mary Beth's blood on the beige carpet.

My mother held a white stick in her hand, crying, and shaking it at the ceiling. "Why?" she shouted. "Why now?"

"Shh," Barton said as he tried to soothe her. "There are people here."

"I don't care," my mother said with her eyes closed and her teeth clenched. "They all know anyway."

"What does everyone know?" I pressed.

Everyone's eyes were on me. My mother seemed to regain some of her composure, but she was still locked inside whatever she was feeling when she started screaming.

"You need to go on, Megara," she spat. "I wouldn't want to ruin your picture-perfect view of your father."

"Too late for that," I shot back.

She considered my words and seemed to roll them around like she was savoring a fine wine. "Well, then, if you think you're ready to know—"

"Sara," Uncle Barton warned.

My mother glared at her brother so fiercely my blood turned cold. She was like a copperhead that had been cornered, and it was coiling up to strike.

She turned back to me. "Your father wasn't just divorcing me because he and I had too many problems." She dropped her head. "It was always that way." She lifted her eyes and moved on, holding up the stick in her hand. A soft pink plus sign appeared in the window of the pregnancy test. My shock must have registered across my face because my mother nodded.

"My sister was pregnant again," she shrugged. She was still processing her find. In her other hand, she lifted a journal with a date just after Thanksgiving on the front cover. "And she had been for months."

Chapter 33

It was then I noticed that the books and papers weren't just household receipts and fiction novels. My aunt had been refreshing her knowledge about pregnancy and writing journal entries about her symptoms and feelings.

I wanted to run out of the room, but I had demanded a place among the adults, and I had to act like one. I said nothing, and when my mother realized she had wounded me, she returned to her self-pity.

Uncle Barton left us so he could attend to the other people in the house. He thanked the guests and led them to the door. I don't know if he gave them excuses or if they assumed their presence was too great a burden for the family, but everyone left peaceably. Imani was gone when we filtered into the living room.

I took Crystal to her room, and she brushed her teeth automatically in the adjoining bathroom. She changed into cat pajamas and settled onto her bed.

"Do I need to read you a story?" I asked her.

"Mommy read stories to me, but she's in the coffin and can't get out."

I repeated my question. I tried desperately not to show my feelings, but it was hard to maintain patience with her.

"I don't want anyone around me," she said, clutching the rocket she said her daddy had given to her.

"You and I are sisters," I declared. "I wish we could be closer."

She looked at me; her features a mask. "I know."

"I'll always be here for you."

She didn't respond, and I closed her door.

When I got back to the living room, my mother, Uncle Barton, Sanders, and Barton were whispering. I pressed against the eaves to hear them.

"She found my shirt," Barton told them. "She's carrying it around like we can't see it behind her back."

"I should have put it in a random dumpster," Sanders responded.

"What's done is done, boys," my mother said. "There's nothing we can do about it now."

"You need to think about how she'll react when she learns the truth," Uncle Barton warned.

"That will not happen," my mother barked.

There was a brief pause. "You have too many secrets," Uncle Barton whispered.

"I'd like to know some of them," I said, stepping into the room. "Starting with why my aunt's blood is on Barton's shirt."

They didn't tell me anything. When it was clear my maturity wasn't benefitting me, I resorted to anger, throwing the shirt at my brother and calling him a murderer.

Two weeks passed, and I had little interaction with anyone. I stayed in my room and only smiled when my little brothers said or did something to tickle one out of me. We stayed in the limbo of moving, with boxes announcing the inevitable shift as our mother searched for another apartment closer to our home county.

Owen sent me text messages, asking me to go out and eat with him, but I refused. He tried to call, but I ignored his attempts. I was thankful for the space he gave me.

Imani wrote messages to comfort me, but she didn't call. I kept expecting her to show up at my house, but she was dealing with her own drama.

Sanders tried to text me, and he spent time with me after his work shifts ended. He joined in the silence that permeated the house when Crystal and I were left alone.

Amazingly, Aunt Tonya picked up Crystal most mornings and took her to brush the horses. She taught her to ride, and some days she opted to care for Crystal all day as they bonded over animals and long hikes.

Even though she'd admitted Crystal looked like my father, I got the idea that she might have thought Crystal was Catfish's daughter. Once Crystal's paternity was revealed through a line of powerful gossip, Aunt Tonya was more willing to interact with the child.

I lay in my father's hammock, looking up at the cornflower sky and wispy clouds until the sky gathered orange and purple hues. I heard the familiar sound of the car, but I didn't move when it pulled into the driveway.

"Hey," Owen spoke.

"Hey," I returned without moving.

He squatted down so he could meet my eyes. "Can I stay with you?"

"Yes."

He tried to get into the hammock with me, but I smiled apologetically and got out. I held his hand and led him to the tire swing at the side of the house. We'd be away from prying eyes and ears there, as anyone in the house who wanted to see or listen to us would have to peer through a small, high window.

"The hammock is special to you," he observed.

I twirled my fingers around the fraying rope that held up the tire. "I used to lie in it with my dad."

Owen helped me into the swing, and he pushed me until we heard crickets chirping. As the night gathered around us, he put his arms around me as if to shield me from the darkness.

"I think I'm falling in love with you."

I tried to make his profession of love mean something to me. On some level, it excited me to be the object of Owen's affection, but I was scared that he'd leave me like my father was leaving my mother. *Or had my father's original plan been to leave one family for another?*

Barton hadn't mowed the grass in over a week, and it was almost to my mid-shin in the places where the boys didn't play. From the higher grass, lights flickered.

"Fireflies," Owen observed as tiny lights drifted up from the grass, flashing their beacons as they rose. "They're one of my favorite parts of summer. I think they're beautiful."

"They're carnivorous," I voiced. I didn't mean to upset the moment, and thankfully, Owen's good temperament persisted.

"I read stories about them," he went on. "Do you remember the little books with facts about insects and animals that the librarians would put out for us?"

I had no recollection of the books. I nodded my head without looking at him.

"I used to read all the ones about fireflies."

I pushed my toe into a bare spot on the ground, and the swing twirled to the left. "My dad calls them lightning bugs."

"I've heard them called that, too, but I think fireflies sounds more romantic."

I glanced at him skeptically. "There's nothing romantic about insects."

He chuckled and kissed my head. "I guess it's all about how you look at things. You see, their lights are part of a mating ritual."

"That's interesting," I said, beginning to feel the romance from the way Owen held me and the soft baritone of his voice. I leaned into his embrace when I realized I'd been stiff against his touch.

Feeling me relax, he continued. "Really, they're part of a great love tragedy. Fireflies rise from the ground and rest in the trees, blinking their love lights as they ascend. They only live a couple of months, find their mate, and die."

"That's almost poetic," I remarked.

Owen reached under my chin and lifted it so he could stare into my eyes. Normally, it made me uncomfortable for him to look at me for so long, but at that moment, it felt perfect.

My lips parted, and I felt his warm tongue in my mouth. We moved in harmony, and the world disappeared. Owen had seen my light blinking in the fading evening. It didn't matter how long we'd be together. All that mattered was that he wanted to be with me, surrounded by fireflies.

Chapter 34

My father was unapologetic.

"I'm not gonna stay with your mother," he said firmly. "Our divorce will be final soon, and we can move on with our lives."

"It's not right," I countered. Owen and my brothers were playing on the sidewalk outside the visitation booth, and their absence emboldened me. "Mary Beth is gone, and you can't be with her. Don't you love Mama, too?"

My father's face softened. "Of course I love your mama. She's been a good companion and a faithful wife, and that's even more of a reason to set her free." He waved his hand in the direction of the courthouse. "The state will find me guilty, and then she'd be married to me the rest of her life, but I couldn't touch her or help with the bills. She can find another husband now."

"I guess I should think of love casually, too."

His eyebrows drew together. "Meg, you need to find a good man who'll love you unconditionally. I don't want you to go through what your mama, your aunt, and I went through."

"I found Barton's bloody shirt," I said suddenly.

At first, he didn't understand me, but then it dawned on him. "Do you have it?" he demanded.

His tone offended me, and I let him know it. I looked away and crossed my arms.

"Answer me, Meg."

"I slung it at Barton's lying face," I spat. "And for someone who didn't get along with him, you're certainly okay with covering things up for him!"

My father relaxed when I told him I'd returned Barton's shirt to him. "I never said I didn't like your brother."

I threw my hands up. "Well, he didn't like you then! I guess he's happy with his stupid father now that he's out of prison." I laughed without mirth. "That's funny. As soon as you go to jail, his father gets out. Maybe they framed you for Mary Beth's murder."

He seemed to startle out of his own thoughts. "Wha—I don't think you know what you're talkin' about."

I had gotten a little carried away, but he hadn't denied covering for my brother. I was tired of the lies and mystery, so I pressed him.

"I found the bloody knife, too."

His voice was grave and firm. "Don't tell your mama."

I was going to tell him that my mother was there when I threw the bloody shirt at my brother, but the door behind him buzzed, and the lower half of a deputy came into view. My father got up, kissed his fingers, pressed them to the glass, and left the room.

I didn't know how my cousin had talked me into standing in the rain on a Tuesday afternoon in a graveyard, but I was there, holding an umbrella over Crystal and me. She allowed me to pull her close, but only because a physical touch was less offensive to her than the rain coming down around us.

I knew where Mary Beth's plot was before I reached it. The ground was barren, and a new stone had been placed there recently. Most likely, Uncle Barton had paid for it.

She could have been buried next to Tom, but the circumstances weren't right. It had been years since he'd died, and she'd filled that time with a lot of lovers. I didn't think she wanted to be buried next to him anyway.

Sanders fell to his knees at the foot of the grave. I tried to look away as he cried, and I fought between whether I should let him grieve on his own or comfort him. I touched his shoulder to let him know I was there if he needed me. He lifted his hand and grabbed my wrist, squeezing once, and releasing it.

The gravestone was polished. It listed my aunt's full name and the dates of her birth and death.

At the bottom of the stone, a poem caught my attention. It read:

"We traveled through peaks and valleys, but you always had my heart. In death, we'll be united, and we'll never part."

It wasn't until I read the author of the poem that I broke down. My father's name stood out in scripted elegance beside his profession of undying love.

I had the presence of mind to press the handle of the umbrella into Crystal's hand before I ran away. Wet branches struck me, splashing water into my face with the sting of their slaps, but I carried on. I finally collapsed on a stone bench.

I don't know how long it took for Sanders and Crystal to find me, but I had started counting the dings the rain made as it hit the bench. I had made it into the hundreds.

Sanders told Crystal to walk to a flower bed just beyond the range of our voices. Once she was there, staring soullessly at the purple flowers, he addressed me.

"I didn't know Ace had put a poem on the headstone."

"Did he buy it, too?" I asked.

"Imani's dad paid for it."

That made better sense to me. Uncle Barton never would have let my father put a poem on Mary Beth's headstone. My father was still married, and my uncle wouldn't have wanted to hurt his living sister.

"He loved her." It wasn't a question.

Sanders lifted my head off the wet bench and sat down, placing my head on his lap. His face contorted in a grimace as it always did before he spoke about my father. I hadn't seen it before I found out Crystal was my sister, but Sanders seemed conflicted about the way he felt about my father. He had good reason, too, as the woman who acted as his mother had loved my father while she was married to his father.

"Yeah," he confided. "They loved each other a lot. They could fight like crazy, but they were always touching. He'd have his arm around her, or they'd hold hands."

"I never really saw him touch Mama," I said. "They fought a lot, though."

"Ace loved them both."

I knew Sanders was trying to comfort me, but it didn't help.

"How long did you know?"

Sanders understood I was talking about the relationship between my father and Mary Beth. "I knew it the whole time. They tried to hide it from me, and she'd sneak him into the house late at night. I purposely stepped out of my room one night, and when they saw me in the hallway, they didn't try to hide it from me anymore."

"Was she with him when your dad was alive?"

Sanders winced like he did whenever his father was mentioned, and nodded in answer to my question. "She was pregnant with Crystal when my dad..."

He trailed off, and I wanted to slap my palm on my forehead for making him tell me something I already knew. I had forgotten.

"Did Barton know?"

He scrubbed his face. "Yeah."

I thought about the way Barton had treated my father. He wouldn't let him teach him anything about mechanics or hunting, and he hardly spoke to him. It wasn't uncommon for my father's sentiments to be followed by a sneer from my brother, and after learning about my father's affair, I thought I knew the reason.

"My mama told him, didn't she?"

Sanders stared at me strangely. "No. Barton followed Ace to the house a couple of nights. He confronted me about it."

"You told him!" My voice rose shrilly.

"He was bigger than me, and he was mad," Sanders defended. "What was I supposed to do? It was Ace's fault, not mine."

"Actually, it was Mary Beth's fault for bringing men into your father's house, and I heard my father wasn't the only one."

Sanders looked stricken. He moved his mouth up and down, but no sound came out.

"Do not talk about my mommy."

We startled sharply in Crystal's direction. She had crept closer to us while our memories and revelations distracted us, and she stood with her hand squeezing the umbrella. I was the first to apologize.

Crystal turned away without acknowledging me, and we followed her. The rain reflected our mood, and the sky had more showers to unleash upon us.

Chapter 35

As much as he had hated my father, I always thought Barton loved Aunt Mary Beth. He used to sit with her for long hours as she mended Sander's clothes or watered her house plants. He seemed genuinely interested in her, endearing himself to her with his knowledge of ferns and succulents.

I never thought he'd kill her.

On the other hand, he adored our mother. He hung on to her words and was the first to rush to her aid when she needed help. He cooked with her, and he helped her with the boys when our brothers were too much for our mother to handle. He had pushed my father across the room during one fight my mother and father had let get out of control, but that was when he was a new teenager, and his hormones had sent his emotions flying out at all angles.

Barton seemed to place the blame for the affair on my father. I put it on Mary Beth.

I couldn't understand why Mary Beth could be kind and compassionate with my mother's children while she slept with her sister's husband. I didn't like to think about the betrayal, but she had hurt us all. Without her, my mother and father would have been able to sort through their problems. If she hadn't existed, my mother would have been less anxious, paying more attention to her children instead of rushing to her bed every night to make sure her husband stayed in it. If Mary Beth had moved away, we could have been a happy family.

I guess that's the reason Barton killed her. He'd found out about the divorce and her second pregnancy, and he'd sought to put an end to it before it decimated our mother's heart.

After all, with Mary Beth out of the picture, we would have been fine. When we were away from her, my mother and father were almost harmonious, and they hardly ever raised their voices.

I could remember one time in particular that we were truly happy. I thought back on it, almost seeing the sights, and smelling the swamp water in the air.

My parents kept our destination a secret until we drove under the banner that announced it. I was the first one to squeal, "Disneyland!"

"Disney World, actually," my mother corrected. "Disneyland is in California."

"The distance between Tennessee and Florida is much closer," my father commented.

My mother brushed his hair behind his ear. "It's still a long drive."

My parents had gotten an unusually large check from the government after they'd filed their taxes, and they'd taken us on a memorable vacation before I outgrew the appeal of the magic. I was nine, and Barton was eleven, so he wasn't really into the idea until he rode rollercoasters that blasted music while they twirled him around and princesses complemented his budding muscles.

I, on the other hand, was completely mesmerized. There were four parks, and I hardly scratched the surface of what they offered before our six-day vacation was over.

We soared through the air on planes and the backs of fantasy creatures, met our favorite characters, and tasted food I didn't know existed. I had a pineapple float every day, and I never tired of it.

"At least she's getting vitamin C," my father said when my mother questioned the daily snack.

My father's vacation fell during the week of Independence Day, so the sun bore down on us constantly, except for the thirty-minute rain shower that always fell after the peak heat of the afternoon. My mother, Barton, and I burned under the rays, even though we applied sunscreen every hour. On the third day, we bought cooling towels and fans, and we could stand in the sun and enjoy the shows and parades. I loved the events in front of the castle, and the kites led along by boats enthralled my mother.

The fireworks were fantastic! The lights and booms amazed me, but I was happier with the view of my family when I sat behind them as colored lights exploded in the air. My mother had her arm hung over Barton's shoulders, and my father held my mother's hand. I took in the scene before I joined them. My father lifted me onto his shoulders and took my mother's hand again. I imagined what other people saw when they looked at our family, and I burned the image into my mind.

When we rode the bus at night, the disembodied speaker expressed the hope that we'd had a wonderful day at every park and welcomed us "home" when we arrived at our resort. Back at the resort, my parents swam close together in the pool and we retired to our room.

Even in the extreme heat, my parents walked closely together, and I caught them blowing kisses at each other, my mother with her lips, and my father with two fingers that he'd placed on her cheek. They shared their plates at dinner, sampling medium-rare steaks and pasta that almost overflowed.

I felt like I was accompanying them on their honeymoon, and it made me happy. My brother seemed pleased, too, answering my father with respect when he asked him a question, and riding next to him on a few of the rides.

For six full days, our family was happy. We drove home singing songs we'd heard all week and sharing our favorite experiences.

When we pulled into the driveway, my heart fell. I don't know why my aunt's presence on our porch bothered me, but I remember being irritated.

She waited until my mother unlocked the door and she told her about a pipe that had burst in her bathroom. My mother was unmoved.

"Call a plumber," my mother had told her sister.

Aunt Mary Beth insisted she didn't have the money, begging for my mother's help. She touched my mother's arm, and my mother shook her off.

"You know I can't fix a pipe. You want my husband."

I didn't understand why my mother phrased it that way, but I wanted my father to stay with us. I would have given every penny I had to keep him at home with us.

"Sanders has to go outside to relieve himself," my aunt carried on, "and I have to use a bucket."

My father had kept one eye on the women during their conversation as he started unloading the car. He put two suitcases on the porch. "I'll fix it."

Mary Beth flooded him with appreciation, and even though my mother took him inside to talk, he emerged and left with Mary Beth minutes later. I watched them cross the lawns to her house, and I felt a sense of loss, even though I couldn't place my feelings.

Now, I understood everything perfectly. Mary Beth purposely wrecked my parent's marriage, and I hated her for it.

Chapter 36

My brother avoided me for a month after our aunt's funeral. I went to his work to corner him into talking to me.

Barton was stocking items from a recent delivery, and I found him with a clipboard and an open laptop in front of him. He looked intent on his work, and the teenage boy with him focused on each box as he counted the contents.

I sat down on the barstool next to my brother. The leather that covered the chair's padding had worn away in places and the cracks poked at my thighs.

"What do you want?" he asked without looking up.

I'd planned my approach perfectly. I leaned over and whispered, "Why did you kill Aunt Mary Beth?"

His head jerked up, and we glared at one another. He continued to stare at me as he directed the teenager to take a break.

Once we were alone, I launched into him. "Why did you do it?"

Barton laughed at me. "You're so oblivious, Meg. I don't know how you've made it this far in life."

I glossed over his insult with the only fact I knew. "My daddy didn't kill Aunt Mary Beth."

He sighed heavily, and it almost seemed like the weight of the world was on him. How had I not noticed the puffy circles around his eyes or the weight he'd lost, leaving more prominent cheek and collar bones?

He shook his head once. I didn't know if he was acknowledging my statement or if he was too tired to give a deeper answer.

"I found your knife," I pressed.

That visibly jolted him, but he remained silent. I wanted him to speak, address my concerns and validate my presumptions, but he wouldn't budge.

"I loved Aunt Mary Beth more than you did," he finally said. "And between people snubbing me over Ace's affair, because they think he's my father and tryin' to make sure everyone from Sanders to Mama to you is okay, I haven't even been able to settle her death into my mind."

I recognized his pain, and I could relate to it. I'd been running around attempting to find my aunt's real killer, and I'd had periods where I was melancholy, but I hadn't really grieved for the woman who had been part of my life. She suffered my mother's disdain so she could be part of our family.

Had she wanted to feel close to her sister again? Is that why she treated Barton and me as her own and slept with her sister's husband?

"Was it an accident?" I spoke softly.

Barton looked up at me as if he were going to speak. I waited, but he wasn't forthcoming. I had to try another angle.

I'd seen lawyers run through scenes in the final climatic minutes of an episode or movie, so I thought I could make Barton confess if I went through what I thought had happened.

"You saw my father turn on the radio for the garden, and you watched as he walked across the yard to Aunt Mary Beth's house. You followed him, and you found them together when you opened the door.

You took the knife out of your pocket, and you tried to stab him, but Aunt Mary Beth blocked you. You didn't mean to stab her, but the knife slid into her body—"

"I used the knife."

We turned toward the voice. Barton rushed over to Cynthia, holding her hand and staring daggers at me.

"Why would you kill my aunt?" I asked dumbly.

"I didn't," she replied, ignoring Barton's attempts to quieten her. "I used it on myself."

I stood on the concrete next to the loading dock and listened to Cynthia's sad story. The teenager came back to help with inventory, but my brother sent him to Cynthia's register, claiming it was her turn for a break.

My brother pulled out his chair for his girlfriend and sat on the barstool beside her. I stood, but I didn't mind. I was full of nervous energy.

"I found out on a Tuesday," Cynthia started. "I remember the day of the week because that's always the day when Mrs. Frazier and her husband come in for fresh produce."

Now that she'd made it clear she wanted to share her story, Barton put a comforting hand on her shoulder. I'd only seen him care so selflessly about one other person: our mother.

She took a steadying breath and continued. "I took a test in the bathroom during my break, and it was positive."

It took my mind a moment to switch my thoughts around from conspiracy to commit murder to the worries of new adults, but when it did, I understood the reason my brother hadn't wanted his girlfriend to speak. "You're pregnant?"

She dropped her head and nodded. "I'm almost five months along now."

My eyes focused on her waistline, partially blocked by the desk in front of her. She noticed my stare as she lifted her gaze.

"That's something your Aunt Mary Beth taught me," she admitted and then waved her hand. "But I'm getting ahead of myself."

She looked up at Barton and back at me. "Your brother was wonderful when I told him about the pregnancy. He wanted to marry me, but my family was against it and your mother hates me, so I knew we'd both have problems with our families if we did.

"I told my parents about the baby, and they flipped. They kicked me out of the house."

Cynthia massaged her arm absent-mindedly, and I wondered how forcefully Cynthia had been removed from her home. Barton followed my gaze and gave me an almost imperceptible nod.

"I couldn't believe my family hated me so much. After work that night, Barton rented a motel room for us. He stayed with me, and every time I rolled over and looked at him, I was reminded of the cruel looks your mother gave me, and I didn't want Barton to lose his family, too.

"I drew a bath while he slept, determined to drown myself, but I saw his knife on the table with his keys and I grabbed it."

Cynthia didn't want to talk about the lines the knife had made on her wrists, but I saw the scars when she brought her hands up. Once I'd understood, she dropped her arms and cried. Barton brought her close to him, caressing her shining hair.

I felt like an intruder as I watched my brother comfort his girlfriend. I thought about leaving a couple of times, but part of me sensed Cynthia hadn't finished telling her story. After she'd bared her soul, I should stay to hear the conclusion.

"Barton broke down the bathroom door," she said, removing herself from my brother's touch. "He was so scared."

"There was blood everywhere," he said, as if he could still see it. "I wrapped her wrist in my work shirt until we made it to the hospital."

"I was discharged three days later, but I see a therapist every week." She looked at Barton and smiled. "She's helped me a lot."

Cynthia moved on with the part of the story that pertained to my accusation. "Barton took me to Mary Beth's house. She let me stay there for a couple of days, and while I was there, she gave me advice about how to care for babies and myself, during and after pregnancy. She even taught me how to sew on a button.

"Your brother and I loved your aunt, and she was becoming close to me. I loved her like she was part of my family. If there's one thing I know in my heart, it's that your brother didn't kill Mary Beth."

My brother amended the story, telling me he had pocketed the knife and slung it down in his room. He didn't plan to carry it again, so it hadn't bothered him when he lost it.

"You know how people talk," she said, grimacing. "My parents heard about what had happened and thought I'd lost the baby. They told me I could come home as long as I agreed not to see Barton anymore. They must have forgotten that he worked with me." She looked at her lap miserably. "If they even paid attention when I told them."

Barton took over for her. "Ace found out about" —he was going to say *the attempted suicide*, but he let the shared knowledge hang in the air— "why Cynthia was staying with Aunt Mary Beth, and he told Mama."

I raised my eyebrow. My father had never been a fan of starting drama. He preferred to keep everything calm and unruffled.

"So, Mama knows Cynthia's pregnant?" I said.

They both shook their heads, as Barton answered me. "No. She only knows about the reason Cynthia was in the hospital. Ace told me it was my responsibility to tell her about the baby."

I thought about the reduced number of groceries available at our house. Barton seemed to read my thoughts.

"That's why I haven't been givin' as much money to Mama," Barton cut in. "I've been saving for the baby, and" —he took a deep breath— "for an apartment for my family."

"You're moving in together!" I exclaimed, not bothering to hide the smile that blossomed on my face. "That's wonderful!"

Cynthia and Barton looked at each other and then back at me.

"That wasn't the reaction I was expecting," Barton chuckled.

"I mean, I'll miss you," I backpedaled. "But I'm glad you've found someone you love and the two of you are going to start a family."

"It's definitely started," Cynthia said, rubbing her growing bump.

I welcomed Cynthia and the baby to the family, and Cynthia let me touch her belly. "We've felt a few kicks," she told me, but I didn't feel anything when she pressed my hand to her abdomen.

I walked home, satisfied that Barton wasn't a murderer. I strained my brain to think of other suspects.

My aunt was promiscuous, so she could have slept with someone who targeted her for her looks or got angry when she'd ended their affair. She was pregnant, and even though it seemed she was clear about the paternity of the child, someone may have worried she would blame them for the illegitimate child.

As my house came into view, my thoughts landed on someone whose marriage would have been destroyed by confused assumptions. My feet led me past my house and higher up Tipton Hill.

Chapter 37

Uncle Catfish welcomed me with a hug that may have crushed a few of my ribs.

"Meg's here!" he called to Aunt Tonya. Then to me, he said, "We've not seen you in a coon's age!"

Raccoons lived two or three years, and I'd been to their house to pick up Crystal the previous week, but I smiled and told him I'd been busy packing for our move. It was a lie, as everything we didn't need right away had been packed up for weeks.

Thankfully, they didn't ask me why I had shown up at their house on a humid Sunday afternoon. My aunt poured me a glass of root beer and reminisced over the root beer floats I'd asked her to make for me during my childhood. I hadn't enjoyed root beer for years, but I let my aunt believe she was giving me a special treat.

After thirty minutes of pleasant chatter, my aunt grabbed her phone and held it up. "You guys can call me if you need me. I'm going to go for a ride."

I was familiar with my aunt's schedule, so I wasn't surprised. No matter what happened, Aunt Tonya would ride one of her horses in the morning and the other in the late afternoon. I had waited for her to leave, so I could be alone with Uncle Catfish.

I expected uncomfortable silence, but I should have known better, as my uncle was adept at making conversation. He spoke to me about my graduation, and he asked me about my future plans.

"I may be going to ETSU," I told him.

He stroked his thin mustache. "Isn't that where your mother wanted you to go?"

I understood the insinuation. Everyone knew my mother could be domineering.

"I was only going to UT because of Sanders," I told him, taking a drink of my root beer. The sarsaparilla aftertaste almost made me grimace.

"Don't you want to go with him now?"

"I do," I answered, "but he won't be able to go to college now that he has to raise Crystal."

His eyebrows drew together, and he glanced away. I had seldom seen him so sober.

"That's a cryin' shame, Meg. That boy has been through enough without sacrificin' his education."

I wiped my finger down some condensation that had formed on my glass. "I'd thought about getting a job at the store where Barton works and raising Crystal myself since she's really my sister. It's not fair for Sanders to be stuck with her when he's not blood-related."

Uncle Catfish's face colored. I could almost feel the heat of his sudden emotions.

He pointed a finger at me. "Now, you listen here, missy. I won't have you talkin' that way. There are people on this hill that don't have an ounce of Tipton blood flowin' through them, but they're treated like family. Blood isn't always thicker than water."

As he'd spoken, my uncle had lifted from his chair and towered over me. It was a side of him I'd never witnessed, and it frightened me.

I had been talking about the relationship between Sanders and Crystal, but my uncle had attacked me from his own perspective. After all, Sanders was a Tipton like his father before him, but Uncle Catfish's last name was Denver, and Aunt Tonya had never assumed it after they were married. They'd been together since before I was born, and she remained Tonya Tipton.

I wanted to tell him I wasn't talking about him, but I couldn't find the words to express it. My legs started shaking, and I held onto my glass like it would help me if my uncle advanced on me. I finally settled on the phrase my father used to end arguments with my mother.

"You're right."

It took several heartbeats, but he blinked and sat down. I expected him to apologize for his sudden temper, and when he didn't, I got more nervous.

He looked straight ahead, reflecting on something he kept to himself. I ran through ways to excuse myself politely, hoping I wouldn't upset him again.

"The truth is, that girl could have been anyone's," he finally spoke.

"Aunt Tonya said she has Daddy's eyes," I said before I realized I'd spoken.

He acknowledged me as if I'd suddenly appeared in the room. He seemed to weigh my words. "Sure, Crystal looks like Ace now, but when she was born, there were a lot of men who wondered if their marriages would be ruined."

As I teetered on the edge of fight or flight, I didn't say what I was thinking. I believed the men he was referencing should have been blamed for their soiled marriages, and I included my uncle on that list. They didn't have to fall for Aunt Mary Beth's charms.

He sighed deeply and rubbed his palms across his cheeks. He reached out for my hand before I saw the movement, and I jumped like I'd received an electric shock. It was then that he noticed the effect of his outburst on me.

His eyes widened. "Hey, Meg. It's okay. I didn't mean to go off the deep end."

I hopped out of my chair, almost making it fall. Walking backward, I inched closer to the door.

"It's fine," I said, hating the shaky quality of my voice. "I'm fine."

In his concern, he tried to hug me, and I almost tripped as I gave him a clumsy embrace. I'd never felt so uncomfortable around him.

"You're afraid of me," he observed, his face crumpling.

In my near panic, I didn't stay to console him. I wanted to get as far away from the man I believed had shown his true colors.

I bolted out the door, not bothering to close it, and I imagined his footsteps dogging me all the way to my house, but when I turned around, no one was there.

For a long time, I sat in my bed, rocking back and forth. No one was there to bother me, and by the time they got home, I'd had enough time to process my feelings about my uncle.

He had been kind and upbeat throughout my life, making me laugh and telling me funny stories, but my uncle had a temper I'd never seen until I had crossed him. *Had the baby in Mary Beth's belly been my father's child, or was there a possibility that Aunt Tonya's husband had betrayed her trust again? Would the baby have been born with green eyes instead of brown ones? If it would have been a boy, would he have developed a tiny mustache when he reached his teenage years?*

After what I'd seen during my last visit, I was convinced my Uncle Catfish could let his temper get out of control. Rage could lead to unspeakable acts, and there's no telling what a man might do to silence someone to save his marriage. I went to sleep that night with a new suspect in my aunt's murder, one I was certain had a motive for killing her and her unborn child.

Chapter 38

"I knew something was wrong with him!" Imani exclaimed.

We'd finally gotten together for a long-overdue girls' night, and she twirled a braided strawberry fruit snack while I crunched one of the cookies we'd almost burned. A movie played in front of us, but too much had happened in our lives, so we opted to kick back on the sofa and talk instead of watching the rom-com.

"I don't know if he did it for sure, but it doesn't look good for him."

Imani looked puzzled. "I know your dad loves his sister, but why would he cover for Catfish?"

I shrugged. "My dad is pretty loyal. He may not want to take the blame, but he won't purposely incriminate someone else."

"It's murder, though," she argued. "Isn't that a life sentence? It seems pretty excessive to go down for that long over loyalty to his cheating brother-in-law."

I considered her argument and shook my head. I was tired of talking about my aunt's murder.

"We need to talk about you," I said, getting serious. "Did you take a test?"

Imani's father had hung out with us during the first part of the night, and I hadn't wanted to mention a possible pregnancy while he could have been within earshot. Finally, he'd gone to bed, waving at us as he ascended the stairs.

Imani didn't seem to follow me, but then she realized I was talking about her missed period. She grinned. "Oh, yeah. I started my period ages ago."

I breathed a sigh of relief for my friend. I'd recently heard Cynthia's story about her unplanned pregnancy, and I had been nervous for Imani. She had a more supportive father, but her decision to have premarital sex would have disappointed him.

"Speaking of the repercussions of teenage sex, how are you and Owen doing?"

Color instantly flooded my face. "Definitely not that well."

"And why not?" she asked, winding her snack into her mouth.

"Because we've only been together a couple of months," I returned. I was a little surprised by how casually she approached intimate topics.

"You've known him your entire life," she said. "Garrett and I couldn't keep our hands off each other after a couple of weeks of dating."

"Imani!" I covered my hands over my mouth when I realized I'd been too loud.

When it was clear her father hadn't heard us, she whispered, "You need to start thinkin' about when you want to do the deed, though."

I laughed. "Yeah. I've been going through a few things, like my aunt's murder and finding out I have a sister. Maybe I'll sandwich it between the next set of traumatic events in my life."

She chewed thoughtfully. "I think you should do it this weekend."

I was horrified. She was talking about losing my virginity like she was helping me arrange a party.

"I like Owen, but I'm not ready for that step."

"Fair enough," she returned. "But *when* will you be ready?"

I'd not given a lot of thought to sex. I was aware people my age were participating in it, but I wasn't interested in something that I'd heard hurt girls the first time. I relayed my fear to Imani, and she rolled her eyes.

"If you're with the right person for you—and you want to do it—it's not so bad."

I shifted my position, feigning interest in my pillow. Imani wasn't going to let me off easily.

"Do you like him?"

"Yeah."

"Do you love him?"

I stopped what I was doing. *Did I love Owen?*

I really liked him, but I didn't move as fast as my friend. I believed feelings of love were built over time, and even though I'd known him since we were little, Owen and I hadn't been hanging out together long enough for me to form a long-term attachment to him. Like any other teenage girl, though, I wanted to hang onto my boyfriend based on the potential for a future with him.

"Yes."

She'd raised her eyebrows, but she relaxed them with my faux admission, rolling from her belly to her back. "Then you should do it."

I tried not to think about it anymore, and we tuned into the rom-com. The wedding scene piqued Imani's interests, and as she pictured herself in white lace and satin, I hoped Owen hadn't had the same thoughts as my friend.

The next night dashed my hopes.

Owen picked me up with the intention of taking me out to eat. Mid-way to Johnson City, he turned the car around and headed back to Erwin.

"Where are we going?" I asked.

"I changed my mind," he said with a wink. "I have something better in mind."

Normally, I wouldn't have worried, but since my conversation with Imani, I dissected his meaning. *Did he want to make out with me in a remote location? Had his parents sent him a text that they wouldn't be home?*

Owen picked up a bucket of chicken and drove to the river. I watched civilization fall away from me, and my hands sweat. He drove down a short gravel road and under a bridge, parking where those who drove by us would only see the top of his car.

I caught him staring at me when he turned off the car. "You're so beautiful," he said.

I thought he was going to grab me, pushing me into kisses that led to more, but Owen pulled out his phone and positioned it slightly above us. I posed for the picture, thankful he hadn't forced himself on me.

At first, I could hardly eat, even though the chicken was good. I kept wondering what would follow when we finished our meal. I continued to take small bites, but when he packed up the remains of our meal, I grabbed another chicken leg.

"You're hungry tonight," Owen commented. "I would have gotten another bucket of chicken if I'd've known you were going to out-eat me."

"Well, I'm a growing girl," I said, cringing at the sound of the words as they left my mouth.

I was acting like a child, even though I was almost an adult. I should be able to participate in an act of love with my boyfriend, but I could only sweat and avoid physical interaction by stress eating.

Finally, the chicken was gone, and my stomach hurt. There was nothing left to do but cuddle Owen under the summer moonlight.

Usually, I would have loved his soft kisses and gentle caresses, but I was scared. My dinner rolled around my belly, making unflattering sounds in the stillness.

"Are you okay?" Owen asked me.

I tried to give him a big smile that may have turned out uncertain. I followed it with a kiss. My thoughts raced, and I couldn't wipe my hands over the tops of my shorts enough to keep them from sweating, so I embraced the situation. Maybe I'd feel better about it if I was the one who initiated our first sexual experience.

I took Owen's hand and placed it on my breast. He squeezed it gently, and I jumped away.

We seemed equally flustered.

"Are you okay?" he said breathlessly. "Did I do something wrong?"

I shook my head, trying to fight for any composure. My heart was racing, but for the wrong reasons. I felt like I was under attack instead of swimming in feelings of desire.

"I want this," I choked out.

He squinted an eye skeptically. "Are you sure, Meg? It seems like you might not feel well."

Could I fake being sick? It was certainly an attractive idea after our last kiss. My stomach was threatening to expel the contents of my dinner, but it wasn't because I'd caught a virus.

"Can we talk about this?" he asked, patting a place on the blanket closer to him. I inched closer, eyeing him like I was walking around one of the copperheads near my home.

"Why do you want to move so fast?" he asked.

I sucked in a deep breath, relieved by the direction of his question. "I thought that's why you brought me here," I answered honestly.

He laughed. At first, it wounded me, but then I realized it wasn't meant to hurt me.

"We've only been together for a couple of months. I wouldn't expect you to do anything like that until you're ready." He reached up and stroked my hair.

I was relieved to hear him say he didn't expect to have sex with me. My fear disappeared, and I melted into him. I kissed him, and I put every ounce of myself into it.

Owen broke away, breathing heavily. "We should stop."

He wanted to end our make-out session, but I was glad he wanted to honor our relationship by allowing me to determine when we moved into a more physical relationship.

There were fewer fireflies closer to the water, but some rose from a patch of tall grass. One landed on my arm, lighting its tail in patterned bursts.

"I think he likes you," Owen joked.

Remembering our discussion about the mating habits of fireflies, I replied, "I don't think I'd be a good wife for him, especially since he only lives a couple of weeks." I lifted my arm, and the firefly left it in search of better prospects. When I turned back, Owen was staring at me.

"I don't know. I think you're perfect."

I embraced him, and we fell into the type of kiss that could lead to more. My stomach disagreed, though, and after my anxiety and overeating, I had to race to the tall grass to spew its contents, and any more thoughts of romance disappeared from my mind.

Chapter 39

My father pressed his swollen jaw, but I didn't ask him about it. If it hurt when they pulled his tooth, I was glad.

"Who are you covering for?" I demanded.

"I ain't coverin' for no one," my father answered in a stern voice that bordered on defeat.

I pressed on. "Did Uncle Catfish do it?"

He met my eyes, and I thought I saw a hint of disbelief before he issued a dry chuckle. "Your uncle couldn't wring a chicken's neck for Sunday dinner."

I understood his reference, but the saying appalled me. My father's irritation with me was apparent in the way he didn't bother to sugar-coat his feelings.

"Who did it then?" I demanded. "I know it wasn't you."

He leaned back in his chair and looked at the bright lights in the room before he responded. "You could take what you don't know and fill the caves in Tipton Hill with it."

I was hurt, but I didn't show it. "That might have been the case a couple of months ago, but I know a lot more now. Besides, I wouldn't have been kept in the dark if the people I trusted thought enough of me to tell me about their secrets instead of me finding out about them on my own!"

I felt like I'd slapped my father with my accusation, and his expression reflected the sting. He pressed four of his fingers to his cheek before he spoke.

"I fell in love," he told me. "Over and over again." He dropped his head and shook it before lifting it so he could meet my eyes. "Mary Beth was the love of my life."

"You're just saying that because she's dead," I spat. I had an overwhelming urge to defend my mother, as it felt like I was fighting for my family. In reality, I may have only been arguing for my perception of it.

"I loved her," he said firmly. "She was my first thought when I woke up and my last thought when I laid down my head at night."

"Even when we were in Disney World," I countered. "What about all the good times you had with Mama?"

He cocked his head. "In a way, I loved your mama, too. She's the mother of my children, and she's a good caretaker of the house. It was easy to pretend she was Mary Beth because they were almost identical."

"Twins usually are," I huffed.

We sat there for a few minutes, my father reflecting, and I with my arms crossed over my chest. I wanted to make him hurt as much as he'd hurt the family, but I couldn't shoot venom at him. He seemed he was on the verge of tears.

"Can you bring Crystal next time?" he asked.

"Yeah. I'll bring your secret daughter."

"That's not fair," he said.

"No, it's not," I replied. "It's not fair that I learned about my sister six years too late, and it's not fair that so many people knew about her before me."

"What was I supposed to do?" he shouted.

His sudden outburst startled me. I could only watch his temper flare.

"I did my duty. I denied myself true love so that you, your mother, and your brothers could live like a family."

"You didn't deny yourself anything!" I shot back. "You got to be married to one woman and sleep with her sister. You had two families for years!"

He bounced up from his chair, and it fell backward. "And I would be with them now if it wasn't for—" He stopped, realizing that he'd almost revealed my aunt's true killer.

The door behind him opened, and our visit was over.

"I love you, Meg," he said softly, recovering from his outburst.

I looked at him, stubbornly refusing to return the sentiment.

He kissed two fingers and pressed them to the glass.

Aunt Tonya placed two cups of tea in front of Sanders and me. We took obligatory sips.

Crystal, Pickles, and Si played in the other room. The sound of rockets, cars, and blocks rattled across the hardwood floor.

I was nervous about going to Aunt Tonya's house, and until Sanders told me he'd been invited, too, I'd worried that Uncle Catfish had confided in her about the way my last visit had ended.

Sanders and I had walked with our younger siblings in tow, neither of us knowing the reason we had been summoned to Aunt Tonya's house on Sanders's only day off that week.

Aunt Tonya sat down and placed her shaking hand on Uncle Catfish's arm. He breathed deeply, imitating the action he wanted her to do, and it seemed to steady her.

"I needed to talk to the two of you about somethin'." She glanced at her husband for support, and whatever she saw in his eyes strengthened her.

"We want to adopt Crystal."

I heard the rest of her words like we were on opposite ends of a tunnel. I could appreciate her kindness, but it was hard to focus on the reasons she listed. I know she spoke about Sanders and me going to college and not being able to have children of her own, but the rest was pushed back as I thought about the way she'd have to prove that she was related to Crystal.

"You'll have to get a DNA test for her," I spoke up, "and that'll prove my daddy is—"

"—her father," Uncle Catfish finished. "We'll make sure she keeps the Tipton last name, and we'll tell her about her parents and siblings."

"That includes you, Sanders," Aunt Tonya said. "There's more to family than blood."

Hearing his wife echo the same words Uncle Catfish had spoken during my last visit rattled me, and I thought about my uncle's temper. *Did I really want him to raise Crystal, a young girl whose special needs could tax a person with infinite patience?*

It dawned on me it was the only time I'd seen my uncle upset, and he hadn't physically attacked me. If I was being honest with myself,

I'd have to admit that Uncle Catfish was dealing with grief in his own way, and he'd tried to make up for his actions as I'd raced out the door.

"I think you know I'm not cut out for raising kids," Sanders spoke. "But I don't want to lose touch."

I startled. I wouldn't have expected my cousin to have given up his responsibility so freely, but since Aunt Mary Beth's death, the people in my family were acting in ways that surprised me.

Aunt Tonya put a hand on his wrist. "Of course not. But you didn't choose to have children. You deserve to go to college and have all the experiences that come with it."

Uncle Catfish addressed me. "You have your daddy's loyalty, and your aunt and I decided we wouldn't let you sacrifice your life either. The children will stay in touch."

Wait! Had I missed something?

My mind parted with its preoccupation with Sanders's eagerness to give up custody of Crystal. "Children?" I repeated shrilly.

Everyone else at the table looked like they'd rather be anywhere else than in the room with me. Aunt Tonya finally opened her mouth to speak, but Sanders beat her to it.

"Mom's baby lived," he explained. "They did an emergency Cesarean section at the hospital, and it was touch and go for a while, but the baby came out of the incubator today."

"Why didn't anyone tell me?" I yelled, staring at all of them in turn.

The playful laughter in the next room ceased, and I was reminded of my younger siblings. I lowered my voice.

"Why in God's name does everyone keep lying to me?"

"We didn't lie," Sanders said quickly. "What good would it have done you or your mama to have known about the baby if it was going to die anyway?"

My rage bubbled over. "If you're going to treat me like a kid, then I'll act like one."

I stood up from the table and walked to the door. "I hate all of you," I said before I slammed the door and walked away from Tipton Hill.

Chapter 40

"It's not my problem," I said to my mother. "They're your kids. Deal with it."

"They're your brothers," she returned. "And I need your help."

I was sitting on Owen's bed, pulling the threads on his blue and white bedspread. I loosened a blue piece and twirled it in my fingers.

"You left your brothers with your Aunt Tonya, and they were scared to death when I picked them up," my mother went on, trying to bring some sense of compassion from me through guilt. "They didn't understand why you'd leave without them."

I rolled my eyes. "They were fine. It's not like I left them with strangers."

She let out a long sigh, obviously tired of the way our conversation was going. "Please come home," my mother begged.

"I don't want to be surrounded by liars."

"What's going on?" my mother demanded. "All I know is that Tonya wanted you to come to her house, and then you stayed out all night."

"I was with Owen," I said.

My mother took another calming breath. "We'll talk about that more later. For right now, tell me what happened."

"Nothing much," I said sarcastically. "Aunt Tonya and Uncle Catfish have decided to adopt my father's illegitimate children."

My mother spoke slowly and deliberately. "*Children?*"

"Yeah, Mama. I guess they kept you in the dark about it, too." I went on unmercifully. "It seems I have another sibling."

"They saved the baby," my mother guessed.

"Yeah." I voiced without inflection.

"I'm so sorry, Megara."

Her apology took me off guard. "Why are *you* sorry? You didn't do anything wrong."

She laughed sardonically. "I'm more responsible for this situation than you realize."

I hung up with her agreeably, but I made no promise to return home. I'd decided Tipton Hill could swallow up all the people who said they had loved me as they'd lied to me.

Owen held my hand lightly as we rocked on the porch swing. The afternoon sun was warm, and the moisture in the air was almost too much to keep us away from the air-conditioned indoors.

"Do you want a popsicle?" Owen asked me.

The icy treat sounded like just what I needed to take the edge off the heat, so I nodded. "But let me get it. I've already imposed enough on you and your family."

"Not at all," he assured me. "I'm sorry things aren't going well between you and your family, but I got to wake up with a beautiful woman in my bed this morning."

I blushed, and he lifted the sweaty hairs clinging to my neck as his hand caressed my shoulders. He brought his mouth to mine for a chaste kiss.

I had insisted on lying on top of the blankets when I had slept in Owen's room. His parents probably imagined that we had been intimate, but what mattered to me was that I hadn't given myself over to Owen in an attempt to feel better about my family's betrayal.

"I'll be right back," he promised, landing another peck on my nose before he lifted off the swing.

I stretched my legs out as far as they would go and swung them back. The gentle motion created a slight breeze I hadn't known I'd needed.

Owen's house was positioned off one of the less traveled streets in town. Occasionally, a vehicle would glide past, but it wasn't often. I didn't know why the black SUV caught my attention, but it seemed out of place on the mostly empty road.

It pulled into the driveway, and I saw Barton in the passenger seat. My first thought was that my Uncle Barton had tracked me down, as the SUV looked a lot like the vehicles he drove, but Dandy climbed down from the driver's side.

He waved at me as if we were old friends, his blond hair swaying as he looked from Barton to me. Barton approached me like he was treading close to a deer, scared that it might run away at any time.

"Hey, Meg," my brother said cautiously.

"Hey."

Dandy rolled his eyes. "What's wrong with you, son? Ask her to come home."

Barton glared at his father. "She's my sister. I know exactly how to deal with her."

"Deal with me?" I raised an eyebrow.

"Your mother can do that," Dandy observed, pointing just above my eye. "It's one of the reasons I asked her to leave the party with me when we met."

"Eww," I said, grimacing and mentally swearing that I would never raise my eyebrow in Dandy's presence again.

Owen picked that moment to breeze out the door. Oblivious to the people at the base of his steps, he carried two vanilla ice creams that were already losing their form with the change in temperature.

"We were out of popsicles," he apologized.

"That's okay," Dandy piped up. "I like ice cream, but I usually eat chocolate."

Owen turned to him, still holding the cones. He hadn't heard the vehicle, so he was surprised to see my brother and someone else interrupting our evening.

"Vanilla's good, too," Dandy said, stepping up onto the porch and grabbing one of the treats. He licked it around the bottom and pointed to the one in Owen's other hand. "You should get started on that one before it's in a puddle at your feet."

The ice cream dripped onto Owen's hand. He looked down at it numbly before he jolted back to life.

"Who are you?" he asked my brother's father.

"Dandy Hughes," he answered, extending the hand not holding the ice cream he had liberated. He dropped it when Owen looked back at me instead of accepting his gesture.

"Do you know him?"

I sighed. "He's my mama's ex-husband. Well, first ex-husband," I amended.

"I heard there was trouble in paradise, but I had no idea how bad it was until they let me out," Dandy said. He let out a low whistle. "I guess that's what happens when you sleep with other people when you're still married."

Realizing that his slight moved beyond my father's infidelities and extended to my mother's unfaithfulness during her first marriage, I wanted to defend my parents, but I could only give it a half-hearted try. "Shut up. You cheated on my mother all the time."

"The lady has a point," Dandy conceded. "I liked to have fun, and I shouldn't have married Sara Beth before I sowed all my wild oats."

"She doesn't like to be called that—"

Owen held up his hand. "Why are your brother and your mother's ex-husband here?" He motioned to Dandy. "And where did he *get out* of?"

Dandy answered the question that pertained to him. "Prison." He took Owen's surprise for lack of understanding. "You know, the pokey, the big house, the—"

"He gets the idea, Dad," Barton interrupted.

Dandy smiled and clapped Barton on the back. I spoke before he could make the situation more awkward.

"My mama sent them to talk me into going back."

I turned to my brother. "You can tell her you pleaded with me, but I wouldn't budge. She'll believe I was too stubborn to go back."

Dandy addressed Barton, jerking his thumb at me. "She's just like your mother, isn't she?" It was hard to take him seriously with the ice cream coating his lips.

"Sometimes," my brother agreed without taking his eyes off me. "Don't you think you're overreacting?"

"How many secret siblings do *you* have?" I asked my brother, pointing to Dandy. "Your father wasn't exactly careful. And what would you do if you found out you had two in the space of a couple of months?"

"Well, there was this one girl in Knoxville," Dandy started, but he closed his mouth and mimicked locking it when we all shot him a threatening glance at once.

"I'd welcome any sibling," Barton replied. "They can't help the circumstances around their birth."

"Spoken like the father of an illegitimate baby," I said curtly. "Did you gain some divine insight after you impregnated your girlfriend?"

Barton colored. "Look, Meg. It's time to go home. I had to take off work today to watch our brothers so Mama could go to her job, and I can't do it again tomorrow."

"That's her problem," I shot back. "I didn't give birth to them."

Barton's temper flared. "You're a stone-cold—"

"That enough, son," Dandy said. His spark of humor had dimmed. "There's never a reason to talk to a lady that way."

I would have been impressed if I didn't think Dandy was an idiot. I liked when he defended me, though. It hadn't happened since my father went to jail.

"I can watch the kids," Dandy offered. "The little sprats seem to like me."

When had Dandy met my brothers? I had only been gone for a day. *Had he been at my father's house while my mother was at work?* The thought repulsed me.

"I'll do it," I said. I didn't know Dandy, but what I did know about him, I didn't trust.

"Do you want me to drive you back?" Owen asked.

I noticed that he'd stopped calling my house *my home* when he referenced it. He'd paid attention, and he'd realized I was conflicted about my idea of home.

"We can take her," Dandy offered. He tried to sound casual, but there was a hint of protectiveness in his voice. *What had Barton told his father about Owen?*

I got to my feet and hugged Owen. "I'll be okay with my brother," I assured him.

Owen reluctantly released me and watched my brother help me into the backseat of the SUV. I waved at him as we drove off.

"Didn't you need to get your stuff?" Dandy asked.

"I didn't bring anything," I admitted. I hadn't had a plan when I'd walked away from Tipton Hill, and I was lucky Owen's mother had given me a toothbrush and shared her shower products with me.

"A wandering gypsy," Dandy mused. "I've done that a time or two."

"It was a last-minute decision," I snapped back. "I'm not like you."

He held up one of his hands. "Okay, young lady. I meant no harm in it."

"You could try to be nice to him," Barton said, leering at me from the front seat.

"Because you've been so good to my dad, right?" I bit back.

"I would have been good to Ace if Ace had been good to my mama."

"I guess a roof over our head and food on the table—"

"Okay, younguns'," Dandy said, shaking his head. He chuckled, mousing Barton's hair. "No more bickerin'. The two of you are worse than two little chickens."

I crossed my arms, and Barton huffed.

"You're gonna be a daddy soon," he told Barton. "You'll need to learn how to get along with your family so the little bugger will be able to know them."

My brother's face was so red that I thought he would explode, but he nodded along. "I know."

"You told him about the pregnancy?" I asked, forgetting that I had mentioned it when I was on Owen's porch. "You haven't even told Mama."

Barton looked at Dandy, but his father kept his eyes on the road.

"Mama's gonna come unglued, and—" Barton started.

"And it will be worse if she finds out Dandy Hughes knew before her," I finished

Dandy turned into our driveway. Barton helped me out of the SUV, and Dandy cracked a joke as we walked through the door.

I looked through the house for my mother, but I couldn't find her or my brothers. I called Aunt Tonya, and when she answered, her voice was hoarse. She croaked out something, but I could only make out the tone of her voice.

"What happened to my Mama?" I repeated until the line went dead.

I had left my mother in a tough situation. What if she'd had to go somewhere, leaving my brothers with one of our distant relatives? Or worse, what if she had taken my brothers with her, only to get hit by a truck as they strolled around a curve?

Her possible loss hit the pit of my stomach and settled there. My fear grew, and I thought about the terrible things I'd said to my mother since my father had been in jail. My father had told me to take care of her and my brothers, and my anxiety threatened to spill over as I realized I'd failed to honor his request.

I called Sanders, but he didn't answer. He couldn't talk or read messages during his shift, so I tried to think of the next person to contact.

"We could look for her," Dandy suggested.

I agreed to ride around with them, wondering if it was futile. As we were climbing into the truck, Uncle Catfish's truck rattled up the road. I went out to wave him down, but he was already pulling into our driveway. He parked at an angle behind Dandy's SUV, and I didn't know he had passengers until my mother got out of the truck, picking up Pickles and Si.

There were few times I had experienced the relief that came with the appearance of my mother and younger brothers. I wouldn't have to tell my father that I hadn't kept my promise to keep them safe. After I relaxed, though, I realized something was terribly wrong.

"What going on, Mama?" I begged. I hoped she hadn't been accosted by someone as she had walked. Some violent people could be brave about approaching an attractive woman, especially when no other adults were within sight.

My mother usually wouldn't have let my brothers ride without their car seats, and it looked like the stroller was peeking out of the bed of the truck. She turned to me, and I took a step back. Black eyeliner and mascara smudged her face. Her eyes looked at me, but they didn't focus. I held her, but I don't think she noticed.

"She was almost at the jail when I caught up to her," Uncle Catfish said soberly. My uncle thought we were privy to whatever had happened. "She broke down on me when I made her stop walking."

Uncle Catfish guided my family to the door, and Barton unlocked it. My brothers were just as stoic as my mother. It was strange to see the lack of vibrancy on Pickles's face. He sat on his mother's lap and put his head on her chest while Si did the same.

Uncle Barton's vehicle glided into the yard, and he parked beside my father's garden. I ran out to him, eager for him to tell me what had happened. He stepped out of his car and hugged me.

"I'm so sorry, Meg."

"No one will tell me what happened to Mama!" I yelled hysterically. "I'll never go away again. I promise!"

He pulled back and looked at me strangely. "Your mother hasn't spoken to you?"

"No. What happened to her? I'll never forgive myself if—"

"Your mama's okay," he said, running his hands down the sides of my head. "At least physically."

"Then why is she so upset?" I yelled at him. "And the boys..."

He shushed me soothingly, bringing me back into an embrace. "He's gone, Meg."

I pushed away from him, the meaning of the words drawing close and slipping away from me. "What?"

"Your daddy," he choked out, failing to hold back his emotions. "Your daddy is dead."

Chapter 41

I'd never known true pain.

Once, when I was playing with Sanders, a tree branch broke, and I tumbled to the ground with it. I thought my broken radius was the worst pain of my life, but nothing compared to the rip that tore through my heart when my uncle told me my daddy had died in jail.

In the coming weeks, I learned his tooth had abscessed. During our last visit, I had mistaken his swollen jaw as a result of a pulled tooth, but my daddy's appointment had been put off again. Imani's father said the abscess had led to a heart attack.

I don't remember walking back into the house, but I assumed Uncle Barton had led me there. I had brief flashes from the rest of the night.

Uncle Barton warmed some soup for Pickles and Si, but they left the bowls untouched. Si fell asleep early, and Pickles volunteered to go to bed early when my mother carried Si to their room. It was my room, too, but I had difficulty thinking of anything as mine since I'd learned that so much of what I thought was simply taking the lies people had told me and using them to build the foundation of my life.

Our phones buzzed and rang. My brother only answered one call, and I assumed it was from Cynthia. I didn't bother to touch my phone, except to turn it off, and my mother stared despondently at hers until Uncle Barton either answered it or silenced the ringer.

Uncle Barton talked to several of my great aunts and uncles, but he spoke to them in clipped sentences. At one point, I heard him assure a caller that we would be out of the house within a week of my father's funeral. I assumed the person on the other end of the line was Aunt Margaret, and I didn't have the energy to hate her for her spitefulness.

After he was certain my mother wouldn't leave the house again, Uncle Catfish slipped out, offering condolences and expressing his need to be with Aunt Tonya. My mother looked after him when he shut the door, perhaps remembering what it was like to have a husband comfort her. Maybe she was just remembering the last time my father walked out the same door.

I had a fleeting thought that Dandy should leave, but he stayed through the night. He walked somberly through the house, hugging my brother and patting my mother's shoulder. I could tell he wanted to embrace her, but he didn't do more than walk around her like he was staring at fine art encased in glass.

Dandy tried to console me, and I don't remember what I said. He didn't appear hurt by it, but he mostly avoided me afterward.

After dark, Dandy brought in a bottle of liquor I assumed he'd had in his SUV. Glasses were passed around, and toasts were offered to my father's memory. My mother drank a glass of amber fluid, but I declined when Uncle Barton offered me a sip of his portion.

Barton gulped two glasses of his father's liquor before Dandy stopped him from drinking more. My brother swayed across the room and landed in the chair next to our mother. He tearfully confessed to her he was going to be a father, and my mother stroked his hair as he cried in her lap. Barton admitted he didn't know what he was doing, and our mother whispered something to him that soothed him.

My river of sadness wasn't as easily dried. I woke up the next day and cursed the sunshine streaming through the windows. Storms should have whipped through the sky to show their anger over the death of a good man.

My mother made pancakes, and everyone ate except for my mother and me. We locked eyes across the table once, two sides of the same coin. Our grief consumed us, but we felt it for different reasons. I mourned the loss of my father and confidant, and she grieved for the relationship she never had with the man she loved.

Dandy had spent the night on our couch, and he stumbled into the dining room scratching his head. His blond hair stood up at odd angles, and he reeked of alcohol.

Uncle Barton had sampled Dandy's liquor, and being unaccustomed to drinking, he had passed out in our bathtub. I had to wake him up when I went to the bathroom, and he wandered into the living room where he claimed the couch Dandy had recently vacated.

I methodically performed housework. I folded clothes, washed dishes, and scrubbed floors. I still thought about my father, but it was much easier to be constructive than to stare at a wall. My mother cleaned the house, too, packing even more as she tidied the almost bare shelves.

Dandy stopped her once. He put his arms around her, but my mother hung limply against him.

"I'll always be here for you, Sara Beth," he promised.

My mother cringed when he said the middle name she had shared with her twin. She pushed herself away.

"I've heard that before," she said, with notes of dryness in her tone. "And I've told you, my name is Sara."

He apologized, but my mother didn't recognize his effort. She grabbed a basket of laundry, and we sat beside each other, folding each piece.

Pickles and Si slept until noon. I supposed depression and grief could affect small children, too.

Pickles was the first to join us. He climbed into my lap and put a thin arm around my neck.

"Is Daddy still dead, Egg?"

I didn't want to answer him, but he expected me to say something. He stared at me like I looked at my Uncle Barton. He knew I'd be honest with him.

"Daddy will be dead every day now," I replied and kissed his head.

"Oh." He looked at his feet and made a circular motion with his toe.

Si toddled into the room, still rubbing his eyes. My mother picked him up, and he latched onto her breast.

Uncle Barton's phone rang, startling us all. He answered it groggily and listened more than he spoke. I stared at him throughout the call. Something told me it was about my father.

Uncle Barton addressed my mother. "Sheriff Watts wants to meet us at the funeral home this afternoon."

"It's already the afternoon," Dandy remarked.

"What time do you want to go?" Uncle Barton asked my mother, ignoring her ex-husband.

"I guess sooner is better than later," my mother responded, lifting herself up with Si still nursing at her breast. "Let me take a shower, and we'll go."

"I'll stay with the boys," I volunteered, even though I couldn't keep up with them if they reverted to their usual energy levels.

"I'm going home to take a shower and down an espresso," Uncle Barton said. "I'll be back soon."

They left me alone in the living room with my younger brothers and Dandy. Grief had mostly muted my emotions, so the silence didn't affect me. My brother's father, however, seemed increasingly uncomfortable, shifting from one foot to another.

Si ran to his toy box and pushed a truck across the floor. Pickles got up and grabbed the truck before it stopped rolling. He slammed it against the wall, and one wheel flew off, striking me on the cheek. Si started howling, and Pickles screamed at him.

"You can't play when daddies die!"

Dandy rushed to check on me, and after I assured him I was fine, he squatted down to talk to Pickles. Si ran into his arms, eager for comfort or protection, and Dandy held him against his chest as he spoke to Pickles.

"Why did you do that to your brother?"

"He can't play anymore," Pickles insisted, crossing his arms.

"Why not? Why do you think you and your brother can't play anymore since your daddy died?"

"Because he might look down at us from heaven and think we don't care he died," Pickles choked out before he burst into tears.

Dandy reached out a hand, and Pickles fell against him. I watched the scene from my place on the couch. I wanted to hold my brothers, but I couldn't interrupt them while they had one arm around each other and their other arm around Dandy.

When Pickles's sobs became intermittent, Dandy held the boy where he could speak with him. "Your daddy won't be mad if you're playing. He'll be smiling down on you from heaven."

"How do you know?" Pickles asked him. "You don't know my daddy, and you've never been to heaven."

I thought the question would stump the long-time felon, but he took it in stride. It was as if he'd already had an answer prepared.

"I didn't really know your daddy, but I know your mama, and she's not gonna marry someone who'd want her children to be sad all the time." He held up a finger. "And heaven is a happy place, so your daddy doesn't feel any pain anymore. He's gonna be happy watchin' over all his children."

"He won't think I forgot him?" Pickled sobbed.

"No, little man. He's gonna be happy he can watch you and your brother grow, instead of hearin' about it while he sits in some prison cell."

The irony wasn't lost on me. Dandy didn't get to see his son grow up because of the choices he'd made when he was young. On the other hand, my father's reasons for going to jail were nobler, as he was protecting someone from a life sentence for Mary Beth's murder. Now, he was dead.

"Did I see a swing set at the side of the house?" Dandy asked Pickles.

My brother nodded. "My daddy put it up for me after he planted his garden."

"Can you show me how high you can swing?"

Pickles's eyes lit up. "Yes!" He ran to the back door, but he stopped. "Can my brother go, too?"

Dandy looked at me for objections, and I gave my consent with a nod. He took my younger brothers outside, and I heard their laughter mingled with the other sounds of summer. It was out of place, yet perfectly right.

Sanders helped me watch the boys while my mother made my father's funeral plans.

Barton had been deeply hung over, but he had gone to work. When he returned, he walked straight into his bedroom, locked the door, and fell onto the bed.

Sanders stayed outside with me, braving the humidity, so my brothers could play. He filled up their pool with cool water from the hose, and they splashed each other until Si got offended over the cascades of water Pickles threw onto him.

"I love you," Sanders told me.

We were sitting in the gazebo. Its shade was our only respite from the heat. I turned my head, but I didn't meet his eyes.

"I love you, too," I returned.

He sighed deeply. He opened his mouth to say more, but Dandy walked out with his empty liquor bottle. A piece of paper had been dropped inside it.

"What's that?" I pointed to the paper in the glass bottle.

He looked down at it. "I have a habit of collectin' bottles, so whenever I drink one around a certain event, I write a little somethin' about the night and who drank the bottle with me. Then I fold up the paper and put it in the bottle."

His explanation hadn't impressed me. My father's death wasn't a party.

Dandy seemed to read my thoughts. "I put a tribute in there," he backpedaled. "I said some nice things about Ace and listed who was here last night." He motioned to my younger brothers and me. "I put you guys down, but I said you didn't drink anything."

Dandy introduced himself to Sanders, and they talked about the weather and local baseball. Dandy extended condolences to Sanders when Mary Beth's name was mentioned, but I'd mostly ignored their conversation, so I didn't know who had brought up the subject of her passing. Death had covered my family like a thin veil, though, so I shouldn't have been surprised.

"It was nice to see you, Meg," Dandy called as he walked to his truck.

Sanders stared at me strangely, but I didn't fill him in on what else had happened. I was content with silence and stillness, much the same way as I imagined my father's corpse as my mother and uncle arranged a funeral for the man who had been my hero.

Chapter 42

I wasn't prepared for my father's funeral.

Unlike Mary Beth's ceremony, people from all walks of life lined up to pay their respects to Ace Tipton. His visitation period ran over, as the preacher was kind enough to delay the service until everyone had approached the coffin.

It was a lovely service, and I remembered most of it. My mother sobbed beside me, and my younger brothers held each other. Barton sat next to our mother, occasionally eyeing the coffin.

My mother hadn't wanted to sit in the front row, an area designated for immediate family. She argued with Barton as he pulled her to her seat, insisting that her husband had been in the process of divorcing her, so she had no place in the family's row.

Aunt Tonya extended her hand, welcoming my mother to the bench. Crystal sat between Uncle Catfish and her. I didn't ask about my father's baby.

Uncle Catfish attended to Crystal, as Aunt Tonya could hardly sit up in her seat. Fresh waves of tears sprung from her eyes every time viewers moved and she glimpsed her brother.

"They did a good job on him," she sobbed. She stared at my mother and me, but we were too shell-shocked to agree. Finally, Uncle Catfish held her hand and made remarks about my father's good coloring and perfectly trimmed hair.

I could see evidence of the abscess that had led to his heart attack. The redness and swelling in his face had been impossible to cover completely.

Ace Tipton had never worn a suit in his life, so we didn't have him dressed in one. My mother picked out a nice pair of jeans, and Barton and I selected a black shirt with patriotic skulls across the front. To most people, it may have seemed inappropriate, but it was my father's favorite shirt. I think he would have been happy with our choices.

My uncle had spared no expense on the casket and flowers, but I got the idea that the flowers were more for my mother since they were all yellow carnations. Her view of them would probably be ruined now, as she'd always associate them with my father's funeral. Uncle Barton hadn't thought that far ahead, though. He'd only wanted to make his sister more comfortable.

Uncle Barton received guests on our behalf. He shook hands with each mourner before they stepped into the viewing room.

I was certain that there were whispers about the love triangle between Aunt Mary Beth, my mother, and my father, but they didn't reach our ears during the service. Maybe there were people who thought my mother shouldn't sit in the section reserved for the family, but thankfully, Uncle Barton or another friend of our family smothered their opinions.

Owen and his parents arrived just before the ceremony started. They wrapped me in hugs and whispered condolences I didn't hear. I tried to smile at their effort, but I couldn't make my lips move.

Imani, Sanders, and Garrett sat behind me. Occasionally, Imani would stroke my hair or Sanders would touch my shoulder. Sanders should have been sitting in the front row, but because of the limited space, he opted to let Uncle Catfish remain with his wife and Crystal.

Sheriff Watts grabbed our hands and shook them lightly as he spoke to each of us. My mother opened her mouth to talk to him, but no words came out, and they embraced briefly before he walked away, wiping tears from his eyes.

I hated him, but I lacked the energy to express it. In my eyes, he was the biggest part of the reason my father died because he didn't take him to have his tooth treated. Of course, I didn't consider my father's dental health had been an issue for him for most of his life.

Dandy Hughes didn't approach my father's casket, but he extended his condolences to each of us. I was a little miffed when he sat beside Garrett in the second row, but he was directly behind Barton, so I tried to rationalize his presence as support for my older brother.

Every person who had sat at our dining room table during Friday Poker Nights gathered into the room, most of them bringing their families. Even men my father had fought crowded around the walls and hung their heads.

Reverend Matteo Sanchez delivered a stirring ceremony. I couldn't really tell you what he said, but I remember everyone's reaction. Aunt Tonya and my mother cried so hard they couldn't lift their heads, and the room was filled with sniffles by the close of his address.

I'd chosen the music for my father's funeral. There were a few of his favorites that played on repeat as pictures of him with our family flashed across the projection screen, but I had requested a song to be played just before the coffin closed.

"Miss You All the Time" rang out louder than the previous songs, and everyone was still as they absorbed the loss of a man who had brought love and light into our lives.

As the last note of the song faded, Aunt Tonya, Uncle Catfish, and Crystal approached the coffin. Sanders stood behind Crystal, giving her a small red and white rocket from her collection.

Aunt Tonya whispered over my father and then urged Crystal in front of her. My sister lifted her rocket and pressed it into our father's hand.

"I'll meet you on the moon," she said.

They turned away, and it was my household's turn to say our farewells.

My brother helped my mother stand on wobbly legs, and she almost slipped. Dandy shot out of his pew quickly, steadying my mother. When he was certain Barton could hold her up, he retreated to his seat.

I hadn't realized I'd been shaky. I was holding Si with Pickles by my side when Imani offered to take Si out of my arms. We transferred him easily, and he waved at our father.

"Hi, Da," he spoke in his sweet voice.

Pickles put his hand on our father's chest. He looked at Imani and said, "I'm ready to go. He's not here anymore."

Imani led my younger brothers outside the room. They joined my aunt, uncle, and sister.

Barton slipped a folded piece of paper into my father's shirt. It disappointed me I hadn't thought about bringing something to leave in my father's casket, and I thought about my class ring.

Mourners weren't supposed to wear jewelry, but I didn't find out about that until later. My mother had been too preoccupied to notice the ring on my right hand, and the only thing I knew about dressing for a funeral was to wear black.

I slipped my ring off my hand and put it in my father's shirt over his heart. My mother placed a lock of her fair hair into his hand.

We cried over my father's body for what seemed like hours, but was probably a few minutes. Even Barton was showing more emotion than I thought he felt for his stepfather.

My mother put her hand on my father's chest, and she lost any remaining composure. She slipped out of Barton's grasp, even though I tried to help him.

"Why?" she yelled at his corpse. "She was gone. Why did you do it to me?"

She was talking about the divorce, and I hoped no one heard her. Uncle Barton pulled her up and almost carried her out of the room. Cynthia had been seated at the edge of a pew with her parents, and despite their warning looks, she rose and followed Barton as he left behind our mother and Uncle Barton.

I was left standing at the casket, and everyone's eyes were on me. I'd been given time with my family before the service to see my father, but I hadn't really told him goodbye. There had been too many eyes on me.

Knowing it was the last time I'd see my father's form made it feel a little less awkward, though. I put my fingers through the hand that wasn't holding Crystal's rocket and my mother's hair, and the stiffness of his palm surprised me. His hand had always been rough and calloused, but it was cold as I tried to express what he'd meant to me.

I thought about our work in the garden, and our long talks in our hammock. I remembered his wise words, and I recollected the times I didn't follow them. I criticized myself for every missed opportunity to spend time with him and wished there were more.

I think I told my father I loved him. Unlike some of the other mourners, I knew our father wasn't in his body, but I believed his spirit was in the room with us. My tears released like a torrent.

"I didn't let your garden die!" I confessed. "It was a lie. I watered it every day, and I played the radio every night. It's beautiful and green, and you should see the tomatoes—"

I must have been hysterical, as I have no memory of anything else I said. I felt an arm on each of my elbows, and I was led out of the room. By the time I focused, I found Owen on one side and Garrett on the other.

Owen sat down on a couch with me, and I buried my head in his chest. I knew they were closing the casket, and I couldn't think about it.

I jumped up and lunged for the door before Sanders stopped me. I pinched at his hands, attempting to dislodge his fingers.

"I got to tell him something." I cried.

"He's gone," Sanders said. He didn't let go of me, but his blue eyes were kind. "Let him go in peace."

I kept fighting him, even when he pulled me into a hug. I didn't stop fighting until Imani wrapped her arms around me from behind. The scent of her buttery perfume flooded my senses and had a calming effect.

The mourners filed out. Some of them approached us, but most of them clicked and clonked their dress shoes on their way out the door.

Uncle Barton drove Barton, my mother, Si, Pickles, and me back to the house. He put the younger boys to bed while Barton sat on the couch with our mother.

Owen and Imani had offered to come over, but I wanted to be alone. After Uncle Barton opened a bottle of liquor, I went to my room.

I didn't bother to undress. I looked out the window at the fireflies as they ascended, and I wondered if my father's spirit was among them, blinking a light to find his way home.

Chapter 43

Everyone was hung over from grief or alcohol when they woke up the next morning.

My mother rushed my brothers through breakfast and a bath, but I stayed in bed and looked at the ceiling until it was almost time to go. Uncle Barton left, and I heard him return, but it didn't move me. I was in no hurry to get to my father's interment.

"You could at least brush your hair and wash your face," my mother commented when she saw I was wearing the same clothes.

Neither of us had the strength to argue, so I complied. I even brushed my teeth for good measure.

When we arrived at the funeral parlor, several people had already lined up in their cars. The funeral procession stretched to the end of the block, but it only amounted to half of the people who had attended the funeral.

Uncle Barton wouldn't argue with my mother about her place, shoving her gently into the funeral home's limousine. "You were still his wife. Get into the car and let the rest of us get through this without dealing with your insecurities."

I'd never heard my uncle speak so harshly to my mother, and I realized it was probably a combination of stress and his prior night's alcohol consumption that had led him to be brisk with her. A tear rolled out of her eye as we were driven to the place my father would be laid to rest, and Uncle Barton took her hand and whispered an apology.

My brothers, Aunt Tonya, and Crystal sat stiffly in the other seats. I stayed close to my younger brothers, worrying that I wasn't giving Crystal the attention she deserved.

Before we started moving, Pickles jumped to an empty place beside Crystal. He pointed to her rocket.

"Are you gonna give that one to Daddy, too?"

In answer, she held it close to her chest, indicating that it was hers. She took a piece of candy when he offered it to her, though, and she turned her head to listen to him as he chatted.

Thankfully, the interment was brief. The heat stifled the people who had worn their finest clothes. The reverend spoke a few short bible verses, extended condolences to the family, and walked away.

My mother, Aunt Tonya, Barton, and my father's children were each given a rose to put on his casket. I was the last one to put down my flower. I wanted to stay until the dirt was thrown over him, but my mother insisted it was time to leave.

I cast a look around me as we left, taking in the mountains and the sound of the Nolichucky River. My father would have been happy with his final resting place, and it'd be a nice place to visit him. He had loved to be surrounded by nature, and now, the forest trees and mountain streams were just as much a part of him in death as they were in his life.

Aunt Tonya received visitors after the funeral, but my mother didn't go. She refused to press her luck with extended family members who thought she should have vacated Tipton Hill as soon as my father had the divorce papers served.

I thought about walking to my aunt's house with my brothers, but I found myself in my father's hammock as gray clouds circled overhead. My sense of duty plagued me until I rounded up Si, Pickles, and Barton, and trudged an eighth of a mile up the hill to Aunt Tonya's house.

Vehicles parked all over her lawn in no discerning pattern, so we made our way through them like we were traveling in a maze. It was the most fun my younger brothers had experienced all day, but Barton and I put an end to it when Si tried to run under a truck on a lift kit.

We were welcomed by Uncle Catfish and seated across from Aunt Tonya in their spacious living room. The western decorations seemed like they were from a happier time, and the dancing cowboys and the smell of comfort food drifting from the kitchen felt out of place. Other than the black attire and crying, it could almost have been a gathering for a holiday or family reunion.

I tried to help my uncle with my aunt and Crystal, but I had to run after Si. Barton had taken responsibility for Pickles, who was usually the more rambunctious of the two younger children, but Si was hungry and tired, so he was burning out the last of his energy at supersonic speed. Every time I sat down, I had to jump up because

Si was tugging on a lady's dress or sticking his hand onto another person's plate.

I had a brief reprieve when I thought he had fallen asleep, but someone clanked a dish in the kitchen, and Si's eyes popped open. It wasn't long before he jumped out of my arms and bolted into every room in the house.

As I chased Si, I stumbled into a conversation I wasn't supposed to hear. I had just captured my toddler sibling, and he was wriggling in my arms. I heard Aunt Margaret speaking to Aunt Jo, another one of my grandfather's sisters.

"She might as well have buried him there, but it's shameful. Doesn't she have any pride?"

Her words washed over me like I'd been hit with a bucket of cold water. I had recognized the cemetery as the one where we'd buried Aunt Mary Beth, but I hadn't looked at the placement of my father's plot. *Had my mother put him beside her sister?*

I tried to think back, but grief clouded my memories. There had been a canopy over my father's casket, too, so it had blocked out some surroundings.

As I stood mulling over my revelation, the sisters caught sight of me. At first, they seemed startled by my presence, but then Aunt Margaret's mouth lifted to one side.

Si moved in my arms, and I ran with him. Thinking it was a game, he clung to me and giggled. I rushed out of the house and stumbled between the parked cars.

The walk back to my house seemed to take longer, and the sun was hotter while my brother's body was pressed against me, making the walk harder, even though it was downhill. Along the way, Si fell asleep, and his head dropped off my shoulder a couple of times before I righted it.

I held myself together until I got home. I even controlled my emotions long enough to put Si in his bed.

I'd seen Dandy's SUV in the driveway, and I found him with my mother in the garden. They were silently picking beans and tomatoes, with my mother on one side and Dandy on the other.

"What's wrong, Megara?" my mother said.

Dandy stood up, dusting the dirt off his knees. He held yellow and red tommy toes in a wooden basket. He took one look at my face and made a hasty exit.

As soon as his SUV pulled away, I let my mother know what I'd heard. She didn't respond, so I yelled at her.

"Did you bury him beside Aunt Mary Beth?"

"I suppose that's obvious," she replied crisply, resuming her search for ripe beans.

I couldn't believe she was going to ignore me. I pulled at the vine my father had fixed to a wire mesh, and it fell to the ground.

"Why did you bury him next to her? Aren't *you* supposed to be buried beside him?"

My mother dropped to her knees, and I thought she was going to keep picking the tangled mess of beans at her feet. Instead, her hands went to her face, and she cried.

I sat beside her, only partially conscious of the damp earth beneath me, as even though the weather had been hot, I had watered my father's garden daily.

"He was always hers," she choked out.

I tried to be patient with her, but my anger was threatening to spill out. I was afraid I was going to lash out at her like Uncle Barton had done that morning, but I restrained myself.

I spoke slowly. "If you don't tell me why you buried my father next to his mistress, I will leave today, and I won't live with you again."

I gave her a chance to collect herself. Even though she was much calmer, my mother wouldn't look at me. Finally, she told me something I never expected.

"Mary Beth didn't have an affair with him. I did."

Chapter 44

"But you were married to him!" I declared.

She started picking beans again and sensing she was going to tell me more, I joined her. I tried not to think of my father planting the beans from the previous year to grow the half-runners I plucked.

"I know you've been told a sweet lie about the way he and I met, but the truth is Ace was Mary Beth's boyfriend," she admitted. "She brought him over to my place a few times before Dandy went to jail, and we all played cards together. After Dandy went to jail, Ace would help me out by driving Barton and me to the store or to visit Dandy.

"I knew how much my sister liked him, and I envied their relationship. It wasn't that Ace was ultra-committed to Mary Beth—my sister and I were still young—but he was consistent. He didn't run off for days and return smelling like another woman."

She took a deep breath. "I didn't know I was going to kiss him, and to this day, I can't clearly remember how it happened, but my sister caught us. Mary Beth screamed at me, and I pointed out her drug trip with Dandy. I think your uncle told you that story."

"I'd like to hear your side of it," I said.

She shook her head. "This one is enough for me right now, and it's not done."

I grabbed a bean too hard, and its contents spilled onto the soil. I could collect the beans for next year's garden, but they wouldn't be planted in the same place.

"I'd read a lot of mythology books," my mother continued, "and I told Ace our love was destined. He'd felt sorry for me when Dandy had treated me badly, and he hadn't been aware that Mary Beth had been with Dandy when she ran off, so he broke up with her and started staying with me."

"I guess that's when I came along," I observed.

"Well," my mother hedged, "yes and no."

I could feel my mother pulling the rug out from under me before she spoke her next words. I tried to stop her. I even lifted my hand to put it over her mouth, but I wasn't fast enough.

"I was already pregnant with you before Ace kissed me."

I think I hyperventilated.

When I came back to my senses, my mother was holding an empty glass, and I was lying on the ground with water rolling into my ears. I lifted myself off the hot earth, coughing.

"I'm sorry, Megara."

It wasn't clear if she was apologizing for throwing a cup of cold water on my face or for admitting to a falsehood she'd continued for almost eighteen years.

I wanted to call her a liar. I wanted to push her away and curse her for trying to come between my dad and me. But I knew she was telling the truth.

"I thought you lost the baby," I said.

Quickly switching gears from caring for me back into our conversation, she asked, "Is that what Uncle Barton told you?"

I nodded, unable to answer her cordially. My emotions were sparking, and they were all ready to fire at her.

"I never told anyone I had a miscarriage," she said. "He must have made that up for your benefit."

A thought struck me as if it had been a box waiting for me to open it. "Is Dandy my father?"

"Yes," my mother replied, holding my gaze.

My world fell out of focus again, and my mother bent down and put a steadying hand on my shoulder. Enraged by her touch, I slung off her hand.

"You're a liar," I accused.

"Ask Dandy about it," she said calmly. "He's wanted to tell you, but he didn't think it'd be respectful since Ace died."

"Good for Dandy," I shot back. "I guess he's developed morals over the years he spent in a federal penitentiary." I rolled my eyes.

"Don't be snarky," my mother said. "I didn't tell him I was pregnant with you when I divorced him, so he thought Barton was his only child until he saw you."

"That was convenient for both of you." It was getting harder for me to reign in my rage.

My mother went on as if I hadn't spoken. "He noticed you had the same color hair as your brother and you both have his forehead."

"I hate you," I spoke suddenly.

My mother startled, and I was glad I'd gotten a reaction from her. I wanted to tear her apart and destroy her calm demeanor. My mother and I had always had a more distant relationship, and I wished she was the one who had adopted me into her life, so I could cut my tenuous ties to her and be done. But fate was cruel, and the unsteady maternal figure before me was my actual flesh-and-bone mother.

"I felt sorry for you when I learned about Daddy's—*Ace's*—affair and Crystal's paternity, but now I see that you're just like the rest of the liars on this godforsaken hill." I threw my hand up. "I'm *glad* you didn't feel like you belonged at his funeral. You took him away from the woman he loved, and you made him make a choice between love and his duty."

I stood up, and the world wobbled, but it righted soon after. "You knew he was a loyal man. I bet you got pregnant with Pickles to make sure you kept him around."

I hadn't given my accusal much thought before I said it, but I already knew the truth. My mother didn't know I was aware of the situation, though, and face paled.

"No," I gasped, pretending it was new information. I could play her game of lies, too.

"Yes," she confirmed. "Poseidon was a surprise, but I guess you can tell when I got pregnant with Pickles."

I'd already mentally calculated the difference between Pickles's and Crystal's birthdays. "You got pregnant with him as soon as you found out Aunt Mary Beth was pregnant."

"I'm not proud of it," she said, hanging her head. "I wish I would have let Ace go then."

"Why didn't you?" I asked.

"I thought I loved him."

"*Thought?*" I asked, raising my voice an octave.

"I loved Ace, but I didn't love him the way Mary Beth did. I was comfortable with him, and he was a good man."

I wanted to scream, but I tried to remain as calm as possible. I knew I was losing my battle when my mother reached out to me again. I backed away.

"It's okay," she told me, giving me permission for an action over which she had no control.

"You kept two people who were in love with each other from being together because you were *comfortable*?" I seethed. "You made Crystal and Sanders suffer, and you let the whole town talk about us, so you could keep a *good* man?

"I remember him cheating on you when I was younger. You didn't think about leaving him when he cheated on you then, so why would it bother you if he cheated on you with Aunt Mary Beth?"

The answer to my question was right in front of me, as if it were waiting for me to pluck it from the air. "You kept him because your sister wanted him. She had hurt you, and you wanted to get back at her."

My mother didn't have to confirm my suspicions. We both knew I was right.

"And so, I hate you," I said evenly.

I walked away from her, not caring that she cried my name. I went into the house and silently gathered a few outfits and some of the special things I couldn't leave behind. I stuffed them into an old tote I'd used for forgotten dance classes.

Si opened his eyes and stood on his bed, holding his tiny arms out for me. I scooped him up and slung my tote over my shoulder.

He dipped his head into my neck until I passed him to our blubbering mother. His confused eyes flitted from her to me.

"Egg!" he yelled, adopting the nickname Pickles used for me.

I hugged him, promising that I'd see him soon. I hoped I'd be able to keep my word.

I walked out the door, fully expecting to leave Tipton Hill. As I walked down the road, I spotted a copperhead in my path, making me veer into Widow Silvers's yard. After I was pledged to my detour, I saw the snake move off the road, and its course made me think of somewhere I needed to visit before I left. I was determined to uncover every secret in the bed of lies my parents had made for me.

Chapter 45

"Did you know?" I yelled at Sanders.

He stared at me. "Know what, Meg? What's going on?"

He was so bewildered I almost believed him. I had to be sure he hadn't buried the secret in a trove of lies like the rest of my family, though.

"Dandy is my biological father." A stream of sobs followed the admission.

His eyes widened. "No way. Who told you that?"

"My mama!" I yelled at him, trying to control the tears that flowed down both my cheeks.

"She's just mad because of the affair. It can't be true."

"You've seen Dandy," I said. "She told me I have the color of his hair and his forehead, and she's right."

Sanders seemed to mull over my words. "Your mama's blonde, too."

"But Barton and I have the same shade, and ours is darker."

"But why would Ace say you were—" He cut himself off.

"You and I both know why my father" —I waited for a beat and corrected myself— "*Ace* would say I was his daughter. He wanted to marry my mama and have everyone on Tipton Hill accept me."

"Do you think they knew anyway?"

I waved my hand. "Of course they knew, especially Aunt Tonya and the older aunts and uncles. I was an outcast, and I was too stupid to even realize it."

I sobbed more heavily, and Sanders drew me close. I hardly felt his arms around me as I cried.

"It's going to be okay," he soothed, running his fingers down a strand of my hair.

"How can you say that?" I demanded, trying to push him away. "Nothing like this has ever happened to you!"

I'd thought I had every right to be upset and think terrible thoughts about the people who raised me. My cousin offered another point of view.

"You may be mad, but at least someone *wanted* to be your father."

I was surprised. I'd always believed Sanders thought highly of his father.

He stared at his feet. "My dad was pretty good when he was around, but he always seemed to have one foot out the door. When Mary Beth asked him to play with me, he'd go through the motions, but I'd catch him staring at the television or out the window."

"Maybe he was easily distracted," I offered.

Sanders scoffed. "No. My dad was happy to see us when he came home, but after the initial welcome, he just sat on the couch. He didn't want to go anywhere or do anything with us. The only place we could drag him to was your parents' Friday Poker Nights, and that was getting harder to do."

"He traveled a lot with his job," I countered, trying to play the devil's advocate. "He was probably happy to be in one place."

Sanders tilted his head. "It was more than that. It was like he was trying to spend time around us, like he was fulfilling a requirement, but he wasn't *with* us. He was like a mostly silent houseguest, but the day he left for another assignment, his face would light up like it was Christmas."

"I'm sorry." It was the only thing I could think of to say.

He shrugged. "That's why I said what I did to you, though. You had Ace raise you as his own child. He didn't treat you differently than the rest of his kids. If anything, he may have treated you a little better, but you were older, and you were—"

"—his little protégé," I finished for him.

"Ace may be gone," he continued, "but now, you got this guy who wants to start a father-daughter relationship with you. The best part is, he didn't know you were his kid, but he guessed it, and so you can't be mad about him not being there for you."

Sanders had a point, even though I wanted to ignore it. Dandy hadn't known about me, making it impossible to claim he had willfully abandoned me.

"I guess you're right about that part," I conceded.

Sanders rested his arm on my shoulder. "Of course I'm right."

We sat in the silent house for a few minutes before I spoke again. "Is Crystal still with Tonya?" I'd always called her my aunt, but it didn't feel right anymore.

"Yeah. Crystal took all her rockets and her rug over there. I guess she's fully moved out of here."

"What will happen to this place when you go to UT? Are you going to sell it?"

He laughed. "I actually thought about renting it to your mama or Barton."

"It might be a nice place for Barton," I agreed. "He loved Aunt Mary Beth."

"Did you love her?"

His question threw me off guard. "Yeah. I loved her. I told her I did all the time." I raised my eyebrow. "Why?"

"Because she knew Ace was married to her sister, but she lured him up here every time my dad was gone. Your mama's marriage never really had a chance."

"He was Mary Beth's boyfriend first," I told him. "My mama took him from her."

He sighed. "But we're talking about over a decade of adultery. Did your mama ever cheat on Ace?"

I thought back. "My mother was always busy with Barton and me, and then Pickles was a handful—"

"So, no." His mouth lifted at one corner as he realized he was making his point.

"I guess not."

Sanders watched me fidget. "I think you picked sides when you were young, and you chose Ace."

I brushed away his accusation. "I didn't pick sides. I didn't even know what was going on."

"That's why you chose Ace."

I didn't want to think of my mother as a selfless person who gave up her happiness so I could have a good relationship with the man I thought was my father. "No. Mama is the reason for all of this. If she had left Ace alone, then he would have married Mary Beth."

"She made one mistake," he said. "Don't you think she's suffered enough for it?"

"No," I said stubbornly.

He sighed and shook his head. "Then you don't deserve her forgiveness."

As I walked to Owen's house, I tried to remember my cousin's mother had left him, and he may have developed a different idea about the way a mother was supposed to behave. It was my mother who didn't deserve me or my forgiveness.

All she had done was lie from the moment of my conception. She didn't tell Dandy he had another child. She only told Ace so he could help her build upon the fabrication of my paternity. She lied to everyone.

But that wasn't quite true. She had only really lied to me. Everyone else seemed to know I didn't belong to Ace, and they kept her secret so I would live with the sting of her lie.

Uncle Catfish's laughter and Aunt Tonya's long talks were muddied by the revelation I wasn't really a Tipton. My whole life I'd felt like I had a place on Tipton Hill, even when Aunt Margaret told us to leave our home, I thought I'd be back to live in one of my relative's houses one day, but the joke was on me.

As if on cue, a sparkling SUV pulled up next to me. I kept walking, trying to ignore it, when the driver rolled down the passenger window.

"Meg!" Dandy called.

I stopped abruptly, and the SUV rolled several feet ahead of me. I made him reverse back to where I had planted my feet.

"Get in the car," he said.

I crossed my arms, indicating that I wasn't moving, even though the late afternoon sun beat down on me and breathed its humid breath in my face. Dandy got tired of trying to talk to me through the window, and I couldn't hear him anyway, so he jumped out of the driver's side after putting the vehicle in park.

The street was rarely used, but his SUV was blocking traffic on one side. I hoped a car didn't come down the road while he was talking to me.

"You're as hard-headed as your mama!" he said, clearly irritated.

I glared at him.

"Sore subject?" he asked, chuckling good-naturedly. "Okay, then. Why don't you tell me where you're goin'?"

My temper flared. "Oh, so now that I know you're my father, you're going to try to act like one. Save it, *Dad*. You weren't there for Barton, and I don't need you around either!"

I brushed by him, knocking him on the arm as I passed. His shoulders were like small boulders; he was unmovable.

"You may be right."

I should have kept walking, but I turned around. "I *may* be right? You ran around on my mama and slept with her sister. You got yourself put in jail, and you let Ace Tipton raise your children. Barton and I are adults. We don't need you anymore, so you can go ruin another family because you already broke mine apart."

I wondered how true my words were as I said them. *If Dandy hadn't slept with Mary Beth, would my mother have stolen her sister's boyfriend?*

"I won't deny my mistakes, but I didn't sleep with Mary Beth."

I raised my eyebrow, but I put it down when I remembered it was one of my mother's playful features that Dandy had liked. "There were pictures of you two in the same bed."

He colored. "I know how it looked, but our clothes were on. I thought of her like a sister. Just like I was supposed to."

"You expect me to believe you didn't sleep with her when you cheated on my mama dozens of times?"

He held up a hand. "I don't expect you to believe anything. My head has been spinnin' since I realized you were my daughter, so I can't imagine what you're goin' through. Both of my parents were murdered just before I turned eighteen, and I never really got over it. I may not know exactly how you feel, but I know what it's like to lose a parent."

"My grandparents are dead," I said, trying to make the information mean something to me. I hadn't known them, though, so I only felt sad they had been murdered.

He nodded, taking a step toward me. "They would have loved you and your brothers, especially little Pickles."

"Pickles isn't their grandson!" I barked.

He pulled air deep into his belly and exhaled it slowly. "Meg, you have this weird idea that family has to be blood. I'd think when you learned Ace had raised you like his own, you would have felt differently. I'll bet most of the folks on Tipton Hill treated you like you were a blood relation, and those that didn't weren't worth your time."

Dandy had a point. Aunt Margaret had been standoffish to me, but I'd always assumed it was because she was sore that my family lived in her house. My paternity certainly explained her reluctance to grant my request for my father's bond.

Dandy put his hand on my shoulder, and I allowed it. We stood together uncomfortably, each one thinking about something more to say.

"Are you goin' to that boy's house?" he asked.

I rolled my eyes. "His name is Owen."

"Can I change your mind?"

I shifted my feet, unwilling to look at him. "What do you mean?"

It was his turn to be uncertain. "My parents left me a piece of property when they died. I put a trailer on it when I turned eighteen, and your mama and I lived there." He chuckled. "You were probably made in—"

"Eww! Stop!"

He laughed outright, watching my reaction. His tone was a little lighter when he continued.

"I arranged for a realty company to manage my property while I was locked up. Renters trashed the trailer over the years, so I had it carted off when I got out. I bought one of them manufactured homes, and it has five bedrooms."

"Why did you get such a big house?" I asked.

He put his hands in his pockets. "To be honest, I grew up in a big house. And I may have hoped your brother, his girlfriend, and my first grandchild would move in with me."

"Still, that's a lot of rooms."

"You don't miss a beat, do you?"

I shook my head, happy to hear a compliment that didn't compare me to one of my parents.

"I have a confession," he admitted.

My mood shifted, and my smile disappeared. Seeing my changed expression, Dandy waved his hand.

"It's not a big deal," he assured me.

I waited for him to tell me whatever he thought related to our conversation. I hated to be so skeptical, but recent events had jaded me.

"Once I thought you might be my daughter, I hung out by your house and spied on you a couple of times to be sure. I wanted to approach you about it, but you were always with your mother, Owen, or that Tipton boy."

"Sanders."

"Yeah, Sanders. Does he know he's not your cousin?"

"Yeah. But we were raised that way."

"He treats you like he's your boyfriend," Dandy observed. "But that's a discussion for another day."

He jumped back to his stalking. "So, I hid behind a maple tree."

"We saw you!" I remembered. "You ran off when we tried to yell after you."

"I sure did," he laughed. "Have you ever seen your mama when she gets mad? I had no business on her property, and I wasn't ready to tell her I thought you were my daughter."

He opened the door on the passenger's side and motioned for me to step inside. "I'd like to take you to my house. We could have dinner and catch up on lost time."

"You just told me you stalked me. I don't think I should." I giggled and couldn't stop. Once I started laughing, it spilled over from an untapped reservoir.

Dandy joined me. "I'm not offerin' you a ride in a van without windows, so you may be alright."

Dandy's manufactured home was almost as beautiful as the ones built by hand on Tipton Hill. I went around it in awe, as he showed me the crown molding and oak cabinets.

"There were only four bedrooms," I commented.

"The family room can be closed off pretty easily," he said. "It'd make a good place for a lady and two little boys."

"You want my mother to move in with you?"

He put two glasses of tea on a cherry table and pulled out a chair for me. I sat down and he moved to the seat facing me, holding his tea glass with both hands.

"I want to help her," he said.

"You still love her." It wasn't a question.

"Yeah," he said miserably. "I know I don't deserve her, and she could never love me again, but I couldn't think of us as divorced. I still feel like she's my wife."

"You want us all to live together," I realized, shaking my head. "That'll never work."

"Why not?" he asked. "There's plenty of room here. I could help with the younguns', and you could save money on rent and utilities while you're goin' to college. I couldn't help you and Barton when I was in jail, but I can do somethin' to give you guys a better adult-hood."

"What will happen when Mama doesn't want to give you another chance, or you decide to chase after other women again?"

"Meg, you may not believe me, and I doubt you want to hear it, but your Mama was the last person I was with before I went to jail, and she's all I think about now."

I covered my ears. "TMI!"

When I opened my eyes and uncovered my ears, he was looking at me jovially. "Will you stay in one of the rooms?"

I thought hard about the situation. I could get along with Barton, and his girlfriend seemed nice, but I couldn't live with my mother again. I explained my feelings to Dandy.

"Oh," he said, crestfallen. "I didn't know you and your mother were at odds."

"She's the reason everyone had to lie."

He pondered my words, running his fingers over his chin. "I don't think so. I think everyone has their own reason for lying. Ace didn't want to lose your love and respect. Mary Beth didn't want Ace to quit seeing her, even if it was on the sly, and your mother just wanted to keep her family together. I'd already messed that up for her the first time." His mouth turned down into a frown, showing deep lines around his mouth.

I didn't want to think about his points. I wanted to be mad at someone, and Mary Beth and Ace were dead, so I couldn't be angry with them. That only left one person to hate for the unfairness.

The light was disappearing from the sky. Dandy stood up and patted my shoulder.

"Well, your mama's not here tonight, so why don't you stay in one of the guest rooms?"

I agreed and put my tote in the room closest to the living room while Dandy put two steaks on the grill. He had soaked them in a marinade, and I wondered how he had known he'd be cooking for two. He froze when I asked him about it. I thought he was going to tell me about a canceled date, but he surprised me when he said, "Your mama called me and asked me to find you. I thought we could end up back here and you might be hungry."

Of course my mother had called him. *Why else would Dandy have been driving down the roads on the other side of town?* I could have face-palmed myself for not thinking of it sooner.

Despite periods of awkwardness, Dandy and I spent an enjoyable evening on his back deck. When the night settled in, and the temperature cooled, he brought out a blanket for me, claiming he was too "warm-blooded" to need one, too.

"When did you find out my mama had had me?" I asked.

He looked up at the sky. "I hadn't been moved from the jail to the prison for long when someone sent me an envelope with Sara's wedding announcement and your birth announcement. I didn't put two and two together, or I would've done the math. I just thought someone wanted to hurt me."

"I bet it was Aunt Mary Beth," I said. "I don't think she wanted to hurt you, but she loved Ace, and maybe she thought you'd ask for a DNA test."

"Why are you callin' him Ace?" he asked me, his eyebrows drawing together like a set of curtains. "That man was your daddy."

"It just doesn't feel right anymore."

He leaned forward in his chair. "Ace raised you, and he deserves the title. To tell you the truth, I couldn't be mad if Barton called him *daddy*, too. I wasn't there for your brother. Not really."

I didn't like the turn in the conversation, so I asked to use the bathroom. Dandy told me to use the bathroom in his room since the handle was stuck on the toilet in the guest bathroom.

I splashed some cold water on my face and noted his simple blue-green hand towels. They contrasted with his sanguine shower curtain.

The towels seemed dirty, so I opened the cabinet under the sink to get another one. I jumped back when I saw the gun.

I don't know how I knew it, but I'd found the gun that had murdered my aunt.

Chapter 46

I stared at the gun for a long time without touching it. It was almost like when you see a snake on television, but it looks more threatening when you spot one several feet away.

The silver metal shined in the light, making the weapon seem colder and more deadly. A black gun may have been easier for my mind to process, as I had seen them depicted that way in television shows and movies.

No blood splatted across the gun, and I'd never learned what had killed my aunt, but I was sure that the murder weapon was in the cabinet under Dandy's bathroom sink. It was a strange feeling, but also a very certain one.

At first, I'd pinned Mary Beth's murder on Barton. After I'd discovered the reason for the blood on his knife, I'd entertained the idea that Uncle Catfish had killed her to keep Aunt Tonya from believing the baby my aunt was carrying belonged to him. My mind had flickered to my mother when she was telling me the story about betraying her twin, but she seemed to feel guilty about her past actions and not justified by them, and she didn't have the confidence of a killer.

Dandy, on the other hand, had an inflated ego. He was happy and carefree. *After all, who would have suspected him?*

My thoughts raced to motives. He wanted my mother to live with him, so he had to get rid of any obstacles. He must have framed Ace for the murder, knowing that the man who raised me would feel guilty for not being able to save his mistress. Dandy had admitted to watching our house, so he'd noted when my father left to visit Mary Beth at night so he could time the killing perfectly.

Crystal had said she saw her father there that night, but she hadn't mentioned actually witnessing the murder, so she may have seen her father bent over her mother after she'd been killed. It made sense.

Ace had left the house when Sanders showed up, leaving as my cousin made it inside. Then he just continued with life as normal until Sheriff Watts picked him up.

I'd spent a considerable amount of time in the bathroom, so I closed the cabinet door, flushed the toilet, and stepped out. I almost ran into Dandy.

"I was just about to ask you if you needed anythin'," he said awkwardly. "I don't have a lot of female things here, but I can run out and get some stuff if you need it."

He had misunderstood my lengthy bathroom time, and I used it to my advantage. "I don't need anything like that, but my stomach is a little upset. Do you have something I could take for it?"

He held up a finger. "I'll be right back."

After he turned away, I flitted into the bathroom and opened the camera on my phone. I took a picture of the gun. I had just closed the cabinet and stuffed my phone into the pocket of my shorts when I heard a voice behind me.

"What are you doing?"

My blood ran cold. *Had he seen me take the picture?*

I decided to play innocent until he completely called me out for whatever he'd seen. "I thought I might throw up, so I came back to the bathroom."

He nodded, but his features were skeptical. *What had he seen?*

Dandy held up a small cup of pink liquid. "I get a lot of indigestion. I keep the pink stuff around to help with it, but it should do for an upset stomach, too."

I swallowed the medicine, only realizing afterward that it could have been poisoned. I shook that thought out of my head. Until he came back and saw me in the bathroom, Dandy had no reason to suspect that I knew anything about his part in my aunt's murder.

"If you need anything else, we can drive to the store."

I couldn't look at him. I was too afraid I'd reveal my feelings, but I knew I had to say something.

"I think I need to lie down."

He followed me to the bedroom where I'd left my tote. His thick fingers grabbed the wood around the frame, and I wondered if my aunt had been his first victim. He'd mentioned that his parents had been murdered, too. I tried to erase the thought from my mind as I pulled back the counterpane and climbed onto the full-sized bed.

"I never thought I'd get to do this," he said.

Dandy advanced on me, and I closed my eyes, waiting for him to strike me. There was no running away. I'd missed my chance when I'd laid down on the bed.

I felt a tug beneath me, and the sheets were pulled down and then over me. They reached my upper arm, and Dandy patted my shoulder. I jumped at his touch, and he recoiled.

"I'm sorry," he said, backing up to the door. "I think I got carried away with the whole *dad* thing. You told me you were sick, and I thought I could be the hero."

I almost bit back that my father was my hero, but then I remembered Dandy was actually my father. I shifted in the bed, trying to think of an appropriate response.

"I love you," he said, and then hastily defended himself. "I know it seems like it's too soon, but it's almost like part of me knew somethin' was missing, and there you are. We get along well, and you understand my humor, and I'm happy you know the truth and I can tell you that you're my daughter."

In any other situation, I might have felt sorry for him. He seemed to be lonely, and he was really trying hard to show me he cared for me, but I was still trying to process the gun I'd seen in his cabinet.

Dandy saved me from more uncomfortable words by closing the door.

Once I was alone, I flipped over, kicking the cover down that Dandy had placed over me. I stared up at the ceiling, weighing my options.

I texted Owen, but I didn't get a response. He was probably in bed, and the boy could sleep through an earthquake. I messaged Imani, and when she didn't answer, I tried Garrett. They must have been together, as neither one of them got back to me. I felt desperate when I sent Sanders a text. He returned my message right away.

I asked him to pick me up from Dandy's house, and he told me he was still at work. I begged him to get me after he finished up, but

Sanders hesitated. He reminded me I was lucky to have someone who wanted to be my father, and he wasn't going to interfere with it. I was typing back to him when I heard footsteps outside my door.

I turned on my side, shoving my phone under the pillow. Dandy opened the door and stepped inside. I tried to regulate my breathing to the rhythm I'd heard from Imani when we'd have sleepovers and she'd fall asleep before me. I felt a gentle breeze as the cover settled back over me.

Dandy stalled near me. I could feel his breath on my skin, and I hoped he wasn't planning to smother me with the bedsheet. Just before I decided to scream, he kissed me on the top of my head and went out of the room, pulling the door closed behind him.

I let out a breath I hadn't known I'd been holding. I battled with the cover, pushing it off the bed.

Dandy's possible motives for killing Aunt Mary Beth and his checkered past kept me up well into the night. I thought about leaving, but if Dandy checked on me again, he'd simply track me down before I made it anywhere.

I was on the verge of a fitful doze when I woke to the sound of whispering. Dandy had been in his room, but I heard his muffled voice as he breezed down the hallway. I crept to the door and lay flat, trying to hear anything through the crack at the bottom. There were measured gaps between vocalizations, so I gathered that he was on the phone. Most of what he said was too distant to hear, but I could make out a few snatches of his side of the conversation.

"I think she knows."

He had to be talking about me. He may have seen me close the cabinet, or worse, take a picture of the gun.

"You know what will happen if you tell her."

Was that a threat? Obviously, someone else knew about his crime. Maybe that person wanted to tell me the truth, but Dandy had issued a warning.

Who was the other person? Was it someone he'd known in jail, or could it be my mother?

Maybe my feeling had been right. Perhaps she had used her ex-husband to get rid of her sister and husband. Even as I thought about it, I realized my idea was far-fetched, but my tired mind continued to run with it.

My mother could have stumbled upon the truth after Dandy killed her sister. They had spoken on the phone, and she had requested that he talk to me after I'd left. That was pretty chummy for people who had been divorced for almost eighteen years.

I didn't hear anything else, so I climbed back into bed. My heart raced until the wee hours of the morning, but at some point, my exhausted mind gave out, and I didn't wake until it was almost noon.

When I opened my eyes, Dandy was standing over me.

Chapter 47

Sanders let me into the house, and I hugged him, looking for Crystal, even though she was with Tonya and Catfish. When I saw her rug and rockets were still gone, I ran to the windows. Dandy's truck was backing out of the driveway.

Dandy had encouraged me to eat breakfast with him, and I'd choked down the cinnamon sugar doughnuts he'd made for me. After breakfast, which had been more like lunch, I'd asked him to take me to see Sanders. Fearing that he'd make me stay if I didn't give him a reason to believe things were still going well, I promised to come back and stay another night, leaving my tote in the room where I'd slept.

"I only have a few minutes, so listen up," I commanded as I released the curtain and rushed back to my cousin.

"I need to know how she died."

Sanders paled. "What?"

"How did my aunt die?" I asked again. "I've tried to spare everyone's feelings, and it felt too weird to ask the sheriff, but I need you to tell me what killed her."

Sanders let out the reason and his breath all at once. "She was shot."

"I knew it!" I said, a little too triumphantly.

Sanders sat on the couch. It seemed I had knocked the wind out of him.

"I'm so sorry," I said, rushing to his side. "I shouldn't have asked you."

My cousin had found his mom after he'd come home from work. In my haste, I had been completely insensitive.

I took his hand in mine. He rubbed my thumb with his forefinger. "It's okay. I know you're under a lot of stress, too."

"I still shouldn't have asked you," I said. "I probably would have punched someone if they'd have asked me how my daddy—I mean—Ace died."

"He's still your dad," Sanders said. "Ace raised you and he loved you. Do you think he saw you as less than his daughter?"

Sanders's question provided me with a new perspective. Nothing had really changed except my knowledge of my paternity. Ace Tipton hadn't treated me any differently, and I knew he loved me.

"You're right," I realized. "He's still my dad."

Satisfied that he'd solved an internal struggle for me, Sanders looked up and smiled. I hated to erase his happiness, but I had to get to the real reason for my visit.

"Dandy killed her."

Sanders startled. "Killed who?"

I rolled my eyes and squeezed his fingers, willing him to keep up with my train of thought. "Aunt Mary Beth. He killed her."

Sanders was completely baffled. "He wasn't even—"

"I know what you're thinking, but I found the gun in his bathroom." I showed him the picture I'd taken of the gun inside the cabinet. "See?"

Sanders had gone completely white. When he spoke, he stuttered through an explanation.

"L-lot's of p-people keep guns around for p-protection."

How could I tell him about my feeling? I explained based on my suspected motives. When I ran through them all, even the part that included the imagined role my mother played, Sanders still wasn't convinced.

A knock sounded at the door, making us both jump. I looked out the window, and Dandy's SUV shined in the afternoon sunshine.

"It's him," I whispered, pushing Sanders away from the window.

Sanders rolled his eyes. "We have to answer the door. He already knows you're here."

Sanders went into the hall, and I followed, holding onto the back of his shirt. I tried to compose myself before Dandy came inside, but I must have appeared frightened, as Dandy asked if I was feeling well twice before he excused himself to the bathroom.

Barton stepped out of Mary Beth's room, surprising me. His hair was disheveled, and he'd barely thrown on his pants before he'd opened the door.

"What are you doing here?" I asked.

Cynthia tugged on his arm, but he held up a finger, and she went back to bed. "I had a fight with mama, and she told me to leave. Cynthia told her parents that she was spending the night with a friend so we could stay together last night."

"What did you fight with Mama about?"

He opened his eyes wide. "You, of course! And maybe a little about the baby."

"I didn't see your car when I came inside."

"It's parked behind the house. I didn't want Mama to walk around lookin' for me and find it."

He glanced back at the room where his girlfriend waited and scratched the back of his head. "We had a late night, so we're still pretty tired."

Cynthia called for him, and he waved before he ducked back into the room. I thought it'd be hard to stay in a place where a close family member had died, but I guess someone had to sleep there eventually.

I dragged my cousin back to the living room. "You can't let me go back with him! Make up a reason that you need me to stay with you."

"Meg—" Sanders started.

"I told you she'd picked up on somethin'."

I froze. My breath caught in my lungs and my legs shook.

It took me less than a second to put together that Dandy had been talking to Sanders when he was on the phone the previous night. My eyes filled with tears as I silently begged for it not to be true.

"Sanders?"

My cousin took my hand and led me to the couch. "I need you to stay calm and listen to me."

I was too busy trying to connect his association with my murderous father. I could hardly concentrate on more than the sound of his voice.

"Did you hire him to kill my aunt?" I asked. "Did you secretly hate her?"

I thought about all the kindness Mary Beth had shown Sanders, from adopting him to caring for his every need. She'd hugged him with tenderness, and I thought he'd felt an equal amount of love for her.

"You've got it all wrong," Dandy said, taking a step into the room.

"Why do you have a gun in your bathroom cabinet?" I asked him, finding my nerve. "And don't try to tell me it's for protection."

"I have the gun, but—"

"And my aunt was shot!" I yelled, jumping to my feet. "And you did it!"

Dandy took another step into the room. "I think we're gettin' carried away."

"I bet you do," I said, pulling my phone out of my pocket. "Why don't we call the police and see what they think?"

"Hang on!" Dandy shouted. "I'm a felon. I'll go to jail for the gun and every bullet in it!"

"I'd think you'd be more concerned about going to jail for the bullet that's not in it," I said, laughing hysterically as I looked up the number for the police department.

Dandy addressed Sanders. "What did I tell you, boy? I won't go down for this!"

My fingers couldn't click fast enough as they slipped off my phone, sending it to the floor.

Dandy stood across from my cousin with his fists clenched. If it were possible, my cousin was even paler.

Without thinking, I ran at my father, attempting to knock him off his feet. "Run!" I yelled to Sanders.

Dandy hardly moved when my body crashed into him, and I landed in a pile at his feet.

"Meg!" Sanders cried.

He fell on the floor beside me, pulling me into his chest. I stayed wrapped against him as his tears fell.

"It was me!" he sobbed into my hair. "I killed her."

I stared up at Dandy, and he looked down at my cousin with sympathy. He squatted beside us and put his hand on Sanders's back. When my cousin could speak coherently, Dandy said, "I think it's time you told her."

I tried to wait patiently, but I didn't know how I'd keep my emotions in check. Thankfully, Sanders was ready to purge his crimes.

"I got the gun from a kid at school." He looked at me for validation. "You know, Freddy."

I shook my head once. I wasn't familiar with the boy.

"Anyway," Sanders went on. "I'd gotten off work early, so I hid in her closet. I waited until they closed the bedroom door, and I popped out."

He hung his head. "My first shot missed, but my second shot hit someone."

He squeezed his eyes shut, and his face contorted. "It hit the wrong one!"

My mouth went dry as it all came together for me. "You were trying to kill my daddy."

He glanced up urgently, grabbing my hands. "I know I was wrong, but I was convinced Ace wasn't going to leave your mother. I didn't know he'd already filed for a divorce. I thought my mom would be left raising another one of his children while the town laughed at us."

I pulled my hands away from him, and before I knew what I'd done, I slapped him. Sanders grabbed his cheek, but he didn't lash back at me.

Dandy intervened, pulling Sanders onto his feet. I stayed on the floor, battling rage, disbelief, and frustration.

"Why did you let my daddy go to jail for what you did?" I clenched my teeth and stared at my fists, so I didn't lunge at him.

Dandy answered for Sanders. "It wasn't his idea. Ace decided to take the fall."

I looked up at them and slammed my fist into my leg. "You don't make any sense." I pointed to Sanders. "He was going to kill him, so why would my father care what happened to him?"

Dandy held up a hand. "Ace understood why the boy did it, and by the time Mary Beth died, I don't think Ace cared a hill of beans about what became of him."

"He didn't want Sanders to lose his opportunities," my brother said.

Barton was standing in the doorway, leaning against the frame. He'd put on a shirt, but it was mostly unbuttoned. I don't know how long he was there, but he'd probably heard whatever he hadn't seen.

"You knew, too," I gasped.

"Ace called me," he confirmed. "He told me to bring bleach and plastic bags. I had to swear Pickles to secrecy, but I made it out of the house without waking up Mama."

My father had stored little tidbits of information over the years, and he'd once told me that bleach would clean gunpowder off skin and surfaces. It was knowledge I hadn't expected him to use.

"I didn't expect to find Aunt Mary Beth dead," Barton went on. "I tried to revive her before Ace stopped me, and then I hit him."

"Barton got blood all over his shirt," Sanders said. "So Ace made us clean up with bleach and take showers."

Dandy stuck his hands in his pockets. "Barton took the gun, but he didn't know what to do with it when the sheriff picked up your father, so he brought it to my house. I haven't touched the thing since Barton laid it in my bathroom cabinet."

"My father was protecting *you*," I seethed, glaring at Sanders. "*You* ruined all our lives, and you get to go on like nothing happened."

Sanders put his face in his hands. "I know. I've been thinking about turning myself in."

Dandy put his hand back on Sanders's shoulder. "That's all well and good, but you've made us all accessories after the fact. I have the gun, Barton helped you clean up the evidence, Sara took the shirt and shredded it, and even Meg could be charged now that she knows what happened."

My association with the crime seemed to wake Sanders from his thoughts of self-absolution. "But shouldn't I turn myself in?"

Barton bounced off the frame. "Yeah. You shoulda turned yourself in that night. You shouldn't have let Ace take the blame, especially since you're gonna waste his sacrifice. He went to jail and died for nothing." Barton stuck his finger in Sanders's chest. "All because he believed you could do bigger and better things."

My father may have thought Sanders was going to move away and make a big name for himself, but he shouldn't have covered the murder. I voiced my opinion to the others.

"His life was over after she died," Barton said grimly. "He was barely a shadow by the time Sheriff Watts picked him up."

I thought back to the moments before the sheriff's car turned onto our road. I'd been lying with my father, sharing a piece of chocolate. I'd noted the bruise on his cheek, but he had always been getting into a scrape for one reason or another, so I hadn't given it much thought. He'd been contemplative, but I'd misunderstood his melancholy mood for the silence we usually shared.

My father made the decision to take the blame for Sanders's actions. He may have done it out of duty, grief, or both, but as his daughter, I had to honor my daddy's decision.

At the end of an afternoon that seemed to go on forever, we all agreed that Sanders should go to school at UT. He'd be allowed to live his life, and his would be another secret we buried on Tipton Hill.

Chapter 48

"There's no way to know if someone would've told you that Ace was really your stepfather. You'd already found out so much, and I didn't want someone else to tell you."

"Yeah," I snapped. "You wanted to be the one to ruin my life."

My mother stared at me coldly over her cup of cooled tea. At Dandy's suggestion, we'd been at his table for hours discussing the events of the past few months and the secrets she'd kept from me during my childhood.

Dandy had taken my younger brothers to an indoor play area. I hoped he'd be able to keep up with a toddler and six-year-old while they bounced on trampolines and ran down bowling alleys.

It was good practice for him since he had decided to pursue my mother. She hadn't officially told Dandy that she would give him a second chance, but she'd moved into his house, and they'd shared long nights on the back deck while talking and holding hands.

One of their favorite topics seemed to be me, and Dandy expressed his desire to see our relationship mended. I doubted holes from years of lies could be patched up in a single evening.

Owen had driven me out to Dandy's property, promising to pick me up whenever I was ready to go back to his house, where I was staying until I could figure out someplace I could go permanently. I decided to try to build a new foundation in my relationship with my mother. I was still bitter, though, and it showed.

"I did what I thought was best at the time, Megara," my mother said, looking defeated. "I was only a little older than you when I married your father."

"Which one?"

"Don't be snarky with me, young lady." Her voice was firmer, and she'd stopped trying to placate me. "I've loved two men in my life, and I didn't know the repercussions of my actions. I thought I was doing what was best for you." She spread her hands out in front of her. "I believed I was giving you a father who would be there for you."

She glanced out the window in the direction Dandy's SUV had been before he had driven away. "I know he likes children now, but your dad wasn't a good caretaker for babies."

It still made me inwardly cringe when my mother referred to Dandy as my dad. I'd tried to call him Dandy, but it sounded so much like daddy, that I decided to call him dad. He was delighted by the change, but my mother met the difference with pressed-lipped acceptance.

"Uncle Barton and Aunt Mary Beth told me the story," I said.

She shook her head. "I love my brother, but I wish he'd mind his business." She refused to address her sister's part in the retelling of her past.

My mother took a deep breath and stretched her hands. Clear polish caught the light in the room. "Tell me what I can do to make things between us better."

It was a reasonable request, but it took me a moment before I could answer her. "Stop lying to me."

"I can do that," she said a little too quickly. "Anything else?"

"I want to know the truth about Daddy," I said, looking straight into her eyes. "Did you love him?"

Her eye glazed with tears that she blinked away. "I loved him so much. I still do."

"Then why did you bury him next to Aunt Mary Beth? Don't you want to be buried next to him?"

She took my hand, and I allowed the touch. "As much as I loved Ace, it didn't mean that he loved me. I'm sure there were moments he cared deeply for me, but he loved my sister. In burying him next to Mary Beth, I did something for him in death that I never did for him while he was alive."

She reached under her chair and brought out a leather-bound book with frayed pages. I recognized it as my daddy's book of hand-written poetry. She passed it to me quickly, as if it burned her hands.

"I guess you know what that is."

I nodded. "Are you giving it to me?"

"Yes," she answered. "And I'm glad to be rid of it. Every time he wrote in it, I knew he was writing about my sister and the life he wanted to have with her."

"Why did you keep him?" I opened the book and waited for her reply.

My daddy's script seemed to jump off the pages, and it almost took my breath. I flipped through the pages of poems to my aunt and realized the descriptions of the woman he loved could have been mistaken for my mother, as she was Mary Beth's twin, but some phrases about their laughter and love were clearly about my aunt. When I glanced back up, my mother was staring at the book with her mouth quivering.

"I was selfish." She cried into her hands, and I watched as sobs shook her body. I didn't offer comfort, but the ice in my heart started to melt. "I already had one failed marriage, and if I let him go, I would have had to tell you he wasn't your father, and I didn't want everyone to hate me."

"Barton loves you."

"For now," she scoffed.

"Why? Have you lied to him?"

She shook her head. "He knew all of it, except your paternity. If he would have known you were his full sister, he would have made me leave Ace the first time he cheated on me."

"He was five when it first happened," I countered.

"You know what I mean."

I understood her point, and I moved on. "Why did you want to hurt Mary Beth?"

"She slept with my husband." She looked up at the ceiling and laughed. "Both of them."

"Dandy said he didn't touch her."

My mother narrowed her eyes. "You can't believe him."

"I do," I said and found that I was telling the truth.

My admission gave my mother pause. She must have had her doubts over the years, but she was unwilling to voice them to me. I hoped she'd talk to Dandy about her feelings.

"What should we do now?" I had an anticlimactic feeling. We'd resolved to have a better relationship, and she'd offered me her confidence, but I didn't feel weepy or deeply resolved. We'd had always been that way, though. We showed love through acts of kindness, like when I'd swept the floor for her on chaotic nights or she'd put a chocolate bar in my school lunch bag, and we'd never really touched or said endearments often. "Do you want to hug or something?"

My mother reached out for me, and I walked over to her side of the table. She stood up, and we embraced. I hated to admit it, but her touch soothed me.

My mother had her faults, but she loved me. If she was willing to be honest with me in the future, then I could forgive her.

After all, if I didn't absolve her then I'd be carrying around more pain and guilt than she would have to bear. It would be more like I was punishing myself than hurting her.

I may not have been able to change the past, but I could move forward with my future. And I wasn't going to let any of my family's secrets cause me to have regrets.

Chapter 49

Owen brushed my hair behind my ear. "You're going to have a great day."

I wish I had his confidence. East Tennessee State University crowded around me, and I was in front of a math building that was three times as big as the main building of my high school.

"Just sit down next to someone and give them a compliment," he advised.

I grinned. "Okay. I'll compliment the first guy I see."

He draped his arms over my shoulders. "I think you know what I mean."

We touched our foreheads together. It was a big day for both of us, and although he seemed self-assured, Owen needed encouragement, too.

"You are going to blow the history department out of the water!"

"I doubt it," he said, releasing me and some of his bravado. "There are a lot of students who have studied more about the Industrial Revolution and—"

I put my finger to his lips and let it drop to my side. "History is a big landscape, but you have a very clear picture of World War Two."

Owen stared in the direction of his building. "We're both going to do just fine."

My mind flitted to Sanders, and I hoped he was doing well as he navigated the campus at UT. He'd begged me to go with him and follow the plans he and my daddy had made for me, but I'd declined. Things were too weird between us now that I knew he had tried to kill my daddy, and he was still having trouble getting over his part in my aunt's murder. Once he'd moved to Knoxville, we'd sent a few obligatory texts, but I doubted I'd hear from him very much after Christmas. I wished him the best, though. My daddy had taken the blame for a crime Sanders had committed, and I hoped my cousin wouldn't squander the opportunity to do better with his life.

Owen could tell I was somewhere else, and he pulled me back to the moment by caressing my cheek. He kissed my forehead, and I stepped into my first day of class. It wasn't the way I'd imagined it, but in some ways, it was better, as I was having experiences based on my own decisions.

When I came home from my classes, everyone was waiting for me. It hadn't been hard to think of Dandy's house as my home when I'd moved into it, as most of the important people in my life were already there, and I'd learned that bricks and wood made a house, but they didn't make a home.

Cynthia and Mama had already set the table, and Barton was chasing Si away from the counters. My little brother liked to climb on them and run his fingers through the potatoes and grab the tops off of the biscuits. We didn't mind him eating the food, but he'd had a cold, and most of our immune systems couldn't take the hit.

Pickles sat next to my dad on the couch in the living room. His eyes focused intently on the show, but he didn't seem to enjoy it.

He paused the movie. "Hey, sweetheart! How was the first day of class?"

"It was good," I responded cheerily. "What are you guys watching?"

He looked down at Pickles. "We were watching a movie about dinosaurs takin' over a city, but I think we're gonna switch it to a cartoon."

"Where the dinosaurs act normal," Pickles amended.

I laughed. Of course my six-year-old brother thought carnivorous animals were actually friendly animals, who helped each other and the humans around them.

My older brother pulled out a chair for Cynthia and she balanced herself into it. She had a month before we'd meet our newest family member, and we were all anticipating the birth. Even though he'd been with my mother when she was pregnant with Barton, Dandy didn't remember a lot about pregnancy and babies, so he kept thinking every ache and pain Cynthia vocalized was the beginning stages of labor. My mother could calm him, though, not unlike the way she had done with my father.

My mother and Dandy weren't together, but it was only a matter of time before he convinced her to give him another chance. He could make my mother laugh like she was a butterfly opening her wings for the first time. There was a lightness to her step and easiness in her smile, and I didn't want to see it change. She'd always had to manage hard times, financially, mentally, or emotionally, but I didn't think she'd have difficult situations with Dandy. His light-hearted approach to life was contagious, and my mother had already caught it.

Pickles and Si liked living with Dandy, and he enjoyed spoiling them. He seemed more like an overgrown playmate to them, but I could see Dandy passing on advice to them in the future so that their relationship could grow into one with mutual respect. I hated to admit it, but Barton had been right not to give up on his father.

My brother and I didn't revisit Aunt Mary Beth's death. It was a hard subject for both of us, and it made it easier to avoid it now that we were away from Tipton Hill.

I still visited Aunt Tonya, Uncle Catfish, and Crystal once a week, and Uncle Catfish kept our conversations light and fluffy. Crystal was flourishing with them, and I was glad they finally had the opportunity to be parents. My uncle's humor and my aunt's grit were the perfect combination.

I'd met the new baby as soon as he'd come home from the hospital. I'd unwrapped the blanket swaddled around him and counted his fingers and toes.

"They're all there," my uncle had chuckled.

The baby had no signs of the challenges Crystal faced, but the doctors wouldn't be certain about that issue until he was two or three years old.

I had stared down into his brown eyes and noted his nose that already looked so much like his father's nose. Our father's nose.

Ace Tipton was still my father. My dad was nice, and we were blood-related, but Ace—my daddy—had raised me with a strong set of values. He had firm hands that taught me how to work, and a conflicting sense of love and duty that had led to his undoing.

"What did you name him?" I had asked my aunt, watching the baby focus on me for the first time.

She had looked at her husband and they had spoken at once. "Ace."

Chapter 50

"And he has your nose," I said, giggling. "It looks a little big on him now, but I think he'll grow into it."

I didn't want to do a disservice to Mary Beth, so I added, "He's blond, like you and Mama. That may change, but it's so cute on him."

I stayed silent as some mourners who had been visiting another end of the cemetery came within several feet of me. We didn't acknowledge each other. It seemed like the only place where a person was safe from social obligations. No one expected a greeting and a hearty handshake while you sat at your family's graveside.

After the mourners' car drove away, I was left with the wind blowing through the trees and the whispering river. We hadn't experienced a lot of rain, and the water had receded. There seemed to be a storm in the darkening clouds, though, and the ground would welcome the precipitation.

My aunt and father were gone, but their gravesites were as good as any other place for talking to them. I didn't want to evaluate whether they heard me. It was easier for me to imagine my aunt patting my leg and my father putting his arm around my shoulders as I told them about the woes of a young adult.

After my first day of college, when I was feeling nervous and insecure, I had gone to their plots every day, but as the weeks passed, and my life felt more stationary, my visits were less frequent. It was hard to look at their knee-high tombstones without feeling the sting of betrayal.

There were so many lies, and neither one of them was guiltless. Gone were the days, though, when they could cover up their deeds. Everything had been laid bare, and after the town raked my family across the coals, we'd emerge from the fire as stronger people.

My father and Aunt Mary Beth weren't the only ones to blame in their strange love triangle that seemed more like a square when I added Dandy to it. However, their influence over the lives around them had been diminished when they had drawn their last breaths. I wasn't angry with them anymore. They were dead, and if God could absolve them, I could be the good Southern girl my father raised and forgive them, too.

My father's headstone had been delivered the previous week. Aunt Tonya and I had gathered the money to get it, and there was such a community outpouring for Ace Tipton that my heart had overflowed with gratitude.

My father's gravestone was simple. It stated his name, nickname, birth and death dates, and an epitaph. Before the divorce papers had been served, it may have read: *Loving husband and father*, but my mother had asked me to drop the *husband* part.

I included *father* but added one of the lines from his book of poems to the bottom, duplicating the words on my aunt's headstone under her designation as a loving aunt and mother.

Many people may have argued that I shouldn't have connected them in death, as he was married to my mother when he died, but my father's heart had belonged to Aunt Mary Beth, and I couldn't let go until I'd done my part to unite them in some small way.

At the bottom of the stones, my father's words were scripted: "I see your light in the night, drawing me to you. I fly to it and my soul rests. For in your arms, I am home."

I had wrapped up my father's hammock and taken it to Dandy's house when we'd moved. Two trees in his backyard supported my weight when I climbed into the hammock. On sunny afternoons, I'd rest in it and look up at the sky, wondering if my daddy looked down on me.

Did he know that I'd found out my paternity? Would it change the way he felt about me?

I could only speculate, but I doubted he would think less of me. I imagined that he'd hold me just as closely as Crystal or any of my brothers.

My mother gave me the option of altering my father on my birth certificate, but after talking with my dad, I declined. Everyone agreed that Ace Tipton had raised me, and my surname should remain unchanged.

It was hard to settle my mind on the reality of the situation. I had believed my father was my father and my existence was as simple as my mother's buttered biscuits and catching fireflies with Sanders in the backyard, but my life had been thrown into a whirlwind, and even though I was safe on the other side, it was still hard for me to process some of the decisions the older people around me had made for the sake of keeping secrets.

All I could do was resolve to live a better life and create more trust-centered relationships. I was tired of dodging copperheads and lunging for fireflies as they flitted away. Their secret lives had been exposed, and after helping clean up the pieces, I knew that secrets hurt the ones you love. I'd learn from my experiences on Tipton Hill, but I wouldn't let them rule my life. My future was full of promise, and I couldn't wait to see where I'd go.

Did you enjoy the book?

If you liked the story, please consider leaving a review on Amazon, Goodreads, and/or BookBub. Your review can help me a lot, even if you write, "I liked it!"

Thank you so much for reading my book. I hope you enjoyed The Secret Lives of Copperheads and Fireflies!

About the Author

Courtnee Turner Hoyle lives her dreams every day. She's the parent of seven children and loves each of them dearly.

She lives in Northeast Tennessee, where the hills are alive with a thousand stories waiting to be told. The secrets run deep, and many times people will do anything to keep them buried.

Courtnee has a few fancy degrees, but none of them reflect her personality or commitment to her family. She might be intelligent, or she could have been gifted at telling her professors whatever they wanted to hear. Whatever the answer, she walked away from formal education with two undergraduate degrees and one master's degree. She should have held out for a PhD. I know. She was a total slacker.

She's content writing, reading, watching her younger children grow, and beaming with pride over the accomplishments of her older progeny. They make her life worth every moment.

Acknowledgements

As always, I appreciate my eldest daughter, Tosha for her contributions. She is one of the strongest people I know, and even though she had her own paternal drama, she chose a path few Southerners follow.

Thank you, Mama, for reading my work. It delights me to write stories you enjoy, and I was happy when you told me you'd miss the characters in this story. It let me know I'd written a memorable family with an interesting story.

I wrote the story before my mama passed, and I thank God she was able to read it and share her thoughts. The twin sisters and my mama share the same middle name.

My older children inspired Megara's character, and my younger children are present in the actions of Pickles and Si. Readers could never guess how many of their funny statements and hijinks were true, and that goes for the older children, too!

My community has supported me as I've written my books, and I appreciate them. I write about the area in and around Erwin, Tennessee, as the scenery and local people are inspiring. The beautiful mountains and kind people will continue to be my muses in future novels.

Sweet 15 Designs, LLC designed a lovely cover. At first, a snake wrapped around a broken jar of fireflies, but it was too dark for the tone of the story. Thank you for redesigning it with fireflies, Ace's hammock, and the copperhead hidden in the leaves.

My reviewers in Book Bindings are some of the best readers in the world! They are kind, but I have received honest criticism from them that has encouraged me to become a better writer.

I appreciate all the people who have read this book. Whether you have plucked it from the shelves of your local library, or you have picked it from a long list of electronic options, I thank you.

I hope everyone enjoyed The Secret Lives of Copperheads and Fireflies, and even though we may have left Tipton Hill, there are many more secrets to uncover hiding in Pale Woods or sinking to the bottom of the Nolichucky River.

Mary Beth's Peanut Butter Pinwheels

Prep time: 15 minutes
Refrigerate: 1 hour

Ingredients

- two to four tablespoons of peanut butter

- two cups of confectioners' sugar

- one teaspoon of vanilla extract

- three to five tablespoons of butter (depending on the amount of confectioners' sugar used)

Procedure

1. Melt the butter.

2. Add the vanilla extract and stir before sifting in the desired amount of confectioners' sugar.

3. The mixture should form a ball that can be rolled flat with

a rolling pin.

4. Spread a layer of peanut butter from end to end and then roll the dough lengthwise, Keeping the peanut butter on the inside.

5. Cut the log of dough into pieces and place them in the refrigerator for at least one hour.

6. Enjoy!

Author's note: Mary Beth's pinwheels are also known as potato candy. Potatoes have been omitted, but you may add mashed tubers to the mixture if you prefer the consistency. Just remember to let the potatoes cool before you use them!

Potatoes will soften the sugar in the mixture and bind it, but if you enjoy sweetness and buttercream flavor, leave them out.

Also by Courtnee

Pale Woods Mystery Series
My Brother's Keeper
Book One
Courtnee Turner Hoyle

Seventeen-year-old Jerrod Miller has struggled with the guilt of his actions for an event that took place almost a year ago. His friends have abandoned him, his family ignores him, and he lost his best friend. To make matters worse, he was unable to access records that may have revealed his father's whereabouts. His sister, Ella, guides Jerrod as he tries to learn and accept secrets his family has tried to hide. However, a sinister spirit may be influencing Ella's actions, and it has an agenda of its own.

Also by Courtnee

Finding Emma

Amazon #1 Best-Seller

What if the only anchor to your identity was a tattoo with a name?
David Winsome answers the door for a beautiful woman who can't remember how she ended up on the hill near his family's home. The woman assumes the name on her tattoo, Emma, and blends into the community while questions about her past plague her.
Why is the town familiar, even though no one seems to know her? And why does she feel an intimate attraction to David, even though she just met him?
As Emma accepts her new life and begins a loving relationship with David, a person who claims to know her enters her life. Does this person hold the key to Emma's past, or is there a mystery much deeper than Emma's identity?
Someone has manipulated the events in his favor, and he has a much larger plan in mind.